the infidelity diaries

Love,
betrayal,
revenge

the
infidelity
diaries

Anonymous

ALLEN&UNWIN
SYDNEY·MELBOURNE·AUCKLAND·LONDON

First published in 2015

Allen & Unwin
83 Alexander Street
Crows Nest NSW 2065
Australia
Phone: (61 2) 8425 0100

Email: info@allenandunwin.com
Web: www.allenandunwin.com

Cataloguing-in-Publication details are available
from the National Library of Australia
www.trove.nla.gov.au

ISBN 978 1 74331 9208

Internal design by Christabella Designs
Set in 12/17 pt Sabon by Post Pre-press Group, Australia
Printed and bound in Australia by Griffin Press

Extracts from *The Kite Runner* by Khaled Hosseini © Bloomsbury Publishing UK

10 9 8 7 6 5 4 3 2 1

MIX
Paper from
responsible sources
FSC® C009448

The paper in this book is FSC® certified.
FSC® promotes environmentally responsible,
socially beneficial and economically viable
management of the world's forests.

The characters and events of this story are entirely fictional.
Characters described in this book are not based on any real person
whether living or deceased and any similarity is purely coincidental.

Zara

Zara

She was standing at the end of the hall in the late afternoon light, her back arched against the wall, between two landscape paintings. Closing her eyes, she ran her hands up and down the red dress clinging to her curves. The dress had been designed by a genius. Its neckline was low enough to be provocative, but the hemline was below knee-length—too long for Leo, the husband of our hostess, to commit adultery there on the spot. But he was still open to temptation, breathing hard in a fashion that suggested he'd been just about to grab her.

Both of them saw me at the same time.

He froze. His seducer laughed.

'The bathroom's just opposite us,' she said, without any sign of embarrassment. 'Leo was just showing me around, weren't you, Leo?'

Leo muttered something about needing to check his voice messages, and fled.

There was nothing for me to do but walk into the bathroom as if nothing had happened, although I was hoping that she would be gone by the time I came out.

But she hadn't gone. She was still there, smiling at me and wiggling her shoulders and breasts in some sort of performance over which she had no control; only right at this moment it was also an act of supreme mockery—and intent—as both of us knew perfectly well.

⚬————⚔·⚔————⚬

The canoe came from behind one of the towering limestone peaks in the sea off southern Thailand. There were only two occupants aboard: the boatman, and a woman too far away to see clearly, who was holding a pair of binoculars up to her eyes. I watched as she turned and spoke to the figure paddling behind her, pointing an arm in our direction—and within seconds the canoe started heading straight for us.

Even today, writing this in the country where I live now, it's difficult to describe the sense of dread I felt at that moment. I was so overwhelmed that I thought I was going to faint, but not realising what was occurring, I put it down to the fierce afternoon heat. It was impossible to imagine in such an enchanted setting a malevolence that was about to change the course of our lives.

In retrospect, I believe that what I experienced was more than instinct: it was foresight. The ability to believe in the mysterious has no place in our rationalist society, but I have no doubt what happened that day verged on the unreal. It was purely a physical sensation. I didn't 'see' into the future, or connect the sense of dread that I felt with the woman travelling in the canoe. And only very

4

gradually, over a few years, would I realise how damaged she was.

Sergei, my Russian husband, and I were in Thailand on holiday in December 2005. We were staying at a hotel close to Phang Nga Bay, which is where this story begins. On the afternoon in question, we'd set off on an old Thai boat with a huge wooden hull, crewed by a group of genial locals, to explore the stretch of water best known for the peaks and islets rising vertically from this corner of the Andaman Sea.

We sailed for almost an hour into the bay until we reached a cluster of the giant rock formations that, from a distance, looked like mountains separating our world from another just beyond. There were sea caves hidden in the shadows of some of the islets, which we wanted to see close up. The crew dropped anchor and we climbed into one of the canoes that had been provided for us, accompanied by a young Thai man who spoke broken English and was acting as our guide.

It was only once we were on the water that we began to get a real sense of the scenery around us. As our guide turned the canoe towards a majestic islet close by, dozens of monkeys began scrambling down the cliff face to a sunny ledge close to the water. There, they lined up in a row—like a council of ancients—eyes fixed on the strangers approaching.

We asked our boatman if we could just drift for a while under the gaze of the primates, and he nodded and smiled. From under his seat he produced bottles of mineral water. 'No ice!' he joked, handing a bottle to each of us.

It's pointless wondering what would have happened if we hadn't taken that decision to drift along the base of the cliff, and instead had paddled into one of the sea caves, then out the other side and gone on back to the boat. In all likelihood, we would never have encountered Caitt coming around that limestone peak.

The dramatic beauty of Phang Nga Bay made the moment more vivid. But we were going to meet her sooner or later, if not in Thailand, then in Sydney where we all lived.

Neither Sergei nor I was born in Australia. I was seventeen when I moved to Sydney from Canada in 1977 with my parents and two slightly younger sisters, Lili and Eve, and our older sister, Lori. Sergei, an architect, was from Moscow. His parents had managed to get him and themselves out of the Soviet Union in 1973 after the emigration policy had eased. Most of those allowed to leave were ethnic Jews. But Sergei's father, a history teacher, had been in trouble with the authorities for encouraging his students to read the work of 'dissident' writers. They were glad to get rid of him, Sergei always said. He was twenty-two years old when he left the Soviet Union and, with his parents, went to live with a relative in London. There, they became part of the Russian diaspora and he enrolled in architecture studies.

The two of us met in 1983, on a ferry that was going to Tallinn, the capital of Estonia—then still under Soviet occupation. I always liked the fact that we met in a part of the world that was out of the ordinary and even a little mysterious.

Sergei was visiting the land where his mother was born. I was fulfilling a dream of spending part of the European summer in Finland, in the Land of the Midnight Sun, where I'd been invited to stay with old family friends in Helsinki.

These friends threw a party for me one evening in their huge old apartment in the Kruununhaka district, which is in the oldest part of the city, next to the sea. One of the guests arrived with a Swedish visitor, who told me he did 'business' in Tallinn. He was intentionally enigmatic; I was young, and didn't ask questions. After dinner we sat on the ancient balcony and talked.

In a city where it's still light at 10 p.m. for a couple of months a year, anything seems possible. So when he suggested that, instead of going to Lapland, I should travel behind 'The Iron Curtain' and see life in a country run from afar by the Kremlin, I agreed. Estonia was just a ferry ride away, across the Gulf of Finland, and foreigners were allowed to visit—although they couldn't go outside Tallinn. I planned to meet him there in a week's time.

Then fate intervened.

The Swede got my arrival day wrong. I only learnt this a long time afterwards and by then I'd almost forgotten him altogether. Sergei was on the ferry to Tallinn, and struck up a conversation with me soon after we sailed. At twenty-three, I was a hopeless romantic. Sergei, at thirty-two, seemed very worldly and had an enchanting Russian accent to boot.

And so, thanks to that missed rendezvous in Estonia, here I was, almost twenty-two years later, sitting in a canoe off the Thai coast, watching the woman who was about to carve her initials over our marriage approaching us over the flat, pale blue sea.

As she began to close the distance between us, Sergei suddenly said, 'I think I know who it is.'

The moment he said this, I knew—although I can't explain how—that our life had just jumped tracks.

'Who?' I asked, still battling what I thought was heatstroke. I opened the bottle I was holding and sprinkled some of the water over my face.

'Caitt. Joe's sister-in-law,' replied Sergei. 'It *is* her,' he added, squinting into the sun at the blonde who was now waving—at both of us, as I first thought.

Joe was an English friend of Sergei's from London, who had also graduated in architecture. He came to visit us in Sydney in the mid-1980s, and liked the city so much that he decided to emigrate to Australia. The two of them had often discussed setting up an architecture practice together, although I think they were both happier working alone.

We never knew that Joe, whose wife, Sally, was a good friend of mine, had a brother who had also moved to Sydney. The first we heard of his existence was when Sergei said that we were going on holiday to Thailand, whereupon Joe mentioned an older sibling, Michael, who had left for Thailand the previous week. He was a yacht broker, married with no children, and was travelling with his wife and a friend of theirs, a film editor called David.

Another coincidence. We knew David casually. He lived in our street.

When Sergei mentioned that we'd booked into a quiet hotel on the northwest coast of Phuket—far from the tourist-trap towns on the island—Joe laughed.

'That's where they're staying as well,' he'd replied. 'God, what a coincidence!'

So we were definitely fated to meet. That much is clear.

Joe explained later that his brother and Caitt, who was South African born, had only recently moved back to the city from a small town in the New South Wales Southern Highlands where they'd been living for years, which explained why we hadn't met them before.

Soon after this conversation we left for our holiday. We didn't expect to meet Joe's brother and sister-in-law immediately, but on our first day at the hotel in Thailand, Sergei ran into David during a brief trip back to our room. I wasn't with him; I was already in the sea, swimming.

David introduced Sergei to Michael and Caitt, who were there in the lobby with him. They were all waiting for a taxi to take them to the airport, he explained. Caitt wanted to spend some time in Bangkok, and Michael and David had decided to go with her. Plans were made on the spot for us all to spend an evening together when they got back at the end of the week.

When Sergei returned to the beach, he told me Caitt was a speech pathologist who worked with autistic children.

'She sounds interesting,' I commented. But there the subject had rested. We hadn't talked about the trio again.

'I remember now,' Sergei said, as the canoe carrying Caitt glided towards us, 'they were due back last night. I wonder where the others are.'

'Perhaps they're on that big tourist craft we passed a little while ago,' I replied.

I'd barely finished speaking when the monkeys that were lined up on the cliff ledge behind us became unusually agitated. Some covered their eyes with furry arms and started screeching. Others scrambled away, vanishing over rocks into the cave beyond.

See no evil? That thought only occurred to me many years later.

Then Caitt's canoe came up alongside and I felt nothing but emptiness. I cannot explain that either.

Women know women. We're meant to have a radar that goes off when predators slink—or sail with bare legs—into view. Was this super-instinct the reason for my feeling of emptiness and my sense of dread a few minutes earlier? I'd never had such a reaction to a woman before, so perhaps it was.

'Sergei! Hello! Imagine running into you all the way out here!'

The stranger, as she still was, spoke in a merry tone while shielding her eyes with one hand. In defiance of the sun, she was wearing neither sunglasses nor hat, and had on a loose yellow shirt that came to the top of her knees.

She looked straight at Sergei as she spoke, without acknowledging my presence. This was my immediate impression of her: that she was shutting me out. My second, strongest impression was the intensity of that stare. Anyone else observing the scene might have assumed that she and Sergei were already lovers, and that this bizarre meeting off the Thai coast was no accident.

As I would learn soon enough, the intense stare and the melting look were two of Caitt's specialties—though not ones that she ever practised on women. She kept her eyes fixed on Sergei as he reached out and held the side of her canoe with one hand. At this point, she and I were literally sitting side by side.

'How did you come to be out here?' he said. 'You're not stalking us by any chance?'

Caitt laughed.

Pale skin with freckles. Pink lipstick. Early to mid forties—we were about the same age.

Still no eye contact with me.

Another large pleasure cruiser appeared from around one of the peaks, creating a series of small waves. As the ripples of water swept towards us, our two boatmen took over, keeping the canoes steady and then talking quietly together in Thai. One had a gold ring in his ear, and both of them wore bandanas tied around their heads, like pirates. It was a good day for a kidnapping.

Sergei, completely oblivious to the lack of communication between Caitt and myself, leaned forward as he slipped an arm around my waist.

'This is my wife, Zara. Zara, this is Caitt.'

Somewhere close by there was a soft splash. There were flying fish as well as turtles in these waters, although we hadn't seen any turtles as yet.

Then everything became still. The monkeys stopped screeching. The breeze died. The heat intensified.

Caitt had stopped laughing.

She was staring at Sergei's hand on my hip. Maybe it was a trick of the light, but she looked furious. As I watched, her mouth started to spasm and I thought she was going to be ill. All of this lasted only a couple of seconds, but it was startling to see.

Sergei, meanwhile, had continued talking in his affable manner. 'This is our first holiday for ages. Zara works too hard. I told her we only had a three or four month window before the wet season starts.'

Only at this point did Caitt look directly at me for the first time. Her face had become totally expressionless.

'Oh yes,' she remarked, in a tone of indifference. 'Joe said that you write biographies. I haven't read any of them, I'm afraid.'

By now she had under control whatever it was that had affected her before and perhaps for this reason showed little interest in taking the conversation with me any further. So I gave her a head start.

'Sergei said you work with autistic children.'

Silence.

'That must be very demanding, but very satisfying,' I went on.

No reaction.

The heat was getting to me. I felt like diving into the sea. Why was conversation with this woman so difficult? Why was she so strange? Where was the breeze?

There was another splash from a flying fish and then, far in the distance, the sound of thunder.

Finally, Caitt spoke.

'Yes, it is satisfying,' she said. 'I work with a team of speech pathologists three days a week. The rest of the time I try to pursue other interests. I did a three-month gourmet cookery class last year, and I'm thinking of taking art classes. A rigid lifestyle isn't my thing. I'm not locked into a career like you, with no time for anything else.'

The first soft slap across the face.

I replied that I wasn't sure any writer had a 'career', since writing falls into a category of its own. Most writers would argue this, I added.

Caitt smiled as if I'd said something amusing. 'But don't you churn out popular biographies?' she inquired. 'It would be harder if you had children.'

I ignored this remark. My sadness at not having children was private, and besides, Caitt didn't have children either. I explained that I had a contract with a publisher to produce two short-form biographies a year, although they still needed to be informative and well written. But I was starting to feel tense.

Why should I have to justify my work?

She wasn't going to give in.

'Joe said you're always working and that you're often

away. I seem to remember you were in your room working the day we met Sergei in the hotel.'

'I was swimming,' I replied.

'I did tell you that,' interrupted Sergei, sounding puzzled as he addressed Caitt.

'So you did. I forgot. I must have got the wrong impression of Zara.'

Never has an apologetic remark been so loaded.

And then she smiled, and changed the subject.

'I'd like to invite you over for Sunday lunch when we get back to Sydney. You live very close to us, I think.'

You . . . Singular? Plural?

'*Spasibo*,' Sergei thanked her. 'Zara and I accept your invitation to lunch with pleasure.'

He may as well have not added that last sentence, since Caitt started talking well before he had finished.

'I'm going back to Sydney tomorrow,' she announced. 'Some family friends have had a skiing accident. They've each broken a leg and they need help with the children. I'm going to fill in until a relative takes over in a few days. They live close to where we are so I can go back and forth as I need to. We were due to go back at the end of this week anyway, so it's not a big problem. Luckily the airline won't charge me extra.'

'Very admirable,' I said. And I meant it, even though I was growing tired of being the woman who wasn't there.

Caitt paused.

'Anyone would do the same. They've both been very kind to me in the past. I'll be free again by the time you get back,' she answered, still looking at Sergei. The way she managed to get across the impression that it was Sergei who had just spoken—and not me—was remarkable. It took the art of ignoring another woman to new heights.

'I was determined to see Phang Nga Bay before I left,' she went on. 'You mentioned getting a boat the day we first met. I checked with the booking clerk this morning and he said you'd gone to the bay. That's what gave me the idea.'

'So you *were* stalking us!' joked Sergei.

This time Caitt gave him her melting look—one that suggested they already had secrets.

'It's complicated, don't you think?' she asked in mock despair. 'Having another Russian in my life.'

'As long as Zara has no trouble distinguishing me from your husband, where is the problem?' Sergei replied lightly.

He grinned as he made this remark, but I saw immediately what he did not: that Caitt was completely thrown by what he'd just said.

She was starting to spook me a little. Her bewildered reaction was unnatural. I began to wonder if this was an act, too. If it wasn't, then you had to wonder about the state of her mind. It took her a few seconds to recover her composure and come up with a punchline that would have been funny—if she'd been joking.

'Now there's an idea,' she purred.

It was probably fortunate that her boatman broke into our conversation at this point and said in English that they needed to get back to their boat.

Before your sunstroke gets worse, I should have added *sotto voce*. But didn't.

Caitt glanced at her watch, before deciding that she hadn't quite finished the act.

Tilting her head to one side, she began wriggling her shoulders like an old-fashioned Hollywood vamp. It was so unexpected, and so out of context, that I was taken aback. Even more startling was the fact that Caitt very clearly wasn't playing for laughs. Her concentration as she performed this extraordinary come-hither routine prompted a sudden, uncharitable thought on my part: is she this bad in the bedroom, too?

'See you soon,' she said breathlessly, with a last, lingering look at Sergei.

Then she and her boatman were off. She didn't say goodbye to me. She didn't look back.

I glanced at my husband. He was watching her go, his face thoughtful. Neither of us said anything as our own boatman picked up his paddle and we began moving once again over the flat sea.

'I can't make her out. What do you think?' I asked after a while.

'I think Joe is right. He said that she loves being dramatic,' Sergei replied.

There we let the subject drop. Sergei seemed genuinely incurious about Joe's sister-in-law and, in any case, I didn't know what more we could have said about her at this point.

That night, Sergei and I went out for dinner to a local cafe just down the road from our hotel. Around 11 p.m., we realised that we were the only diners still there. The family running the cafe seemed to have vanished, and no one came when we called out.

So Sergei went off to find someone who could give us the bill. He left his phone on the table. When it began ringing, I didn't recognise the flashing number—although I sensed who was calling even before I picked up.

'Hello?'

Silence.

I waited a second or two and was about to hang up when the voice at the other end said curtly, 'What are you doing, answering Sergei's phone?'

Stunned, with no idea how to answer, I waited a few seconds, trying to stay calm. I'm not sure which disturbed me the most: the hostile tone, the rudeness, or the possessiveness that I also distinctly heard in Caitt's tone.

There was something else as well, which I couldn't immediately put my finger on.

'We're at dinner,' I replied. 'Sergei is paying the bill. That is you, Caitt, isn't it?'

'Yes it is,' came the crisp reply. 'I just wanted him to have this number so that we can arrange a meal back in Sydney. No matter.'

'Would you like my number?' I asked. 'You can call me to organise a date.'

'If you like, Zara,' replied Caitt, sounding amused all of a sudden. 'Can you text it to me? I'm in a bit of a rush right now.'

She hung up then, without another word—and a few moments later, Sergei returned.

'I think I'm only just included in the invitation,' I commented, after I'd told him about the call.

He looked momentarily bemused. 'Oh, she's a flirt,' he replied. 'But she's harmless. Come on. Let's go back along the beachfront.'

Thailand had been in the grip of a heatwave all week, and it was still stifling even at this time of night. Sergei's suggestion made sense. The breeze blowing in from the ocean and through the small bushes lining the beach—where lizards hid during the day—was invigorating.

Perhaps it was the breeze that sharpened my brain because while we were still making our way along the path at the edge of the sand, I suddenly realised what it was about Caitt's phone call that I hadn't been able to work out.

It was her astonishment. She had been so taken aback when I answered that she hadn't bothered to pretend otherwise.

That's when it came to me in a flash: here was a woman who regarded Sergei's life up until the moment they met as totally over and done with.

You see, in Caitt's eyes, I was already redundant.

——✦——

As we walked back to our hotel, I felt more strongly than ever that the life we'd had up until then had just ended, and that nothing would ever be the same again between Sergei and me.

This would turn out to be true. Something that had been unique and enduring despite the tensions that existed in our relationship—and which are also part of the story—started going into retreat from this point.

An erosion began.

In time, our encounter with Caitt in Phang Nga Bay would take on special significance because of the way that she appeared as a figure in the distance before coming gradually into focus. But even then, nothing about her was clear—and it still isn't. Sometimes I try to picture her face and all I get is a blur. Blonde hair, blurred features. All these years later, there's a good chance that I wouldn't even recognise her anymore if she suddenly materialised in front of me.

Caitt was a stealth operator *par excellence*. Sure, she sent plenty of signals from the start about her intentions towards Sergei, but I chose to minimise what was happening—or I tried to—in order to play down her significance in our lives. She knew that I did not want to make her my enemy and she exploited that to the max. The sense of disquiet that I always felt in her company never vanished completely; but in a complicated way we did, for a short time, forge a friendship of sorts, despite endlessly circling each other.

Caitt, always with her eye on the main goal: getting closer to Sergei.

Me, waiting to see her next move.

This 'friendship' began when Michael left her at the start of April 2006, five months after the holiday in Thailand. I now realise that Caitt switched from being sinister to cordial because she didn't want to be regarded as the prime suspect when Sergei's relationship with me started to deteriorate. She could safely flirt with him while Michael was still around—but not afterwards. The thing she most wanted was for outsiders to regard the collapse of our marriage as inevitable, and her own, growing 'friendship' with Sergei as a natural development. However, for this to happen, she had to put a carefully planned structure in place, and be patient.

Both of us put on a show of amiability, which wasn't completely contrived. Whenever we met, which was often— for Caitt made sure we became part of a circle of people she knew—we fell easily into conversation. We shared similar political views. We liked the same books, the same films. Caitt could be charming and funny and often I had to remind myself that she was calculating and false.

There were a few occasions when I caught her watching me with an unpleasant glint in her eyes, especially if she'd had a couple of glasses of wine. She would turn away immediately—hoping, I suppose, that I hadn't noticed anything amiss. And similarly, I could be accused of putting on a double act in the sense that I never spoke the truth to her face, that I didn't trust her one inch.

Sergei and I had been together for almost twenty-two years when we met Caitt. She wasn't stupid; she knew the power of time, and that she couldn't rush the seduction process since, in order to separate Sergei from me permanently, she needed to create the one thing she didn't have—which he and I did.

A history together.

She went about it methodically, even 'dating' a couple of available men after Michael left her, to make it look as if she was enjoying the single life again. We went out with Caitt and her boyfriends a couple of times for meals, although Caitt never allowed these relationships to last longer than a few weeks. Her dalliance with Leo, the husband at the start of this story, was more risky. I think she may have had a brief fling with him, without ever wanting anything to come of it.

Leo and the others were only needed for as long as they were useful. Sergei was her work in progress.

Much later, when the disturbing side of her personality re-emerged, I couldn't help wondering when it was that Caitt first suspected Michael was going to leave her. Maybe she dreaded being alone, and that was a factor in her behaviour.

Caitt and Michael had been together for almost as long as Sergei and I when their marriage ended. Who can't understand the fear of loneliness that comes after separation, divorce—or worse?

The single knife and fork on the table. The empty chair at night.

So I continued to give her the benefit of the doubt, despite my disquiet and my suspicions, for the simple reason that there is another sort of loneliness that's rarely talked about: the loneliness that results from suspicion, and which is worse than suspicion itself.

I had no idea back then about how, one day, I would be confronted in the most horrific fashion by Caitt's determination to be the centre of attention. Nor that it would be Joe who would try to explain her behaviour during what became one of the darkest periods of my life. He said that Caitt needed drama the way other people need air to breathe; witness, he said, the way that she played up to men in front of their wives. She enjoyed the tension this created because she felt a natural urge to 'fight' other females in her territory, although at the same time she took it for granted that any man—all men—would find her the most desirable.

Behaviour which was wearying for everyone. But you have to be philosophical about women like Caitt. And it wasn't her extreme coquetry that was the issue. As I would find out, it was the diabolical thing that drove her to make it incredibly, ruthlessly clear that no matter the circumstances, nothing would stop her from trying to steal attention back to herself.

Joe laid bare her character in such brutal fashion, when that time came, because he was in shock; otherwise I suspect that he would never have been able to say something so honest about the woman who, as he would also admit to me, had once told him that she'd always secretly loved him—and not her own husband.

———— ⟿⟾ ————

When people make lists of great, life-changing events, they never include their own acts of infidelity. But they should because, even if they don't want to admit it, infidelity, whether it's discovered or not, always has consequences.

Nine years into my marriage to Sergei, I began an affair which lasted for just over twelve months. The anguish this caused him in turn caused me anguish for years. Confronting a very hard truth, as I eventually did—that I was capable of hurting someone I still loved—made me question what sort of person I was, or had become. It changed me forever, and ultimately made me grow up, although it's also true that I struggled with the notion that you could be in love with two men at the same time or, at least, love one, and become infatuated with another.

There was no particular reason for me to look elsewhere; in fact, I didn't—not intentionally, anyway. The man in question chased me hard during a complicated period of our life when Sergei never seemed to be at home very much. Is this a justifiable reason for being unfaithful?

Old friends of Sergei's were visiting Australia and the more time he spent with these people, who were dealing with ghosts from their past, the more melancholic he became. The extreme cynicism of one of the drinking friends—a brilliant man, but with a poisonous mind—began to affect my relationship with Sergei in ways that are hard to describe.

21

Or am I simply making excuses? I had an affair that I didn't break off, even though I knew Sergei was suffering.

I told him the truth about what I was doing. He loved me—and I made him suffer.

Sergei was devastated when I went off to join my lover in a Middle Eastern country that would soon experience great political upheaval. Even today, I cannot believe I simply up and left.

We didn't see each other for several months, although, before I left, I gave him the phone number for where I would be. Despite the extraordinary emotional turmoil that had taken over our lives, the idea of not staying in contact simply didn't occur to either of us.

Except that the phone number was incorrect—which I didn't know at the time.

Sergei rang me continually, as he told me when we were back together again. I also tried to ring him. But in the place where I was spending most of my time, communications were poor; whenever I tried to ring Sergei, the line invariably cut out and all either of us ever heard was a sound like wind rushing through forests.

There was also something else that Sergei later told me: that he had begun to wonder whether I'd given him the wrong number deliberately. And what he added still leaves an echo: 'I thought you'd disappeared forever.'

Sergei and I went to Thailand thirteen years after the events that I've described. Calm had been restored between us. Or so I thought. But when you have an affair, there is always blowback—and when it comes, there's no predicting the consequences.

Would Caitt have become the terrorist in our marriage if I'd been faithful to Sergei? I'll never know the answer to that, just as I will never be sure that Sergei's affair with her began in October 2006, as he later claimed.

⸱─────⸱✠⸱─────⸱

'Sergei!'

A familiar figure in faded blue jeans and a white linen shirt broke away from her guests and hurried over the lawn, as if fearing someone else would get to him first.

It wasn't a big crowd at Caitt's house that Sunday. Or rather, the house where she lived with her husband. Odd, how I thought of her from the start as a single woman.

'You look so well!' she cried, almost skipping up the steps onto the terrace where we were standing, and embracing Sergei as if he had just crawled out of the desert or survived a horrific ordeal.

'Why wouldn't I be?' he replied humorously.

'Joe told me that you have high cholesterol. I thought about all the prawns you just ate in Thailand and started worrying. So I intend taking charge of your diet in future. Oh, hello Zara,' Caitt added, as if she had just become aware of my presence. 'You made it.'

There are opening shots, and there are throwaway lines— and there are lines that are carefully plotted beforehand to create rifts and fractures and small wars. I decided not to bite ('But Caitt, weren't you expecting me?'), and took what I considered to be the classier option: smiling into the middle distance without responding.

'Sergei mentioned that you often work at the weekends,' Caitt went on. 'So I thought . . .' She shrugged when I still didn't reply.

'Caitt messaged me this morning, asking whether we were both coming to lunch,' explained Sergei.

Couldn't he see that this was exactly what she had wanted him to say?

'I said yes, that we'd both be here, although you sometimes write at the weekends,' he added.

I made an airy batting-away gesture with one hand, as if at a troublesome fly.

'Well, anyway,' said Caitt, turning to Sergei, 'you've come, and that's all that matters.'

We'd been back from Thailand for a week. Caitt had rung—Sergei, not me—the same evening that we got home. Now she was watching with glee as this particular scene, obviously planned in advance, played out exactly as she had hoped—except that I was ostensibly refusing to bite.

'We need some champagne,' she continued, waving at a good-looking man who had just walked into the garden with some bottles of bubbly. I assumed this was Michael, although we still hadn't met. When Caitt left Thailand early to return to Sydney, he'd gone with her.

'Darling, come and meet the incomparable Zara!' she called out to him in a very loud voice, and with a great show of affection put an arm around my shoulders.

Heads turned in the garden. I saw Joe and his wife Sally, who waved. Sally took a camera from out of her bag and captured the moment as Caitt, Sergei and I stood like the best of old friends on the terrace.

Years later, a puzzled Sally took out that photo to show me, remarking, 'I'm not sure what happened.'

Out of the three of us, Sergei was the only one who could still be seen clearly. Caitt and I were indistinct, ambiguous figure, unidentifiable in every way.

The past is a foreign country. It's a much overused line, from the novel *The Go-Between* by L.P. Hartley, but I've always loved it. And these days I regret not asking Sally for a copy of that photo, because I now live in a foreign country and somehow that photo belongs here, too. I could have placed it in the crack by the window facing the road leading east, where people walk endlessly past through the dust.

There was still dust in the air that Sunday at Caitt's, whipped up as a result of the hot northwesterlies that had blown over the city the previous day. She and Michael lived in Sydney's Inner West, about twenty-five minutes' drive from our own place in a still semi-bohemian network of small streets in McMahons Point on the lower North Shore. Theirs was a surprisingly characterless house with an interior so bland and plainly furnished that I was astonished when I first saw it. Where were Caitt's theatrical instincts? There was far more atmosphere in the garden, despite the dust that we could all taste in our throats. I remember people joking later on in the afternoon that only champagne took the edge off the sense that we were inhaling parts of the desert.

It wasn't the dust that made the day so memorable, though. Nor was it the moment when Sally took the photo of the three of us on the terrace. It was what came later.

Sergei announced that he was going off to say hello to our host. He had to hurry to catch up with Michael, who was already heading back towards a door at the rear of the house, from where he'd originally appeared.

Caitt, who hadn't taken her eyes off Sergei, seemed about to follow him down into the garden when she was hailed by a woman with very short, bright red hair who had just walked through the French doors onto the terrace.

'Tobie! You're just in time!' Caitt exclaimed, beckoning the newcomer over.

'In time for what?' queried the redhead, who was wearing a tennis dress, or something very similar. It was white, it was short, and it showed off her legs.

'Just in time to keep Zara occupied,' replied Caitt.

'Zara, meet Tobie,' she added. 'My very good friend and genius computer consultant.'

Tobie chuckled, as if Caitt had said something funny.

'Not anymore,' she said obscurely. 'Hi, Zara. I saw you arriving. Your husband is very handsome. Caitt told me about him when she got back from Thailand.'

Her voice, smooth as silk, was filled with amusement.

I said nothing.

'Caitt and I go way back,' Tobie continued, after exchanging looks with her friend. 'We used to go on holidays together and chase men. We didn't mind if they were married or not. Remember that summer in Sicily, Caitt?'

'Do I!' exclaimed Caitt, and burst into laughter.

I saw Sergei glance in our direction. He was talking to Joe and Sally. All three were drinking champagne and I wondered where Michael was. I needed a drink, too! At exactly that moment, Caitt's husband walked through the French doors carrying more champagne and a couple of glasses, which he placed on a small table that had been set up on the terrace.

Caitt, who had her back turned to the French doors and seemed unaware of her husband's presence, grabbed Tobie's hand—and the pair of them took a step closer to me like two spiteful puppets.

'Tobie and I have a history of fishing for men. We catch them, play with them and then we throw them back,' she chanted.

'You *never* throw them back,' said Tobie, with emphasis. 'You keep reeling them back *in*.'

Striking a pose she began singing softly. 'Row, row, row our boat, gently down the stream. Merrily, merrily, merrily . . .'

Life is but a dream.

'I can get any man that I want with a snap of my fingers,' said Caitt with a swagger.

The atmosphere had changed. Something unpleasant was happening.

Tobie was grinning, but Caitt's whole demeanour had altered. She had become scornful and hard, and she repeated the line almost in anger.

'*I can get any man that I want with a snap of my fingers!*'

Then, just as suddenly, her laughter returned; flicking her hair back over her shoulders, she turned and walked down into the garden with Tobie in tow. Just before she reached Sergei, she looked back at me and briefly we stared at each other. At that moment I saw a woman standing in sunlight who seemed perfectly ordinary; perhaps, for a few seconds, she was the person she'd once been.

The sensation was very real, and made me wonder— not just then, but several times in the future—whether something had happened to Caitt earlier in her life, which had turned her into a predator.

I could have asked her, of course. Sometimes, when we were together, I sensed an underlying anxiety, a fear, an uncertainty about everything.

But I never did ask—and maybe that's why she showed me no mercy.

There were many more Sunday lunches at Caitt's. Sergei and I became a fixture at these feasts in the garden, until Caitt's invitations to us as a couple dried up. But the first lunch was easily the most memorable.

When she said that she could get any man that she wanted with a snap of her fingers, Caitt was being deadly serious in exactly the same way that she had been in Phang Nga Bay when she performed her come-hither routine in the canoe.

Every woman that I know, including my sisters, Lili and Eve, would only make such a remark as a joke. I was still musing over the incident when Michael came over and handed me a glass of bubbly and said, 'This is champagne! You drink it!'

He was friendly and funny, and completely different to Caitt; however, as we chatted about Thailand, I wondered what he had made of the scene that had just taken place on the terrace. I was also conscious that we were both watching his wife as she played up to Sergei at the edge of the lawn. When all of a sudden Caitt took Sergei's arm and led him away from the others towards the ground floor of the house, Michael paused mid-sentence before continuing with what he'd been saying.

A few minutes later, Caitt and Sergei walked out onto a long upstairs balcony running the length of the house.

I glanced at Michael. 'That's the balcony off our bed-room,' he said casually, his expression unreadable.

I think there's a good chance that Caitt plotted the balcony scene even before she left Thailand—because when she took a step forwards and held up a small object that flashed in the sun, I suddenly understood the point of the exercise.

At the sound of the dinner bell ringing from above, all the guests in the garden looked up.

'Hello, everyone. Finish your bubbly, because very shortly we're serving lunch!' she cried, once again linking arms with Sergei.

There was laughter and a scattering of applause. Caitt reacted to this by taking a bow. But the joke was on her unsuspecting audience, because she was thanking them for something entirely different.

An image had just been created of Caitt and Sergei that would stay etched in people's minds.

Their first official appearance as a couple.

The garden setting may not have been as spectacular as Phang Nga Bay although, in the bright sunlight that Sunday, everything seemed to have taken on extra dramatic appeal: the long wooden table, already set with wineglasses and plates, the deckchair in front of the Japanese bamboo.

As the buzz of conversation resumed below them, Caitt and Sergei left the balcony; shortly afterwards, Sergei came back out onto the terrace. Caitt, he said, was preparing pasta for lunch.

Michael went off to help her, and we joined Joe and Sally on the lawn.

I assumed that Caitt would relax after the triumph of her balcony scene. But I assumed wrongly.

At about the same time that everyone began to make a move towards the table, our hostess suddenly appeared with Tobie and Michael—all of them holding large bowls of pasta—and planted herself in front of Sergei. 'I want you to sit with me at the head of the table,' she said, handing him the huge bowl of linguine in her hands.

'Oh dear!' exclaimed Tobie in a loud voice. 'Where will you sit, Zara?'

At this, Sergei turned and gestured to me to join him—whereupon Caitt, who had already led him over to their seats, called out with a great show of solicitousness, 'Oh, Zara, you don't mind if I sit next to Sergei, do you? Will you be okay on your own?'

Even Sally, a scientist with an academic's dreamy demeanour—I constantly teased her about being away with the fairies—raised incredulous eyebrows when Caitt said this, and I think Caitt realised that she'd just made a mistake.

I didn't *need* to sit next to Sergei; he didn't need to sit next to me. I wasn't at all concerned about 'where' I would sit. Such an overt display of nastiness was instructive, although I was surprised at Caitt's apparent lack of concern about how others might regard such an obvious act of malice.

And perhaps I was making too much of the entire incident, since it seemed doubtful that anyone else took much notice of what had just happened. Most of those present, nearly all of whom turned out to be members of Caitt's extended family, were too busy talking.

'Zara, there's a seat here,' said Sergei, tapping the chair on his left. 'Come on!'

I didn't look at Caitt as I sat down next to my husband although, when I did glance her way, she was not looking pleased. By now everyone was sitting down and helping themselves to the pasta. Tobie seated herself on the opposite side of the table to me and, to my surprise, since I assumed she was there to cause mischief, promptly launched into an entertaining story about her new job as a tour guide for a company specialising in trips to the Baltic Republics.

Caitt tried—unsuccessfully—to distract Sergei's attention. But my husband, naturally, wanted to tell the story of how he and I had met en route to the Estonian capital when it was still under Kremlin control—and how I'd never made the rendezvous with the Swede.

'Of course, once she'd met me she forgot all about him,' Sergei added facetiously, leaving out the real facts of the story. 'Besides, Swedes can't compete with Russians in the bedroom.'

'I'll never know,' I commented, equally facetiously, at which point Caitt knocked over a bottle of red wine she'd just opened.

It was Tobie who jumped up and dashed off to find something with which to mop up the puddles of pinot between our bowls of seafood linguine, lemon rissoni and smoked salmon fusilli. So much for Caitt's concern about Sergei's cholesterol, I thought—although it didn't seem wise to say this aloud.

'What a waste of good wine, Caitt,' I said cheerfully, and was rewarded with a furious look from our hostess.

'Yes, it is,' agreed Sergei, getting to his feet. 'I'll go and fetch a couple more bottles.'

That was the first and last time Sergei and I sat together at one of Caitt's Sunday lunches. There were place cards at the second lunch we went to—and the third, and the fourth. On each occasion I was put safely out of the way at the far end of the table, but at the third lunch, Caitt put me next to a relative of hers, a single man who'd been divorced for a number of years and who, she said suggestively while introducing us, was looking for a new relationship.

At the end of the afternoon, after he'd left, she inquired whether he had taken my phone number.

There were no witnesses to this scene. There never were during those moments—and there were several—when Caitt allowed me glimpses of the twist in her personality.

It's part of the reason why I damn Caitt in this story far more than I do Sergei—because he did not have a poisonous nature and the cynicism he increasingly displayed towards life was partly caused by the damage that I did early on to our relationship. I'm certain of this.

The morning after I'd admitted to having an affair, I woke up next to him and saw to my shock that he was weeping. I'll never forget it. Nor what he said.

'What a waste.'

I am certain that it was this fatalism that in part drove his ultimate infatuation with Caitt. Sergei was a good man, who had once loved me unconditionally. My infidelity was his undoing.

To this day I can't decide whether Caitt's malevolence was due to some sort of desperation, or despair about how her life had played out, or whether she got a kick out of trying to unsettle me because that was just part of her nature. Even when she reached the stage of not caring anymore about crossing the line and making it obvious that she was throwing herself at Sergei, she was careful to keep in check the venom that I suspected she kept in reserve for any woman who got in her way—and which, in the end, she was unable to control.

I doubt that I was the first woman to have found herself in Caitt's way. In fact, I know it. But to provide any more details would be to betray someone who asked me never to repeat what she told me because, as she put it, she escaped from Caitt's grip—even if her own husband didn't.

All I can say is that this woman, who was married to a friend of Joe's, warned me about Caitt the first time we met. 'Be very careful before you let that one into your house,' she told me quietly.

Four years after that particular conversation, one sad evening as I was walking towards the large For Sale sign outside our house, I thought I caught a glimpse of the same woman in a car driving away down the street. Then, on the doorstep, I found a beautiful bunch of flowers with long stems; I particularly remember the long stems because I had to search out a vase in the packing.

There was no note with the flowers. But I knew who had left them. And why.

———— ✥ ————

The Sunday lunches became such a regular event that we soon structured our weeks around them. I didn't make a fuss about going to them, because I suspected that Caitt was hoping I would, and that any such reluctance on my part would play into her hands. My sister Lili, who lived in London and came to visit us in March, missed one of the lunches by only a day, because her departure date was a Saturday. This was probably fortunate, for while she was in Sydney she would 'meet' Caitt, without having a clue who she was—and would instinctively loathe her.

Lili came on her own, leaving her husband, Will, behind in London. He'd begged off the visit, pleading pressure of work. Lili and I joked in our emails to each other that, obviously, he had never recovered from his first visit to Australia, years earlier, when, looking increasingly haggard, he never stopped complaining about the noisiness of Australian birds at the crack of dawn.

The night before Lili was due to arrive, Sergei and I had our first argument about Caitt.

33

I had decided to have a break from work so I could spend time with my sister, and at breakfast that morning Sergei had suggested that the two of us should meet at the little wine bar a few streets away from our house where he met Joe most evenings after work for a glass of wine on the way home.

'It would be nice if you came with me for a change,' he added pointedly.

So I said yes, of course I would come—aware that I'd been spending long hours in my home office, reading through material for a new biography that my publisher was thinking of commissioning me to write.

The first person I saw when we walked into the wine bar was Caitt.

'There's Caitt,' I said, somewhat idiotically.

'Yes, she started coming to the wine bar a while back,' replied Sergei. 'We have a drink together most evenings.'

Caitt turned around at that moment and her dismayed expression told me everything. This was her territory with Sergei. I was the intruder. How dare I come here?

'And that's Clara,' said Sergei, as one of the women that Caitt had been talking to, turned around at the same time. 'She's one of the speech pathologists Caitt works with.'

'I didn't know you'd met Caitt's colleagues,' I commented. 'So they've just started coming to the wine bar as well?'

Before Sergei could reply, and before Caitt could stop her, Clara came over to where we were standing.

'Hi, Sergei,' she said, and added curiously, 'Who's this?'

'This is Zara,' said Sergei.

We shook hands. I had a fairly good idea what Clara would say next.

'How do you two know each other?'

'I'm married to Zara,' said Sergei, genuinely surprised.

Clara glanced towards Caitt. 'But I thought . . .'

She didn't finish the sentence.

A couple of people I knew from the publishing industry were at the other end of the wine bar, and I thought this might be a good moment to go and talk to them. So I did. Out of the corner of my eye I saw Caitt approach Sergei, embrace him briefly, and then leave. Clara left soon afterwards, after throwing a few more questioning glances my way.

'It seems that you and Caitt are regarded as a couple,' I said evenly, once we were back in the car, driving home.

'Not at all,' replied Sergei. 'It was just a misunderstanding. I always tell people about you.'

I knew that to be true. Sergei did tell people about me. But nor could I overlook Clara's reaction. It was blindingly obvious, I persisted, that Caitt was letting people think that they had a relationship.

The conversation went nowhere. Sergei refused to countenance the idea that Caitt was doing any such thing. 'Why would I ask you to come to the wine bar with me, if that was happening?' he asked. Sergei had a point, but giving in at this point wasn't possible.

'Because you're naive,' I answered. 'You can't see what's happening. Caitt is bringing her friends to the wine bar and introducing them to you, because she's trying to draw you into a life that's separate to the one you have with me.'

'Then you should come with me to the wine bar more often,' retorted Sergei, logically enough.

We spoke in monosyllables to each other for the rest of the evening.

However, by the time Lili arrived the next day, we'd forgotten our quarrel and the three of us spent Lili's first night in Sydney—a Monday—sitting up late, drinking champagne and talking about old times. When Sergei eventually went off to bed, Lili and I decided to ring our other sister, Eve, who lived in Shanghai. But the phone switched to voicemail and we left a drunken message instead.

We discussed ringing Lori, our older sister. But we knew that we wouldn't. And besides, she probably wouldn't pick up the phone. Lori led a quiet, reclusive life on her own in a small country town outside Sydney where she worked for a Christian charity organisation. She had kept herself at a distance from the rest of the family for years, a situation that saddened my parents although ever since Lori had joined a bizarre religious group in her twenties, she had been a difficult person to get on with. She stayed with the group for almost a decade before departing abruptly—giving no reasons—and moved to the town where she had lived ever since. Eve, Lili and I had all gone to see her on separate occasions, but it was obvious that Lori preferred her own company and after a while we had all stopped making the effort, opting to ring her occasionally instead. Lori never rang anyone. She remained aloof.

Once a year she would visit our parents, although never at Christmas, which was a relief. The only time Lori *had* come at Christmas, she had rebuked us for drinking champagne and sat grimly at lunch, without talking, as the rest of us pulled crackers and made rude remarks about turkeys.

It wasn't that we were disrespectful of Lori's religious beliefs; far from it. But as I once tried to explain to her, it was important to find joy in life, too. Lori had shaken her head when I said this, and rather than let old grievances surface—such as the way she had always ignored Sergei, on the rare occasions when we saw her, snorting at his accent whenever he spoke—I dropped the subject immediately.

Eve and Lili had similarly tried to get through to our sister, without success. Only once, when she suddenly turned up unexpectedly in Sydney and asked if she could come and stay for a few days did I wonder whether she might be lonely. But when I broached the subject as delicately as I could, she took great offence and once again I backed off. She startled me, though, by saying that she was considering becoming a nun. However, this hadn't eventuated.

'I'll ring Lori before I go back,' said Lili uncomfortably. 'It's too late to talk to her now, anyway.'

Which was true. We turned to other subjects in relief.

My spirits lifted, having Lili in the house. We took her out somewhere different every night, with the result that she begged Sergei to take her to the gym with him before she went off to stay for a few days with our parents who still lived on the peninsula north of Sydney.

'I haven't done any exercise all week, except pour myself huge glasses of champagne,' Lili quipped.

The following afternoon—a Wednesday—I dropped her off at the gym at 4 p.m. Sergei had organised for Lili to check in as his guest, and would meet her there later, after work. Then I went home to begin cooking. Some friends were going to join the three of us for dinner.

When my sister walked through the door a couple of hours later, I knew immediately that something was up.

'A weird thing happened,' she said as soon as Sergei had disappeared to take a shower. 'I went to the room where all the exercise machines were. The place was pretty much deserted. There was just some guy, and a girl who was leaving, and me. I was on the cross-trainer when a woman came in on her own. She just stood there and stared at me—and kept staring. I don't know what her problem was, but that look of hers was so awful that I crossed over to the other side of the room, and used the equipment there. I could feel her malevolence. It was coming off her in waves.'

I chose my words carefully.

'Then what happened?' I said.

'She got on the running machine and a few minutes later Sergei arrived, and that was the really off-putting part,' added Lili. 'Sergei knew her. The moment he walked in, she stopped exercising and went and kissed him hello. Sergei called out to me to come over. But I didn't. Who on earth is she, Zara? She didn't want to meet me—that much was obvious. She left almost immediately.'

I was trying to work out what to tell Lili, and was on the verge of giving her chapter and verse about Caitt, when Sergei walked into the kitchen and we both changed the subject.

At the end of the night, after our friends had left and Lili had gone off to make a phone call to Will, I asked Sergei whether Caitt had been at the gym.

'Yes. Did Lili tell you?' Sergei replied. 'Of course she wouldn't have known who Caitt was. I'd already told Caitt that Lili was there, and suggested she should go and say hi. You both look alike, so I knew she'd easily spot Lili.'

'But they didn't meet,' I pointed out.

'No, they didn't,' Sergei answered easily. 'Caitt had to go somewhere else. She said that she didn't want to interrupt Lili's exercise routine.'

Lili returned from her phone call at this point, excited about her conversation with Will. He'd told her that he'd found some beautiful old doors for the house that the two of them were restoring in the village of Gümüşlük, in Turkey. I forgot about Caitt, and got some more champagne from the fridge. We spent the rest of the evening toasting future holidays on the Aegean coast.

The following evening, Sergei and I drove Lili to the old family house in a beautiful if more distant part of the city, on the northern peninsula—or more precisely, on the cliff top at the northern end of Whale Beach. When we all moved to Australia from Canada, this was my parents' first choice of 'suburb', and there they stayed. A few days later, I drove back to the peninsula to collect my sister for the trip to the airport and her return to London and, while we were stuck in a traffic jam en route, she started talking again about the incident in the gym.

That was when I told Lili that the woman she'd seen was Joe's sister-in-law—married to his brother Michael—and that she and Sergei had become good friends.

Lili raised her eyebrows. 'She's not after Sergei, is she?' she demanded.

'Why do you say that?' I hedged, with a sideways glance at my sister.

'I forgot to tell you, but just before she left the gym she embraced Sergei and put her head on his chest and closed her eyes as if they were old lovers from way back. I mean, honestly! Does she always behave like that?'

'Well, yes,' I replied. 'She does. All the time.'

'Why do you put up with it, Zara? I wouldn't,' said Lili. 'Did you tell Sergei that I disliked her intensely on sight?'

'No. It would only cause tension,' I replied. 'I can get on with her and anyway, I don't feel I can tell Sergei not to see her anymore.'

'Why not?' Lili retorted, deliberately ignoring this reference to my own past. 'She's trouble.'

Luckily the traffic started moving again or else I might have blurted out that the situation with Caitt was by no means straightforward, and that nothing had been the same since we'd met her four months earlier. I had never told either of my sisters about what had happened in Thailand, and I didn't want to tell the story now, in a rush.

But later, driving away from the airport, I kept thinking. About the way Lili had reacted to a woman of whom she knew nothing when she'd first set eyes on her at the gym and, more to the point, about the word that she'd used when this woman, a complete stranger, had stared at her.

That was the extraordinary thing. Both Lili and I had exactly the same feeling on our first encounter with Caitt. For Lili, it was when Caitt walked into the gym. And me, when Caitt's canoe came around the peak in Phang Nga Bay.

Malevolence.

Everyone was taken aback when Michael and Caitt split up at the beginning of April. Certainly, Michael seemed to have been absent from home rather a lot, and he'd been missing at the last two Sunday lunches that Sergei and I had attended. But there was no reason to think that something was wrong. We knew that he often went away sailing for days at a time as part of his yacht brokerage business and Caitt seemed fine whenever we saw her.

Which was all the time.

Then, out of the blue, she announced that their marriage was over.

There was no animosity. No one else was involved. Michael hadn't met another woman. They would always remain friends.

At least, this is what Sergei told me when he got home early one evening from the wine bar. Caitt had arrived and given them the news, he added.

My immediate reaction was sympathy. The end of a marriage can be devastating, and perhaps this one had been deteriorating for a while without Caitt giving anything away. She may have been deeply unhappy but hiding her feelings from friends. It might even have explained her flirtatious behaviour with Sergei.

However, when I suggested that he ring her immediately and invite her to spend the evening with us, Sergei replied that Caitt had gone home to pack. She was going away the next morning to the Freycinet Peninsula in Tasmania for a break.

We didn't see Caitt for the next fortnight. Then one Saturday morning, we were having a coffee at a neigh-bourhood cafe when Caitt suddenly walked past. She was accompanied by a girl of about seventeen, a stranger I hadn't seen before.

Sergei jumped up and called out to them, but Caitt kept walking—unusually fast—until he hailed her so loudly that she had to turn around.

Hadn't she seen us? Apparently not.

To my surprise, her pretty companion greeted Sergei warmly and then looked at me, obviously puzzled—whereupon Caitt introduced us in an oddly rushed manner. 'Zara, this is my god-daughter, Caroline,' she said, adding urgently in the same breath, 'Zara is married to Sergei.'

'Really?' said Caroline, clearly startled. Her discomfort at the situation was telling. She thought that Sergei was her godmother's new boyfriend; it was written all over her face.

It was also clear that Caitt was panicking. The last thing she wanted was for Sergei to catch on. If he realised that Caroline was under such an impression, then Caitt would have some explaining to do.

I wasn't surprised when Caitt pleaded some urgent shopping as an excuse not to join us for coffee.

Only when she and her bemused god-daughter were gone did Sergei explain that Caitt had phoned him a couple of days earlier, asking if she could borrow one of his cameras while Caroline was over from London. Her own camera was broken, she had explained. He had dropped off the camera on his way home the next evening, which was when he'd met Caroline, he added. 'Perhaps we should have them over for dinner,' he then suggested.

I couldn't refuse, for how could I tell Sergei what I'd observed? A certain look on a teenager's face? Caitt's consternation? The way in which she had almost gabbled that he was married to me?

We duly invited the two of them over to dinner—and that night, I met a dramatically different Caitt. Gone was her flirtatious, suggestive manner with Sergei, her habit of acting as if there was no one else with him. She behaved normally, and with great warmth towards me, as did Caroline.

I can only speculate that Caitt must either have confided in her god-daughter about her game plan—which was unlikely—or had pleaded some temporary bad behaviour, because she'd been so unhappy with a marriage on the rocks and a husband ready to leave home. Ultimately there's no way of knowing what she told Caroline and it's not relevant to the story.

The dinner is, however, because it marked the moment when Caitt changed her tactics. For the next few months, she worked diligently to create the impression that she and Sergei were no more than good friends. She did this in public, but also in private, in front of me, whenever she came over for dinner or we saw her socially. This was the period when, as I've already written, there were moments when I sometimes imagined that we'd become allies.

Perhaps she even thought the same about me. Perhaps, in other circumstances, we *could* have become friends.

Consequently, it didn't seem untoward when she mentioned one day that her regular tennis partner was being posted overseas, and asked Sergei if he would play tennis with her on Saturday afternoons instead.

Caitt knew perfectly well that I liked to spend that time writing, and that I probably wouldn't object. And I didn't. It was about the only time of the week when I could sit down over fragments of writing—separate from my work—that I hoped were slowly turning into a novel.

Little did I know how I would come to dread the solitude and shadows of an empty house. Nor how much time I would spend reflecting on the part I played, however unintentionally, in shutting Sergei out during all those weekends when I entered the realm that all writers know: total immersion in a place where fiction and life merge.

I thought he understood the 'illness' of writers: that we have to write, and that we write despite everything, and that the act of writing is necessarily selfish. Besides, Sergei had his own artistic pursuits, too. He would often disappear for hours on end with his cameras and photograph the sea and the landscape.

I thought that we understood each other.

By the end of May, the Saturday afternoon tennis games had settled into a routine. Caitt let me know from the start that she and her previous partner always played doubles with the same couple, and that this pair didn't want to change the arrangement. I realised this was her way of letting me know I wasn't welcome to join in—which contradicted the idea, of course, that we'd become allies. But it also meant I could use the time to write.

Caitt wasn't a common-or-garden seductress. Her 'ownership' of Sergei beggared belief. Over time I began to question her emotional stability, but in many other respects she was more 'normal' than I was, in the sense that she had a more practical nature. I remember being totally bemused by a conversation that I had with her once, about the benefits of having a phone app to keep track of her spending.

Bemused, because many writers merely pretend to understand the strings attached to everyday life, and I was no different.

Caitt did not live in her imagination as I did a lot of the time. She did not forget to shop for dinner. Or to put petrol in the car. And she knew how to change the cartridge in the printer, which always ran out of ink because of my aversion to poking under the bonnet or lid of anything.

Printer, car, pressure cooker.

More importantly, Caitt never left anything to chance. Men, especially.

The tennis courts where they played were next to a gym, and in no time at all, Caitt suggested to Sergei that the two of them should join up. This gym had a better swimming pool, she said, and they could use the change rooms to shower after tennis rather than wait until they went home.

I realised that this was a ploy, a way of bringing Sergei closer into her orbit. I belonged to a gym in the city and Caitt knew this—and knew it was unlikely that I would change memberships. She was right. Apart from anything else—as she also knew—I rarely swam in swimming pools, preferring to swim in the ocean. Sergei loved the sea, too, and before he started vanishing at weekends for hours at a time—in the latter part of 2006—we often went for a swim together when he came back after tennis in the late afternoons, driving to Manly and walking along the beach afterwards once the crowds had begun to thin out, and when the light started to soften and the waves hit the sand with a particular rhythm.

Caitt occasionally accompanied us when we went ocean swimming. So the gym change-room excuse was a bit weak. In the meantime, she had a beach of her own planned for Sergei, one hidden away in Middle Harbour and where no one they knew would see them. I'm guessing that eventually they started going there straight from the gym, by which time Sergei and I were spending more and more time apart.

Coincidentally, Sergei had often taken me to the same beach. It lay in a pretty curve of cliffs, with pale grey rocks and a lagoon at one end. I'd seen a painting of it once, years earlier, and it turned out to be just as magical. I love swimming, but can only lie on a towel for so long before I get bored, even with a good book. This little beach, though, I loved. It had wild flowers, and the only noise came from the gulls and the cries from the sea eagles we occasionally spotted circling in the sky overhead.

When Sergei suddenly seemed to lose interest in keeping up our trips to that beach, I didn't think anything of it, even though it was quicker to go there than to Manly. Then, one weekend, I suggested that instead of sharing the ocean with half the city, given the crowds that Manly attracted, we should revisit our enchanted beach instead.

Sergei went blank. He didn't answer. At the time I put it down to lack of interest. No big deal. It never occurred to me that it could have something to do with Caitt.

We saw her a lot. More often than not, we socialised for part of each weekend with Michael's ex-wife. If she missed her marriage and Michael, she never said so.

But as time went on, she started to have more and more difficulty controlling her emotions when I was around.

One night Sergei and I went out for dinner with Caitt and one of her temporary boyfriends—whom she went on to virtually ignore for the entire evening. The four of us arrived at the restaurant at exactly the same time and were shown to a small table for four people. I took the chair next to Sergei, and Caitt's boyfriend took the one opposite him. Caitt, white with anger, pushed the remaining chair away from her, hard.

She did this so forcefully that a waiter came over and asked if anything was wrong. Aware that Sergei and her boyfriend were also looking at her askance, Caitt went into damage control and claimed that she thought she'd seen a spider on the seat of the chair. She even managed a forced laugh. Sergei looked at her strangely but said nothing. Caitt avoided looking at me altogether. The atmosphere remained strained and I think we were all relieved once dinner was over and we could go our separate ways. She broke off the 'relationship' with her boyfriend the next day.

This incident marked the moment when our civility to each other began to slide. I think Caitt was put out by my presence that night because, by this stage, she and

Sergei had begun having the occasional meal together if I happened to be away overnight—as I had been a few times, interviewing people in preparation for the new biography that my publisher had indeed commissioned me to write.

Sergei told me from the start about his dinners with Caitt. They ate in the brasserie that was attached to the wine bar, so it wasn't as if they went anywhere special, he said—for the first time sounding a touch defensive about his friendship with Caitt.

We had just entered the danger zone, and still I didn't react. Apart from anything else, Sergei always rang me whenever he got home from these 'dates'. I knew that he disliked being at home on his own, and that he needed people around him. He had always been an extremely sociable man, and it wasn't a problem, in the same way that my work sometimes took me away from home, and this wasn't a problem, either. Or so it had always seemed.

I wouldn't have dreamed of questioning his whereabouts whenever he rang me, which obviously worked to Caitt's advantage. The irony, of course, is that it was Caitt who would turn out to be extraordinarily possessive.

And yet I kept resisting any kind of confrontation and even made excuses for her to our friends, who distrusted Caitt and had started to say so. She was lonely, I said. Her marriage had ended. Sergei was a gallant Russian, and she missed male company. She was lively, a good conversationalist, and could be good fun.

'No,' said a close friend of ours one evening, watching Caitt thoughtfully as she snuggled up to Sergei in full view of everyone who had come over to our place that night to celebrate his birthday. 'She is not good fun. I feel uneasy just being in the same room with her.'

I remember how startled I was when he said this. Our friend was an unemotional pragmatist, not given to making melodramatic statements—nor to exaggerating situations.

And yet, as ever, I pushed his remark away—just as I tried to block out another, even more disturbing image.

Later that night, coming back from the little room downstairs where we kept our bottles of wine, I saw Caitt in the study clutching a framed photo of Sergei and me that usually sat on his desk. She didn't notice as I paused in the doorway; she never knew that I caught my breath when I saw her.

Even at that point I didn't react as most women would have, by confronting her for once and for all. Instead I stole away with the wine I was holding and went back to the part of the house where everyone was talking and laughing, back to an atmosphere of normality that increasingly seemed only to exist when friends were over, because of the distance that had begun growing between Sergei and me.

Whenever I had tried talking to him about what seemed to be happening between us, he refused to discuss it. We had started having fights about nothing. We no longer made love. We hadn't, for several months. When he told me long afterwards that he had discussed our intimate life with Caitt, I was appalled.

The night that I spotted her in the study with our photo would turn out to be the last time she came to our house.

For weeks afterwards, I tried to convince myself that what I'd seen had been an illusion, a trick of lighting— just as I had in Phang Nga Bay, when her face changed so suddenly.

The lamps in the study had been turned low. There were shadows; it was late; she'd been drinking.

So it must have been fatigue that I saw, not ferocity.

But once again, I'm getting ahead of the story.

———— ✢✢ ————

At 11 p.m. one night at the end of July, Sergei collapsed.

We were at home, getting ready for bed, when he suddenly went pale and moaned; he managed to say that he was in incredible pain and that his head was splitting, before his legs buckled beneath him.

There had been no warning beforehand that anything was wrong. Sergei hadn't said he felt ill, or even that he felt nauseous. The agony he was in became much worse as I grabbed the phone to call an ambulance and I remember that my voice shook so much that momentarily I had to stop speaking in order to control it.

The journey to hospital was a nightmare. Even now, I hate the sound of an ambulance siren. The grim expressions of the two paramedics tending to Sergei frightened me, and I kept asking them why they couldn't give him some pain relief, since he was obviously in terrible distress. Maybe they did, but my memory is blank.

Sergei had suffered a bleed in the stem of his brain. Exactly why this happened would remain a mystery. His doctors found no sign of aneurysms, as is often the case in such circumstances. Not knowing the cause would never cease to be troubling.

Ultimately, he would make a good recovery after spending almost a month in hospital, which included a nerve-racking ten days in the neurosurgery intensive care unit. I spent most of those ten days by his side—and I didn't leave the hospital at all for the first forty-eight hours. Only after the medical staff said they were satisfied that Sergei's condition had stabilised did I go back to the house to grab a couple of hours sleep.

'Get some rest. You're exhausted,' said the same nurse who had wrapped a blanket around me as I stood numbly in ICU that first night—or rather, in the early hours of the morning—while Sergei was surrounded by medical staff.

It was close to noon when I arrived home, and I was immediately struck by the notion that I had come to the wrong house. I remember standing outside in the warm winter sunshine, shivering despite the coat I was wearing, and wondering why I had the sensation that someone else lived here.

The house itself didn't look any different. A colony of tiny lizards lay sunbaking, as usual, in the cracks in the stone steps up to the front door. It had been an unusually warm winter and the temperature today was twenty-four degrees. I wondered, all of a sudden, how many summers we had left as a couple, and then immediately tried to pull myself together. Where on earth had that thought come from?

I banished it as I unlocked the door and stumbled inside, feeling utterly alone—and worn out from feeling so alone.

It was a feeling that encompassed far more than what had just happened to Sergei. It was the whole situation between us. A tension existed that seemed to have no basis in anything. The two of us had always had passionate arguments about every subject under the sun, and I could be as infuriatingly stubborn about my point of view as Sergei could be about his. But our arguments now were different. There was no point to them. He had become critical of me in a way he never had been previously, treating almost everything I said with scorn. For some time I'd been feigning a calmness that I certainly didn't feel, not least because Caitt had begun ringing Sergei most evenings, usually around the time we were eating dinner.

One night she rang on the landline and I picked up. Her brusque, dismissive tone of voice annoyed me intensely. 'Zara, is Sergei there? His phone is switched off.'

The conversation between them on that occasion didn't seem to have much point. I remember Sergei grunted his way through it, saying merely, 'Okay, let's talk tomorrow,' before hanging up.

Fed up, I challenged him. 'What was so important that Caitt had to ring yet again when we're having dinner? Didn't she get to spend enough time with you at the wine bar this evening?'

My sarcasm infuriated him. 'We're friends!' he replied. 'She can ring whenever she likes!'

Caitt also emailed him constantly. I had only discovered this when Sergei had his laptop open on the dining room table one evening, and started chuckling over a cartoon she'd just sent him.

'Come and see it,' he called out.

'You had twelve emails from Caitt just today?' I asked incredulously, scanning the inbox over his shoulder.

'So what?' Sergei retorted. 'What's the matter with you?'

Now, in our silent house, in the bedroom where he had collapsed, I told myself to stop it—stop dredging up all of this stuff. There had been a moment in hospital when Sergei reached for my hand as a nurse injected him with morphine. So he hadn't forgotten he loved me, I'd thought. But now, in our bedroom, I felt that I was fooling myself.

The idea of sleep seemed impossible. All the same, I kicked off my shoes and lay down on the bed, with both our phones next to me. I'd left Sergei's phone behind when I'd rushed with the medicos out to the ambulance and it was still lying beside the bed when I got home. I hadn't checked it for missed calls.

Somehow I dozed off while still vaguely aware of a church bell tolling somewhere in the distance. A wedding? A christening? A funeral? I had opened the bedroom windows wide when I first came in, needing to feel fresh air on my face. Finally I was starting to calm down.

Then Sergei's phone started ringing and I sat up with a start.

The disdainful voice at the other end of the line—the flash of memory—made me gasp.

'What are *you* doing, answering Sergei's phone?'

It was Thailand all over again.

'I've been calling Sergei for the past twenty-four hours,' she went on. 'I'm worried about him. You don't happen to know where he is, by any chance, Zara?'

Why on earth didn't I hang up then?

I did hang up—but only after I had answered her question. 'He collapsed. He's in hospital. He's stable. He can't see anyone except me.'

And then I slammed down the phone.

It was impossible to sleep after that. I got up and drove back to the hospital—where I stayed for most of the next ten days, as I've said. My visits home were fleeting. I put my work on hold.

Finally, Sergei was moved to a room of his own in the 'step-down' section of ICU. Only then did I race into the city early one morning to the one place I knew where I could lock myself away and work in absolute peace. The 'eyrie' was a city office belonging to an old friend, a human rights lawyer who was constantly travelling overseas and who had been generous enough to give me a key. I went in there often to write; now I needed to collect some research material as well as a couple of books, before going directly to the hospital. At this time of the morning it had been quicker to drive than take the train.

It wasn't yet nine o'clock when I arrived back in the wing where Sergei was being cared for. One of the nurses on duty that morning saw me walking along the corridor and called me over to the desk.

'Sergei has a visitor,' she said. 'She turned up about five minutes ago. A woman. The same one, it turns out, who has been ringing here every day. She was very insistent about seeing him and became quite upset when I said that you're the only visitor he's allowed. In the end I said she could have three minutes only. Her time is up.'

'Thanks,' I said. 'I think I know who it is.'

The nurse gave me a questioning look, then glanced at the clock on the wall.

'Make sure she leaves,' she said. 'I shouldn't have let her in at all.'

'Yes,' I replied. 'I will.'

Sergei's room was just around the corner. Even though I knew Caitt would be there, I was still shocked by the scene that confronted me. Sergei was sitting on the side of his bed, in his hospital gown, looking dejected. Caitt had her back to the doorway. She was standing so close to him that their two bodies were almost touching. As I watched, she put one hand on her hip and with the other began stroking Sergei's head. He tried half-heartedly to brush her hand away but, as he did so, Caitt grabbed his hand and held it. Then she bent down and kissed him with great tenderness on the forehead.

I always knew that sooner or later I would see something happen between Caitt and Sergei that would be a defining moment, one where I knew that I had to stop giving her the benefit of the doubt. But when it came, I wasn't prepared for it and stood there frozen, feeling utter desolation. And shock.

Sergei caught sight of me then, and smiled wanly.

'Hi,' he said. 'Where have you been?'

Caitt spun around. She didn't look in the least embarrassed. Just irritated.

'For heaven's sake, Zara! Why are you here so early? Sergei needs to rest. Come along, I'll give you a lift home. Or did you drive over?'

She picked up her bag and the long black coat that she had slung over a chair and gestured for me to move back into the hallway. I felt a tap on my shoulder at the same time. Behind me stood one of Sergei's specialists. A bluntly spoken man, who I suspect could see immediately what was happening—having probably dealt with similar situations many times in his career—he didn't bother with niceties.

'Out!' he said. 'You can come back in a few minutes,' he added, to me.

'You can't,' he said to Caitt, who looked stunned.

She pushed past me, not meeting my eyes.

I went over to Sergei and gave him a quick kiss. 'Back in a sec,' I said.

Wrapped in her executioner's coat, Caitt was waiting outside in the corridor. We walked side by side in silence, as far from the nurses' station as possible, and then we both halted. It was yet another odd moment, when I think we both silently acknowledged an odd kind of sympathy for the other.

But then I saw that cold, hard look return to Caitt's face—the one she never let anyone else see. And because—as ever—there were no witnesses, she didn't measure her words.

'I want to explain my philosophy to you, Zara. Not right now. I'm too upset about Sergei. But you and I need to have a discussion in the very near future. I realise that you care about Sergei, but how often *aren't* you there for him? I'll accept for now that you'll try to look after him. However, this is a temporary situation. Sergei's health is now my priority.'

I let her finish. I remained perfectly composed. One of the best things about being a writer is that I know how to self-edit.

'Goodbye, Caitt,' I said. 'I must get back to Sergei.'

And I turned and started walking back to his room, supremely aware that several seconds went by before I heard the clicking of her heels going in the opposite direction.

We both knew that she had just declared war.

⸺⸺⧫⸺⸺

Back in Sergei's room, I sat down on his bed next to him. The specialist had left. 'I think Caitt's in love with you,' I said.

'I think you're right,' Sergei replied.

It was the only time he ever admitted this to me. Later he would always deny that he had ever said such a thing.

During the months that followed, a false calm descended. A false peace if you like. Both Caitt and I knew perfectly well that a line had been crossed in the hospital corridor, although all she said, the next time she saw me, was, 'My feelings got the better of me that morning.'

We both let the subject drop. I don't think either of us wanted a confrontation right then because, ironically, neither of us wanted to cause Sergei any stress. I knew that Caitt was merely biding her time, and I knew as well that she would 'cooperate' with me so that I wouldn't banish her from the house.

So whenever she came over she was careful not to overdo the languishing looks, or the lingering looks, or the wistful if-only glances, that were part of her repertoire.

Still, the false peace couldn't last—and it didn't. Caitt could only keep up her act of appeasement for so long.

The incident in the study, when I discovered her staring at the photo of Sergei and me, took place in September, about six weeks after Sergei was allowed out of hospital. That night—his birthday night—he was almost back to his old self. We had cooked his birthday party dinner together, and he had even given me a hug once or twice. His health scare had shaken him. 'I feel diminished,' he'd said, the first night he was home.

But he'd been given the thumbs-up by his doctors after a second checkup only a week before his birthday, and for the first time in ages he was relaxed. It was good to watch him laughing and joking, even though Caitt spent most of the evening, as ever, trying to monopolise his attention.

I know exactly what triggered that scene in the study.

After the main meal, I had come out of the kitchen with a birthday cake and was bringing it across the room to the table, when one of our friends asked Sergei if he'd been able to eat the hospital food. Sergei replied that I'd sneaked some piroggi into his room, so he'd survived. Just.

There was laughter. Then someone else commented to me that it must have been terrifying, the night he collapsed. As I said yes, and tried to describe the awfulness of those first forty-eight hours, Sergei suddenly reached out and put an arm around my waist, drawing me to his side. It was as if we had suddenly been transported back to a past when we were still happy together. Leaning into him, I felt for a moment that we were a couple again.

Automatically, I glanced at Caitt, who was sitting on Sergei's right. She had gone rigid, just as she had when Sergei put his arm around my waist in our canoe in Thailand. Her mouth was working and her hands, clenched on the table, had become fists. For one moment I really thought she was going to leap to her feet and push me away from Sergei, just as she'd pushed the chair away in the restaurant. I could almost physically feel her wanting to do it.

But then her eyes went to Sergei and her furious expression was replaced by the bizarre, bewildered look that I had also come to know well. *How could you?* she seemed to be saying.

The moment passed. Conversation around the table resumed. Caitt put on a frightful smile, picked up Sergei's hand and held it to her cheek. And later on, I caught her in the study, with our photo . . .

She left before anyone else that night, pleading a headache. Days went by. No visits from Caitt. No phone calls, either—at least not to the house. Towards the end of the month, I asked Sergei whether she had gone into retirement, since she hadn't been over since his birthday dinner. 'A joke!' I said innocently, when he looked irritated by the question.

He'd seen her a few times for a drink, he said, after a moment. And Tobie, too, he added.

As it happened, I had been invited to a book launch the following evening, which Sergei had said he would skip. No doubt it was because of the conversation with him about Caitt that, at the last minute, I changed my mind about going to the launch and rang Sergei at his office, suggesting that we go out for dinner instead.

'Let's meet somewhere.' Then I added, 'And not at the wine bar.'

'There's nothing wrong with the wine bar,' replied Sergei. 'Anyway, Caitt invited me for a quick meal at her place. I'll let her know that we're both coming.'

'Since when has she been inviting you over for dinner?' I asked immediately.

'She did a couple of times, before I became ill. You were off somewhere, working as usual. And why can't she invite me? What's wrong with that?'

His tone had become unusually aggressive.

'You didn't mention you'd been having meals at her house. And I've noticed that she hasn't invited the two of us over to her place for quite a while.'

'She has been very busy.'

'But not too busy, apparently, to invite you on your own.'

How I hated arguing with him like this.

'Don't try to restrict me,' Sergei replied.

'Look, there's nothing in it,' he added. But there was a hesitation in his voice that I noticed. 'I'll ring you back.'

When you've lived with someone for a very long time, and especially if English isn't that person's first language, you become used to the way they use words and phrases and structure their sentences. Sergei had never used this phrase—'Don't try to restrict me'—before. It didn't flow when he said it. It didn't sound like him at all.

He rang back within minutes. I knew what he was going to say, even before I picked up.

'Caitt said she wasn't expecting you, so it's better for the three of us to eat out.'

'Fine,' I replied calmly. 'Where are we meeting?'

Somehow I wasn't surprised, when I arrived at the cafe he'd suggested, to find Sergei nursing a glass of wine on his own. Caitt wouldn't be able to join us for dinner. Apparently something had come up.

'What?' I asked.

Sergei shrugged. 'She didn't say.'

For all his apparent lack of interest, I could see that Caitt's abrupt change of mind had unsettled him, and I think that this was because he knew perfectly well why she had changed her mind—although he wasn't going to admit as much to me.

I saw the same, unsettled look on his face a fortnight later. We had just come home from the party about which I've already written: when I interrupted our host's dangerous liaison with Caitt in the hallway upstairs, the host being Leo, the husband saved from committing adultery on the spot by a brilliantly if frustratingly designed red dress.

I told Sergei about the incident. The story rattled him—it was obvious—but he sprang to Caitt's defence all the same.

'She'd had too much to drink, that was all. She has been flat out all week organising a charity function in aid of the kids she works with. It's the first time in days that she has relaxed,' he added.

Not for the first time, I was made aware of an ongoing, daily dialogue between Sergei and Caitt. It seemed that he knew everything that was happening in her life. It seemed pointless to tell him the rest of the story, about Caitt's expression of triumph when I finally walked out of the bathroom after lingering inside for as long as I dared, to find her standing alone in the hall. That expression was her way of putting me on notice: Sergei next.

'She wants me to go to the function,' said Sergei, interrupting my thoughts.

'Aren't we both invited?' I asked pointedly.

'You'll probably be working,' Sergei replied.

This was new—both the remark, and the accusing note in his voice. I didn't work all the time and, up until Caitt entered our life, Sergei had always accepted that my job, like his, sometimes required periods of intense concentration.

The subject was dropped. And we went to the charity event together.

I admit I was curious to see Caitt in her 'other' life. Would she be any different in manner? It turned out that the evening would include a game of charades. Each speech pathologist would assume an identity and the guests had to guess who it was. Caitt, announced Sergei, as we arrived at the function, had decided to be Batwoman. Some of the kids were going to the function as well and she knew that the Batwoman character was a favourite of theirs.

'We'll get to see Caitt's natural instincts for comedy then,' I commented. It was probably fortunate that his phone rang at the same time.

'She's nervous,' he said afterwards.

No need to ask who 'she' was.

'Really?' I replied in a tone of wonder.

Sergei looked at me sharply but evidently decided not to push it.

The evening turned out to be pleasant enough. Naturally we sat at Caitt's table and naturally Caitt sat next to Sergei. She was dressed all in white and looked very glamorous and monopolised Sergei as usual. But when it came time for the game of charades, I felt almost sorry for her because no one could work out who she was trying to be. People sat in their seats looking bewildered.

Caitt started out by mouthing the word 'bat' and pretended to put on a mask. Then she did lots of furling and unfurling of an imaginary cape. I only knew it was a cape because of my 'inside' knowledge, of course. Otherwise I suspect I would have been as mystified as everyone else as Caitt strode up and down in front of the tables of guests, throwing back her hair and striking various poses. At one point she went down in a half squat, then leapt up in such dramatic fashion that I almost called out, '*Crouching Tiger, Hidden Dragon?*'

At another stage she looked directly at Sergei and me and at that exact moment, Sergei happened to reach over and push back a stray piece of my hair.

It threw Caitt off balance, noticeably so. And as she faltered mid-sentence, I wriggled my shoulders.

She saw it. She got it. She smiled unpleasantly.

And I knew that she was sending me a warning.

At the end of the evening it was Sergei who suggested we not hang around afterwards and join Caitt for a drink somewhere instead. 'I didn't know that was part of the plan,' I commented.

'It was. Sort of,' he answered, and then relapsed into silence.

We were still in the car driving home when he said suddenly, 'She isn't very good.'

I could have replied that, on the contrary, Caitt was very good indeed at playing charades. But I was more preoccupied with the look she had given me—and the three words that I could almost have sworn had formed in her mouth when I wriggled my shoulders.

Just you wait.

⸺✥⸺

Sergei recovered his health. But his near miss with mortality had a profound and enduring effect on him. Our new-found closeness didn't last long; well before the end of that year it had become obvious that his attitude towards life, towards me and towards the future had changed irrevocably.

I have no doubt that Sergei's vulnerability, caused by what had happened to him, was part of the reason for the change in his personality. It certainly played a part in the events that followed. I remember being stunned when he suddenly said out of a clear blue sky after we'd come home on Christmas Eve—after spending part of the evening with friends—that our house and everything we owned together would always be ours and no one else's. He repeated that last line almost angrily.

'What do you mean?' I asked him. 'Where is this coming from?'

'Sometimes I might not live here. I might end up not living with you all of the time. But I'm not leaving either, and I expect you to keep living in the house,' he replied.

When I asked whether this meant we were splitting up, he avoided giving any answers and then, in some awful

62

accident of timing, Lili rang from London to say she suspected Will was having an affair.

I replaced the receiver after the conversation, feeling as if all our lives had suddenly turned upside down. And everything became even stranger as we went through the ritual of Christmas Day and Boxing Day at my parents' house—staying on the peninsula with them—before returning to the city on December 27.

Friends were arriving to spend the rest of the week with us. We got through the days by putting on a good act in front of them, and spent New Year's Eve at a party—sans Caitt—with our house guests.

But it felt as if we were merely fulfilling a pattern of living together because that's what our marriage had become. We had a relationship, and we didn't. Only a few days into 2007, Sergei suddenly informed me that he wanted to spend more time at the weekends with other people. I defiantly declared that I'd do the same thing. We barely saw each other for the rest of January.

I think that ultimately we might have managed to survive Caitt, if it hadn't been for Sergei's brain bleed. It was certainly the primary trigger behind his decision to have an affair—as he himself would admit. The possibility of death had given shape to the disillusionment that had been part of Sergei's makeup since childhood. This was it, he said, when he first got home from hospital. Proof that life had no real point.

And then all of a sudden, from the end of January onwards, I was spending hardly any time at home anymore.

Someone else desperately needed all of my attention—the motionless figure whose bedside I'd been at almost permanently since the moment when I had raced out of the house with the car keys in hand, seconds after a frantic phone call from Dad, and only minutes ahead of a newsflash about an accident that had just taken place on the northern peninsula.

A middle-aged woman had been hit by a car that had sped towards her without stopping as she was crossing a road.

Lori. Our sister.

For weeks she lay in an induced coma in an intensive care unit, terribly injured. The police never found the driver who did this to her. The car had been stolen and was eventually discovered, burnt out, on a road leading off one of the freeways that seemed to go on forever west of the city.

She would spend the rest of the summer, and autumn, and part of winter, in hospital. Eve and Lili flew immediately to Australia to help keep vigil by her bedside—and made return visit after return visit after return visit. In the early days, following the accident, we practically lived in ICU— my parents, my sisters and I—until Lori was allowed to come back to life. We were focused on trying to make her aware that she wasn't alone, especially after seeing her tears as she took in her surroundings, once she had recovered consciousness.

Whenever my sisters temporarily returned to the lives we'd all put on hold, I often went back to my parents' house with my devastated parents and slept there.

Sergei told me right from the beginning that he couldn't bear the sight of my sister lying motionless in ICU, especially after his own stint in hospital—and I understood that, but I still wished that he would come with me to see Lori more often. He came only a few times, usually on a Saturday afternoon, and only if it was 'my' hour to visit, but he always seemed to be in a hurry to get away before my sisters or parents arrived. And if I rang him in the evenings, on the nights when I stayed with my parents, he rarely answered his phone, although he would always ring back by midnight.

I didn't want to think about Caitt, or what might be happening. So it came as a shock when I realised that my mother, with her unerring instincts, had guessed that Sergei and I were adrift.

I know that, because one evening Sergei surprised me by phoning and saying that he'd meet me at my parents' house on the peninsula—and when he walked in, my mother's face lit up with relief and she said, 'It's lovely to see you.'

Neither of us wanted to disillusion her.

This was in March, just after Lori had been moved into the step-down unit of intensive care and had begun to speak weakly but clearly. For the first time in years, we saw a softness return to her face as it began to sink in that she still had a family who cared about her. One night I watched as she hugged our parents—and saw a sense of peace envelop all three of them.

Grief, and relief, can fine-tune the senses, and I think this might have been why I finally phoned Sergei and asked him whether he was having an affair with Caitt—and he said yes.

I no longer knew the man I'd lived with for so long, and this, as I've already described, had been the case for some time. Even before his affair with Caitt began, Sergei had started flying into rages for no reason. Or else he would simply act as if I wasn't present, becoming remote and withdrawn to the point where he had turned into a stranger—most of all, I suspect, a stranger to himself.

Even so, it was me whom he rang early one evening when he was clearly in shock. I had just left the hospital and was on my way home. Lili, in Sydney for three weeks, was keeping Lori company. Sergei told me that he'd just shouted at a woman after she had left her car partially blocking our driveway. Horrified when he saw fear in her face, he'd gone back inside the house, shaking. 'What is happening to me?' he asked.

Despite the mystifying changes in his behaviour, I was completely thrown by this phone call. Sergei had always been the kind of man who drew people to him, who delighted in the company of others. He had a generosity of spirit and a unique personality that captivated everyone he met. He was also a very kind person, one who treated women with an old-fashioned gallantry. His friends, male and female, loved him.

Nothing he'd just said made any sense.

Was Sergei's tendency towards melancholy resurfacing? He had once told me that his father had suffered a depressive illness for years. Amazingly, and probably because what had happened to Lori was taking up most of my energy, I didn't immediately think of Caitt as being the cause of his mood swings, although this probably sounds contradictory.

I know now that she was a lot more manipulative than I had wanted to believe. But I am also convinced that part of Sergei's behaviour was due to his own emotional turmoil about having an affair in the first place.

At one stage later on he rang Eve—after I'd let both my sisters know what was happening—and said that he hated what his affair with Caitt was doing to me. 'Then stop it,' said Eve. But he didn't—not then, anyway. There's good reason to believe that having an affair was causing Sergei a great deal of anguish, while at the same time rekindling memories of the anguish I'd caused him when I'd had an affair. Emotionally, it was incredibly complicated for both of us.

The right time will come in this story when I'll be able to explain what I mean. But not yet.

Long before I knew the truth about Sergei and Caitt, I had asked Sergei if they were sleeping together. Sergei was outraged at the question—and so was Caitt, he said later, when he repeated to her what I'd said.

'We think you have a sick imagination,' he added.

His condemnation hit hard. Before Caitt came along, I had never been suspicious of other women. I wasn't the type. Sergei had a number of female friends, whom I'd always considered friends of mine as well. I would have considered it unnatural if he'd had no women friends!

So when he did finally confess—and added that they were, indeed, already having an affair when I'd first asked him the question—I was devastated that someone who usually never lied, and had always been the most straightforward of men, would have come out with such a twisted response. Sergei had never been malicious and he certainly never played mind games of this sort. In fact, deceitfulness was so out of character for him that I think his statement—'We think you have a sick imagination'—shocked me far more than finding out about the affair, once I had.

It's significant that ultimately Sergei's honesty won out.

I kept thinking about the incident when he had shouted at the motorist who'd parked her car badly. I couldn't get it out of my mind, nor his remark about a sick imagination.

Something never rang true about that particular accusation. And even without all of this, the fact that he was spending more and more time with a woman who had become openly hostile to me was extraordinary. Anyone else in my position would have asked the same question—'Are you sleeping with Caitt?'—long before I did.

Even so, another couple of weeks must have passed after Sergei had shouted at the motorist before I picked up the phone one afternoon and rang him on impulse.

'Are you having an affair with Caitt?' I asked.

'Yes,' he replied. 'It started five months ago.'

'Please let her know that you've told me,' I said. And then, unable to speak any more, I hung up.

Perhaps I wanted to hear Sergei say 'yes' to the question I had asked him. Perhaps I needed an excuse to further distance myself from a situation that had become too difficult to handle, on top of what had happened to my sister. Both Sergei's and my emotions were at stretching point, and as the knowledge sank in that he and Caitt had been sleeping together while I was sitting at Lori's bedside in ICU, I felt a rage at Caitt, and at Sergei. I wanted desperately to vanish. I wished that I could feel nothing, I yearned to be a deserter. I even wished, briefly, that I didn't have a family. But of course I couldn't abandon the one I had.

To this day I have no idea when Sergei's affair with Caitt really started. Perhaps he'd been lying when he said it had begun five months earlier. Perhaps not.

I thought, after making that phone call to Sergei, that he might stay away until late—hoping that I would have driven back to the hospital by the time he came home. But I was incapable of leaving the house—and in any case, he walked through the door about an hour later. I don't think either of us knew what to say. We just looked at each other. Oddly enough, I think we both felt closer to each other at this moment than we had for a very long time—and indeed, we treated each other with great gentleness that evening, almost as if nothing had happened. We mentioned Caitt only in passing. We even watched an old movie on TV. It was bizarre, although I do remember asking at one stage, 'What now?'

'I don't know,' Sergei replied.

Later, I wondered whether he would opt to sleep in the spare room—or whether I should—but we both went into our bedroom as usual at the end of the evening. However, rather than slip under the sheets, I lay on the far side of the bed wrapped in a beautiful old Turkish blanket that I loved for its comforting softness.

Once or twice during the night I looked at Sergei's sleeping figure and wondered what would happen to us in the future. By now Caitt had played such a destructive role in our life for so long that his affair with her seemed almost an anticlimax.

Sleepless for most of the night, I got up at dawn and was out of the house within thirty minutes. It was early summer, and not yet too hot to walk through the empty streets of McMahons Point into the city.

Clearly, I couldn't work in the house. I needed space, and silence, and time.

Climbing the steps leading to the Harbour Bridge pedestrian walkway, I imagined creating a life of impermanence, one that would mean never settling down anywhere and keeping constantly on the move, like a fugitive. The idea appealed to me enormously.

In another good—or bad—accident of timing, I was flying overseas the next day to start a series of interviews with a Brazilian environmental activist whose name seemed to be everywhere all of a sudden. This was the biography that I'd begun researching some time earlier and could no longer put off starting to write. It was an unusual assignment, since most of the biographies I 'churned out' were on Australians. There was only one reason why I knew that I would come back to Sydney, rather than make an excuse to keep travelling.

The still-frail figure of Lori in her hospital bed.

In the end it was Mum who had insisted—as Dad told me—that I must go overseas as planned. Eve was about to return to Sydney. Lili would come back as soon as she could. I would be away for only ten days.

Even Lori, smiling weakly, had told me that I must do my work.

Still, Sergei must have been anxious that I might be planning to stay away longer than planned, because he rang that morning soon after I got to the eyrie. I didn't pick up. Nor did I answer when he rang an hour later. Or when he rang at midday.

I wasn't punishing him by not taking his calls. I literally didn't know what to say to Sergei anymore. I had no idea what he was thinking, or doing, or planning.

I suspect that my not answering the phone was also emotional exhaustion, the result of having Caitt in the background for so long, chipping away at the task of separating Sergei from me with the sort of patience that only someone fanatically committed to the destruction of our relationship could maintain.

At 3 p.m., when I finally picked up the phone, there was no mistaking the panic in Sergei's voice. 'Don't stop talking to me,' he said. We had a civil conversation, although I can no longer recall what we spoke about.

Then I drove to the hospital, and didn't get home till 9 p.m. Both Sergei and I were tense with each other. Despite needing to pack and get to bed reasonably early, I felt that we should talk about what was happening. But Sergei said it was too soon; we'd discuss everything once I was back. I was beginning to feel anger again—and I didn't want to be angry. I didn't want to have feelings about anything.

'Don't worry. I won't phone for the whole ten days I'll be gone,' I said before I left for the airport early the following morning.

'Then I'll ring you,' he retorted.

Sure enough, he rang several times, concerned for my safety because I was in a dangerous part of the world. The calls had to be brief. It was only when I got back that he told me how worried he'd been. 'I assume that you saw Caitt every night all the same,' I replied.

Sergei told me that whether he'd seen Caitt or not was none of my business. Later, though, he mentioned that he'd told Caitt—to her chagrin—that he remained very attached to me. 'What was the context of the conversation?' I asked.

But to this, Sergei didn't reply.

Far harder for me to accept was the explanation that he eventually gave me, as part of his justification for having an affair with Caitt: that he still loved me but, having just confronted mortality, he needed to experience again the same level of sexual passion that comes with a new relationship. In other words, we had been together for too long—and life was unpredictable. And short.

He then said that Caitt had confided to him after he'd come out of hospital that she'd long hidden a terror of sudden, serious ill-health. Ten years earlier, she'd been diagnosed with a brain tumour; luckily, it was benign. But the experience had frightened her badly. As Sergei told it, she had stressed to him that because they had both seen death on the horizon, this set them apart from other people. The normal rules didn't apply to them. They could have an affair in the knowledge that everything was permissible, and should be. She said nothing about how she would have reacted to the same situation if she was in my shoes, although I had a fairly good idea, given her abnormal possessiveness of Sergei.

'And you agree with her?' I asked him now, of her so-called philosophy.

'It isn't a matter of agreeing or disagreeing,' he replied, and went on to talk about the new urgency he felt to seize opportunities—like finding passion again. Caitt was offering him that opportunity, he added.

We were sitting in our courtyard when this conversation took place. The bougainvillea that Sergei had planted at the back of the house looked glorious that year, although it was beginning to spread over the roof and badly needed pruning. Anyone seeing us with our glasses of wine, sitting in its shade that particular afternoon, would never have guessed what we were discussing. Or rather, what Sergei was telling me, since I listened in silence.

There was a reason for this. I understood what Sergei was saying. I even understood his need for a 'last chance'. I still do. These days, whenever I hear of someone whose relationship has foundered following a potentially fatal illness, I think back to everything that happened to us.

But that isn't to say that I coped admirably with the affair, because I didn't. It wasn't just the circumstances, and the timing. My anger grew whenever Sergei repeated to me what Caitt had said about our relationship—when she knew perfectly well, of course, that he would do this.

'She doesn't understand why you're upset because, as she said, it's not as if I sleep with you anymore.'

I think this was the worst of her remarks. I was outraged that Sergei couldn't see her sly cruelty, and I was also shocked that he'd discussed something so personal—and which had caused me great sadness—with someone as manipulative as Caitt.

I painted her character in the blackest terms that I could think of. Every time I did this, Sergei would storm out of the house. It became a regular occurrence. If I mentioned Caitt even in passing, he'd simply get up and leave—almost as if he'd been looking for an excuse to do so. I never asked him, when he returned—and he did always return—if he'd been to see her, because I had begun to shut off.

Only once did I ask him to tell me if he intended to leave permanently, and he looked straight through me and didn't reply. I felt at that moment as if I didn't exist.

It was strangely comforting. Nothing was real. So nothing mattered.

⚬———⇌⇋———⚬

Lori was eventually transferred to a ward where she spent weeks going through an intensive rehabilitation process. She was still stuck in hospital, and desperate to go home. Eve and Lili almost went broke as they continued flying back and forth between London, Shanghai and Sydney, staying at the house on the peninsula with our parents.

Whenever they came back, I took the opportunity to 'vanish', booking cheap hotel rooms in the city and eating dinner in food courts, rather than go 'home' or stay with friends and have to admit what was happening. Lili and Eve always knew where I was, but nobody else did. At times Sergei seemed disturbed by my absences, but he never asked me where I disappeared to on these occasions. I suspect that he had decided, like me, that anything beyond the immediate moment was simply too difficult to deal with.

It was interesting that neither of us moved out of the house, even though 'home' had become an ambiguous word. But it was during this period that an incident occurred which I've never forgotten. It changed my perspective completely.

Late one Saturday afternoon, Sergei and I bumped into each other in the street outside our house. I was coming home, briefly. Sergei was going out. Both of us halted, uncertain whether to say anything to each other, or simply pass each other by.

He looked completely worn out. We both did. We had raged at each other ever since his confession, until eventually a sorrow set in. I felt I had no right to tell Sergei to end the affair even though by this time I knew, or thought I knew, the full extent of Caitt's ruthlessness. I had no idea why Sergei continued to come home—eventually—every evening. Or why, if I was away, he rang me each night once he walked through our front door.

I said without anger that we seemed to be at an impasse, and that I was thinking of leaving him for good, because I felt that he wanted—needed—to be elsewhere. I added that, if he truly felt he would be happier with someone else at this stage of his life, he should follow his heart. I didn't want him to feel obligated to me, or to stay with me through kindness. I wanted him to be happy, if there is such a thing. I wanted him to find peace.

Sergei listened without speaking. Then he said simply, 'Can't you wait for me, the way I waited for you?'

Perhaps he had been searching for an opportunity to say that to me. Perhaps, in our anger at each other, we'd kept missing the right moments to try and communicate. Although, far more likely, it was because we were spending so much time apart.

I didn't know then how these words of his, too, would leave an echo. The softness that had been missing for so long from his face returned briefly and now, while I knew that he wouldn't end the affair immediately, I sensed that Caitt's hold over Sergei's life—and mine—wouldn't become permanent.

I got that drastically wrong, too, only not in a way that anyone could ever have predicted.

<hr />

The footpath incident was the beginning of the end of Sergei's affair, although something else happened a few weeks later that almost did persuade me to leave him for good.

I had been back working in the eyrie, and was walking through the city towards the Harbour Bridge mid-afternoon when I suddenly felt a sharp pain and started gasping for breath. Two alarmed passersby and a security guard helped me into a nearby medical centre where I was examined by a doctor and given blood tests. Apparently I was having a panic attack—a condition I knew barely anything about.

It was a bad one, so they said. I lay on a bed in a room in that medical centre for almost two hours, because I felt faint whenever I tried to sit up—and I tried to keep sitting up because the last thing I wanted was to be transferred to hospital. I'd had enough of hospitals for a lifetime! Eventually, I did feel much better, and a nurse asked if they could ring someone to come and collect me.

I insisted I felt well enough to leave without help and they let me go, somewhat doubtfully.

The noise of the traffic seemed louder than usual, and the light hurt my eyes. I had intended walking to Circular Quay, and then taking a ferry to McMahons Point. But I felt too tired even for this. I went into a cafe, and ordered a lemon squash and a tiramisu, for energy. And then I rang Sergei.

To his credit, he drove into the city immediately, parked illegally (as he told me later), and hurried into the cafe looking stricken. I avoided talking about what had happened, save for a brief conversation—for which I think he was thankful—and the moment we got home, he started getting organised to cook dinner while I rested.

That evening, after I'd taken the medication I'd been given and had gone back to lie on the bed, I heard Sergei's phone ring. He lowered his voice while he was speaking and I knew that he must be giving Caitt an update. A few minutes later he came into the bedroom with a quizzical expression and asked me to show him the plasters that I should have on my arms—if I'd really had blood tests.

At that moment I truly hated both Caitt and Sergei, and I think Sergei realised it, although I was so spaced out from the medication that I merely pushed up my sleeves and showed him my arms. He had the grace to look ashamed for believing, as Caitt had obviously suggested, that I'd made up the whole story.

Thank god for those pills. I was unused to tablets of any kind, and these had what I regarded as a brilliant effect. After that brief flash of anger, all my emotions dissolved. For the first time in ages, I felt no anxiety, no sense of trepidation. Nothing. Now I understood how people could become hooked on prescription drugs. And because of that, I knew that first thing in the morning I should throw the rest of the tablets away, which I did—after a final, wistful look at the packet.

I kept just one pill aside.

I waited a week while trying to make up my mind about whether to just do it, and leave Sergei. Was I hoping that he would suddenly tell Caitt it was over and come home on a white horse, bearing caviar and vodka?

He went away for the weekend—I have no idea where— and on the Monday morning I got up, packed a few things and, shortly before midday, walked out of the house with my suitcase and laptop, not having a clue what I was going to do next. And not caring.

By late afternoon, when the pill—that last one—began to wear off, I stopped aimlessly walking around the city and went back to the eyrie, where I'd left my belongings. I couldn't be bothered finding yet another cheap hotel for the night and, since the office included a tiny bathroom, the logical decision was to sleep on the small sofa crammed between desk and door, and to think about what to do next in the morning.

There was a little Japanese cafe in the street directly below. I ate there. My phone was switched off. I wondered what would happen if Sergei suddenly had another brain bleed, and immediately switched my phone back on. I rang him. The number rang out, so I switched my phone off again.

I ate there again the following night, when once again I was the only person dining alone. I didn't mind. Nor did I wonder where Sergei was, or whether he'd even gone home. I liked the fact that the meal came with wonderful old chopsticks, rather than cheap wooden ones. I ate slowly. The food was delicious. The cafe owner bowed as I left.

Then I went back to the eyrie, where I thought how ridiculous it was to end a marriage in such a fashion, camping in a friend's office in the city. Shouldn't there be a more dramatic finale? What would Caitt do in the same circumstances? Perhaps I should ring her and ask.

I sat at the window for a while, battling despair, and then phoned my parents to ask about Lori, keeping my tone light and breezy. Afterwards, I went to sleep on the sofa, using a wrap that I'd thrown into my suitcase at the last minute as a blanket. At five in the morning, wide awake again, I opened my phone and found seven missed calls from Sergei.

That night we met for dinner in the Japanese cafe. Sergei had his old energy back. I saw it the moment he walked in. He looked refreshed and all the tiredness had gone from his face. Evidently my leaving had invigorated him. This was the new start he needed.

'Where did you go?' he demanded, the moment he sat down.

It was a totally unexpected opening line. Why did he suddenly care? As it happened, I'd slept for a second night in the eyrie, but I didn't want him to know. I shrugged.

Sergei sighed, exasperated, but didn't push for an answer. He asked the cafe owner for a menu, before launching straight into what he wanted to say. Caitt's parents had bought a new house and in three weeks' time they were having a housewarming party. It was going to be a big event, with all of Caitt's family attending. As it happened, both Sergei and I had met Caitt's parents once or twice at her Sunday lunches and we'd met many of her other relatives as well. Caitt wanted Sergei to go to the party as her partner.

Well, of course she did. I wasn't surprised by Sergei's announcement. I almost asked what he and Caitt were planning to buy her parents for a housewarming present. It was the perfect occasion for Caitt to introduce her new beau to her family. Or perhaps she wouldn't need to say anything at all, since obviously I wouldn't be there. The situation would speak for itself.

Fait accompli.

I wondered idly what the expression was in Russian.

'I'm not going,' said Sergei.

I looked away. What a comedy. Of course he was going. I didn't need to hear what I assumed was about to follow: that Sergei would politely lament the end of our marriage and then, after some minutes, would come up with a hollow reason about why, after all, he should accept the invitation.

'I told Caitt that I couldn't go to the party, because you're not invited.'

Sushi, or tempura? I could never decide. Once, in Tokyo, I'd eaten the best sushi in a bar in the very heart of the city, in one of the tiniest streets I'd ever seen, where the tram ran alongside people's houses.

'Zara? Are you listening at all? Caitt said that she wanted to invite you to her parents' party as well, but that it was out of the question because you have a problem with her.'

I almost laughed. Truly, she was beyond belief.

Sergei was still waiting for my response.

'Do you think it's possible,' I asked, 'that she stands in front of the bathroom mirror and practises her lines?'

He considered this. 'Yes. Perhaps she does,' he eventually replied. And the ghost of a grin crossed his face.

We didn't talk about Caitt after that. I actually felt her presence—for the first time—start to fade. Nor did I press Sergei to end the affair, but I knew that it was only a matter of time.

After dinner we went our separate ways—Sergei, back to the house, me, upstairs to the eyrie. But we agreed that at the weekend, after I had been to see Lori, we would drive out of the city and spend three days together.

It was mid-May. We kept to our plan and went to an old hotel by a river that both of us loved—and finally, we started to talk to each other warily, and with curiosity, too. For one entire afternoon, we sat by the river in silence, and that evening we slept like exhausted travellers.

Then we went back to the city and, a day later, Sergei told Caitt that he wanted to remain a friend, but not a lover. He also told her that he wasn't going to leave me. He went to see her, to tell her directly, and when he returned home he looked shaken. I could almost feel her fury following him through the front door.

'She's very angry with you,' he said.

I had a thousand questions for Sergei. I asked none of them. I knew that we had to find our footing again with each other and I hoped that he would be able to gently put Caitt to one side.

I also knew that she would keep phoning him, and that he would still take her calls. It was the right thing to do and I knew that as well—despite initially rebelling against the idea of Sergei and Caitt remaining in contact. It was part of his character to treat people decently, although that may sound contradictory and perverse. He wouldn't discard her. Sergei never discarded anyone. Old girlfriends. Caitt. Me.

There was one thing that I don't think Caitt ever worked out, though. Sergei and I had something important in common. Neither of us was 'good' at infidelity; neither of us was a natural. Our respective uselessness at being able to cope with unfaithfulness was, I believe, one of the things that brought Sergei and me back together—for the time we had left.

———————✷·✷———————

In June, Lori finally came out of hospital. She was much changed, with a sweetness that none of us had seen in her previously. But she remained a frail version of the woman she had been and every day I silently cursed the driver who had taken away her health.

Sergei came with me regularly to visit Lori, who had moved back in with my parents indefinitely, and the three of them, too, found their footing with each other again. We were all fragile. We all treated one another carefully. And I think that Sergei and I found some peace in the old family house at Whale Beach during that period.

I remember the afternoon that we drove away after staying overnight with my parents and looking back and seeing Mum and Dad, and Lori, standing in sunlight, waving. Then Sergei's mobile buzzed. He glanced at the name of his missed caller and tensed.

I should have known that Caitt wouldn't give up. That she would retreat, but not disappear altogether. Sure enough, time would prove that she had no intention of letting me—

or Sergei—off the hook. She emailed him regularly about what she was up to, and once sent a photo of herself sitting alone on a windswept beach, which Sergei showed me.

'Could that be her ocean of tears in the background?' I queried, clutching one hand to my breast.

But Sergei silenced me with a rebuke that I never forgot. 'That doesn't suit you,' he said.

As far as I knew, he was keeping Caitt at arm's length, although she continued to drop into the wine bar where Sergei and Joe still met every evening after work for a drink. She always came over to chat, he told me, and to ask how he was.

'And what do you say?' I asked.

'I say that I'm fine. That we're fine,' he replied.

The game hadn't finished. She had simply changed tack.

In October that year, Caitt began a new relationship with a man whose company carried out polling for political parties. Sergei met him when she brought him into the wine bar one evening. 'She asked if I wanted to come over on Sunday and join them for lunch,' he told me, and smiled wryly. 'Naturally I said that I couldn't.'

He saw Caitt and her new love interest several times after that. I deliberately didn't ask any questions, although I wondered how much the boyfriend knew about Sergei, and whether Caitt had told him that Sergei was married. I half-hoped that we'd run into them somewhere one night, although I suspected that Caitt would make sure there was no chance of that ever happening—especially after Sergei mentioned one evening that she was hoping to get married.

He said this so casually that I was surprised, and he noticed. 'She was a friend. We had an affair. It's over. It wasn't that important,' he said.

But sometimes there's no such thing as the end of an affair—even after it's over.

Sergei and I tried very hard to recover our former serenity. But even though we managed to start edging towards an old love, something had been broken, and I think we both knew it, as hard as we both tried to recapture the magic shared by those two people who met on a ferry on the way to Estonia.

Out of the blue, in November, Tobie rang Sergei. She was staying at Caitt's place, she said, and suggested he come over and have dinner. Caitt was overseas with her new boyfriend. It would be just the two of them.

I was in Canberra, interviewing a relative of the Brazilian activist as part of the research for the biography. As Sergei gave me this news, speaking on the phone from his car early one evening, and adding that he was on his way over to Caitt's right then, I felt as if someone had just punched me in the head. Luckily, at that moment I was in my hotel room and able to pour myself a glass of water and sit down.

'How can you? Don't do this! How did Tobie even know I was going to be away tonight?'

I heard myself shouting, and was shocked. But it's no wonder that, having kept such a tight lid on my emotions for so long, I erupted.

'What's the matter with you?' Sergei shouted right back. 'I just explained that Caitt wouldn't be there!'

He then started to say that Tobie hadn't known anything about my overnight trip to Canberra; she had phoned on the off-chance that he might be free.

'Can't you see that she and Caitt have planned this together?' I said, and then I hung up, before he had answered. It was too much. And in any case, I was beginning to lose my voice. This was something that had been happening a lot recently.

Sergei went ahead and had dinner with Tobie. I almost didn't pick up when he rang only a short time later. 'I'm home,' he said, sounding strange. 'I didn't stay long.'

Tobie had tried to seduce him. 'I suppose you think I'm an idiot. But I didn't expect that,' he added.

He was speaking the truth. I could hear it, although I was amazed that, yet again, he couldn't see the game being played.

'Yes, I do think you're an idiot,' I snapped, or tried to. I could barely speak for huskiness.

We got over this episode by never mentioning the subject again.

I had assumed that Sergei wouldn't want to discuss anything to do with Caitt, or their affair either, but he surprised me by saying that we would talk about it as much as I needed to. 'We'll probably have many conversations about what happened,' he added. And we did, over the months, talking about the past—my past—as well.

'I wasn't punishing you,' he said at one stage. But this time it was Sergei who was fooling himself.

In our anger at each other when he was still sleeping with Caitt, he'd said many times, 'You could do it. So can I.'

Christmas came and went, and by New Year we had started talking about selling the house and spending part of each year living in Europe. Our life was calm. We were calm. It seemed that we had survived.

And then, almost unbelievably, everything changed again.

One evening when we were both sitting reading—I remember it clearly—Sergei suddenly looked up and said angrily, 'Why did you say that?'

Astonished, I replied that I hadn't spoken a word. What was he talking about?

'You know perfectly well what you just said!' he exclaimed, and got up and left the room.

I sat, frozen. Sergei came back and resumed reading. We didn't speak. He went to bed early, without saying goodnight. Were we going backwards?

A week later, the same thing happened again. Sergei accused me of saying something I hadn't. He did the same thing to Joe one night. And to another friend, on a separate occasion. People were becoming bewildered. What were these mood swings? More importantly, why was Sergei imagining that people were saying things when they weren't? I dared to suggest he talk to his doctor about it, but this only upset him. Perhaps he could feel that something was wrong, but didn't want to confront it.

Then one night he said out of nowhere, 'I get the feeling I don't have long.'

The cancer that took Sergei was sudden, just like the brain bleed. A rare cancer that would snuff out his life within weeks. He was diagnosed only a short time after he made that remark about not having long; and within hours of his diagnosis, he told me that everyone in his family always died very quickly and that he expected he would as well.

Death wasn't a certainty when Sergei said this. There was still hope; or was I fooling myself yet again?

During one of the periods when he was out of hospital and at home, we were sitting together on the sofa that faced the windows looking into the courtyard. We weren't talking, only because both of us were lost in our own thoughts about the unexpected, almost incomprehensible thing we were facing, when Sergei looked at me suddenly and said, 'But I don't want to die.'

He sounded utterly bewildered.

He was broken-hearted.

It's a terrible memory, and it has merged with another one—of a small town in Italy where we spent part of one summer a year after we'd first met. One afternoon we watched an elderly couple tottering arm in arm out of a restaurant, clearly having enjoyed a very long lunch. As they walked past us, the pair began arguing about what they were going to eat for dinner that evening. We had picked up enough Italian to have no trouble understanding what they were saying. I remarked to Sergei that the two of us would be exactly like that in our old age—arguing about food the whole time—and he laughed.

He reminded me of that comment after I came back from the Middle East, my own affair over. 'I thought you'd disappeared forever,' he said then. 'I've been imagining growing old on my own.'

But it was Sergei who disappeared forever. Not me.

And I was the one left behind—with Caitt.

⚬————✦————⚬

Sergei died in April 2008, aged fifty-nine.

Within twenty-four hours of his death, Caitt sent me a text message:

'The man who loved me with such passion has gone. I know that his last thoughts were of me. He yearned for us to be together. This ending is beyond cruel. I have suffered so much. How can I live without him? How can I go on?'

I am unable to describe how I felt at that moment. I cannot write it down here. There is a devastation that's beyond words. Suffice to say that Lili and Eve and one of my closest women friends were all at the house when the text arrived and got me through the terrible, gasping panic attack that followed. At least I knew this time, what was happening to me.

It was my sisters who also gently persuaded me, a few weeks later, that we should go through Sergei's emails, in case the only friend of his whom I hadn't been able to contact—who was travelling somewhere in Asia—had sent him an email that he'd missed.

So we opened Sergei's laptop and started searching.

There were no emails from Caitt, which seemed odd. In the first fortnight after his diagnosis, as word spread, Sergei had answered text after text and email after email from friends who either lived overseas or, for whatever reason, were out of the country, and wrote telling him how much they loved him. Other friends visited him at home and during his bouts in hospital, and kept up a similar stream of messages. 'I love you, too,' he always replied. Just one sentence, over and over again, before he became too weak to use his phone or laptop anymore. But it was enough. It said everything.

Only later did I realise that he'd been saying his goodbyes.

I assumed I would find similar emails from Caitt. But, as I've said, there were none. It was strange, but Caitt's cyberspace whereabouts were hardly a primary concern at the time. More importantly, there was no message from Rupert, the friend of Sergei's who still didn't know he had died.

'Let's try again,' said Eve a few days later. 'We may have missed it. Searching Sergei's emails was difficult for you emotionally. Let's be really thorough this time.'

We found them as we were scrolling down through the pages—waiting like snakes coiled and ready to strike. Email after email from Caitt, writing to Sergei just after he'd been diagnosed with cancer.

How we had missed them the first time around was a mystery. Almost all of Caitt's messages were extremely sexual, or else full of passionate declarations of love. She recalled places they'd been together, conversations they'd had together, and even the shopping they'd done together, always with constant references to the future they were still planning to share together, 'once you're well again and Zara can cope with hearing the truth'.

The screen blurred in front of my eyes. Perhaps I was weeping; I can't remember. It was Eve who sent me out of the room while she read the emails again.

'Something's not right,' she said. 'I'm certain they weren't there before. The pattern is all wrong.'

I had no idea what she was talking about. Eve is a brilliant film designer, but she is also a natural geek—someone whose IT skills had always put her on a different planet to Lili and me when it came to technology.

'So?' I said to her dully a short time later. 'What did you find?'

'I've printed them out. Leave it with me for a while,' she replied. 'Oh, and by the way, I've changed Sergei's password. This is his new one.'

She handed me a slip of paper with the new password written down.

I didn't open Sergei's laptop again for months. But

neither could I stop thinking about those emails from Caitt. She had written them even though she was involved in an apparently serious, meaningful relationship with a new man. Then again, her behaviour was par for the course.

The other reason I couldn't get the emails out of my mind was more significant. Before Sergei became too ill to see anyone, I'd asked him at one stage whether he would like Caitt to visit. He had shaken his head and said no.

Now, however, I had to consider the possibility that she must have rung him on the rare occasions when I left him alone to race to the shops to buy food or pick up more of his medication. Perhaps Sergei had rung her. 'Zara has gone out.'

Naturally she would have read whatever she wanted into her conversations with Sergei, although I wondered why he hadn't mentioned them to me—if indeed, they really had taken place. And if they had, he must either have forgotten to mention them, through feeling so ill, or simply didn't think to do so. And why would he? Caitt, if she'd been asked this question, would have been incapable of understanding that Sergei had been focused on his mortality, not on her.

There was another possibility. Sergei and Caitt had decided to get back together, if he recovered. But I doubted that. Instinct told me otherwise.

The emails she sent him after he became ill may have served to keep her ego in check. But clearly, her knowing that he was with me when he died had pushed her over the edge—as her diabolical message to me had revealed.

To mourn someone properly is hard, and it should be. We mourn too briefly, fitting our sorrow into an already time-poor schedule and, before you know it, people are telling you that it's best to 'move on'. A phrase I can't stand.

But you can also mourn for too long and, knowing Sergei, he would have loathed that. And the truth was, I felt a great longing to be alone and to travel, if only for a few weeks.

I took the lightest of luggage, and Caitt's emails. For some reason I was only able to read them printed out on paper. Perhaps seeing them as actual emails was too close to reality, too confronting. My plan was to read them dispassionately over the time I was away, which I did with varying degrees of success in Greece, and then Finland, and finally in Tallinn, Estonia. I sat on a wall and re-read the emails for a third or a fourth time, and afterwards gazed at the view of the city's red roofs and the onion domes of its churches, reflecting on the odd fate that had brought Sergei and me together in the oldest capital in northern Europe.

Another year passed before I took out the emails again. By this time, I'd sold our house and moved into an apartment in the same suburb, in a steep street running down to the harbour. I'd packed the emails at the bottom of a box when I got back from Europe; in the move I discovered that there were small holes where they'd been partially eaten by silverfish. I thought that was funny. And why on earth was I keeping the printouts? I had never deleted them from Sergei's emails, so there was an electronic, silverfish-proof record if I needed it.

Nevertheless, I started going through them yet again, and that's when I discovered that I no longer hated Caitt. On the contrary—and what a revelation this was—I realised that I was grateful to her for providing Sergei with a way of escaping the horror of his cancer, and his terrible loneliness as he faced the knowledge that he was dying. He needed the distraction of her emails; he needed to remember, to dream.

Wasn't his affair—indeed, as he'd said to me later—ultimately of no importance?

He was right. It did damage, but we didn't separate. We stayed together to the end.

Sergei's life was important, not what had happened between him and Caitt.

I should mourn him, not his infidelity.

Eve came to visit and one evening she asked me if she could borrow Sergei's laptop for a few days. She wanted someone she knew well and trusted, a man who had been the brains behind a phenomenally successful ISP, to make sure it was virus free.

I knew that she was going to ask him to check out Caitt's emails for the strange 'pattern' she'd mentioned when we'd first discovered them—and I didn't want this to happen. I felt at peace with Caitt's emails. I didn't want any more shocks. I almost refused.

What did it matter anymore?

But a week later Eve came back from seeing her friend, with the laptop tucked under her arm and an expression on her face that signalled bad news.

'Do I really want to hear this?' I asked.

'I think you have to,' she replied. And then Eve told me that her friend thought there was a real possibility that the emails from Caitt had been sent to Sergei not once—but twice.

The first time, just after he was diagnosed with cancer.

The second time, after he'd died.

Sergei had deleted the emails the first time around, obviously not wanting me to see them. But Caitt had forwarded them all again.

'Can you think of anyone Caitt knows who might have been able to hack into his emails in order to check that the ones she'd sent were still there, or had been deleted? Someone with a really sophisticated knowledge of computers?' asked Eve, before adding that perhaps Caitt had known his password.

I was about to say no, when I suddenly remembered that first Sunday lunch at Caitt's, three years earlier.

'*Zara, meet Tobie, my very good friend and genius computer consultant.*'

Was Tobie the key? She had once boasted of her IT talents, and had even run her own one-woman company for a while, sorting out internet problems for clients. At one stage she had offered to 'clean' my laptop for me, after all sorts of problems started occurring. I declined Tobie's offer—not trusting her—and instead took the laptop to a professional, who discovered that my computer had been infected by something far worse than a common virus—a Trojan Horse.

In the end, I bought a new laptop, and considered changing my email address. But I didn't, mainly for work reasons, and also because I knew that if there was someone out there wishing me ill, it would only be a matter of time before that person tracked down my address. I opted for a firewall instead.

To this day I don't know the truth about Caitt's emails to Sergei. Although, if Eve's friend was correct, then Caitt was even more vengeful than any of us ever imagined.

She had wanted to make absolutely certain that her emails wouldn't disappear, knowing that sooner or later I would find them, because she wanted me to doubt everything that Sergei had told me. She wanted me to wonder for the rest of my life whether he really did end their affair.

And for a while I did wonder, despite finding a brief note in shaky handwriting that Sergei had written to me soon after he became ill. He left the note between the pages of the *Tide Guide*, which he never failed to consult before taking a swim.

He wrote that he loved me, and would never have left me. Everything else that had happened was irrelevant, he said.

When someone you love dies, all sorts of emotions and thoughts come to the surface and then start to recede. Eventually, death takes the sting out of bad memories, which is why—after some time—I've come to regard Caitt's emails in a different light.

Rather than deem them an act of remarkable spite, I've realised that they could also be seen as an expression of the raw grief that she must have felt writing them, guessing that Sergei did not have long to live. If this was the case, then, for the first time since we'd met, she was acting with honesty. She wanted me to understand how much she'd loved Sergei. She was revealing her grief without any filters. And maybe, just maybe, I was right to feel grateful that Sergei had received those passionate, sexually explicit epistles from Caitt. It had been the only way that she could think of to help him. She had been saying goodbye to him in her own way.

One of Sergei's finest qualities was his generosity of spirit. It shines in my memory. He may even have helped me reach this conclusion about Caitt.

And when very unexpectedly, I met someone else two and a half years after his death—a wonderful man with whom I've found great joy, and a sense of completeness—I knew that Sergei would be cheering me on.

At times I've imagined I've heard him speaking to me.

'Live your life. Be happy with him. This was meant to be.'

<hr />

It's now November 2012. The two of us remain deeply in love.

We've made a new life together in a country whose people and landscape have embraced us as if we've belonged here all along. Perhaps we have.

And I've pushed to the back of my mind the moment six months ago when I opened my laptop to check any new emails and found the following message:

'Hi Zara, I often wonder about you, and hope you are well. Can't we meet, and try to heal the wounds from the past? No one wants to tell me where you are living, although I understand that you're with someone new. I'm so glad. He must be so interesting. I'd love to meet him . . .'

Lili

London

We stood shoulder to shoulder, Will and I, as we waited together for the 3.15 p.m. plane from Bodrum, Turkey. We were so close I could feel his breath, soft and treacherous as apricots, drifting across my cheek. But we didn't look at each other once, not even when the display flashed up a delayed arrival time of 5.45 p.m.

Not so long ago, we would have grabbed the opportunity for a coffee together, used the time to plan another trip to the Bodrum peninsula, debated whether we could grab a few days in Istanbul on the way through, argued amiably over whether we *really* needed a visit to the carpet shops behind the bazaar for yet another rug for our villa.

But not this time. Although I let my eyes flicker in Will's direction, he kept his focus ahead, oblivious to my gaze.

For a brief, irrational second I felt incredibly sad that I didn't merit even one glance. But then I had to remind myself—Will didn't actually know that it was me who was standing by his side.

Earlier that afternoon each of us had, separately, prepared ourselves for the arrival of 'our' guest.

In the rickety Georgian house overlooking Hampstead Heath that I had sold him all those years ago, Will had stood for a long time under the shower's rush, washing himself meticulously. A towel wrapped around his waist, he shaved, creating a lather with the badger-fur brush that a previous lover had given him, taking off his bristles with tiny, sharp strokes.

Then he had spread out his shirts on the bed and considered which would go best with the linen trousers I had bought him in Rome last year and which, although stretched slightly thin over his expanding bottom, still made him look deceptively chic. He hovered over a faded Provençal blue-and-lavender striped shirt and an olive-green T-shirt we had chosen together in New York a few years earlier. Finally he chose the striped Provençal, as he was always going to, because it gave him that air of casual elegance—a look that said he had tried, but not too hard. He shoved his feet into his favourite battered deck shoes but, after gazing at them for some time, decided that they didn't fit the look he was aiming for, and changed them for the Ralph Lauren loafers that I didn't even know he owned.

At around the same time, a few miles away in a small terraced house off Edgware Road, I, too, got ready. I showered quickly and tied my unruly hair off my face. I didn't bother with makeup—there was no point. No one would be looking at me. At least, that was the plan. I threw on skinny black jeans and a tight-fitting grey sweater. Then I went downstairs to where Rachel was waiting with my new outfit.

I had bought the *hijab* on the internet, on a website that advertised itself with the words, 'Just because you're modest, you don't have to dress like Granma'. The site offered scarves in a variety of colours, from mulberry to the palest indigo. Some had the most intricate patterns embroidered on them; others had tiny flowers painted in white. It seemed a slightly contradictory choice for women who wore head scarves to follow their religion's dictate of modesty—shouldn't they be wearing plain black coverings, which would indeed camouflage their beauty, rather than delicate, feminine scarves that could only enhance their features?

I recalled the women I'd once met in Sumatra, who had worn defiantly beautiful head scarves intricately decorated with luminescent threads, and who had kept their coats pinned tightly to show off their curves. I loved their tiny rebellion against the repression of beauty, but wondered how they got away with it in their strict Islamic world.

Rachel couldn't explain such contradictions to me. She was, after all, no Moslem herself, but a Cornish atheist married to a particularly secular Lebanese restaurant owner. She only wore the *hijab* for gatherings with his not-so-secular family, who had moved a generation earlier from their palatial villa in Beirut to join the Arab diaspora in London.

If her *hijab* never got much of an airing, neither did her *jilbab*, the long black manteau that cast her body into an anonymous shadow and which she was lending me for this venture.

Buttoning the *jilbab* from top to bottom, I considered myself in the mirror. It seemed more like a particularly shapeless version of my old winter coat than a credible camouflage, and I couldn't see how it would do the trick.

But then we put on the *hijab*, the midnight blue scarf scattered with tiny stars, folding it low over my forehead and then wrapping it over my head, so not one hair was visible. It was clipped into place around my face. Without the hair framing them, my facial features looked different—nothing like the person I was used to seeing in the mirror.

Out of context, would I recognise the crooked nose, the tiny scar above my right eyebrow, the slight overbite I had never been able to correct?

More importantly, would Will? I was not convinced.

Then Rachel folded the end of the *hijab* up over my nose and mouth, pinning it in place at my jawline.

And with that one gesture I disappeared. The person who was me was now nothing more than a pair of eyes and untidily plucked eyebrows peering out of the folds of cloth.

I was ready.

❖

As I walked into Heathrow Airport, my heart fluttered against my ribcage in terror, a moth trying to flee the flame. I saw Will leaning against a pillar, gazing at the arrivals board. He turned for an instant and I was convinced he would know that it was me walking towards him, even though every part of me, apart from my eyes, was invisible.

Rachel had warned me that, even wearing the *jilbab* and *hijab*, sometimes even wearing the full *chador*, you could occasionally be recognised by those who knew you best—by the way you walked, the way you stood, even by the tilt of your head.

I had taken every precaution. I had borrowed a pair of her shoes—black, sturdy, low-heeled—as mine were too recognisable. Not one stray tell-tale red hair had slipped from under the *hijab*. I kept my eyes down, in case the anguish in them gave me away.

And the precautions seemed to work. Will looked my way for a splintered second, and there wasn't even the tiniest flicker of recognition. His gaze was as blank as childhood, and it swept over me and around the terminal before settling once more on the arrivals board.

Shaking invisibly, I went over to him and stood centimetres away. He shifted slightly so he had more space but, apart from that one small movement, he didn't even acknowledge my presence. I was completely invisible to him.

I shouldn't have been surprised. I'd been pretty much invisible to Will for months. My sharia disguise was only hiding me from someone who had stopped looking for me a long time ago.

As the arrivals board flashed up the news that Flight TK1985 from Bodrum and Istanbul had landed, Will straightened up and began to peer more expectantly at the people trickling through. I could smell his excitement coming off him in waves of musk as he leaned forward, his eyes fixed on the gates.

You can always detect the passengers from Bodrum. Half of them look like Dolce & Gabbana models—half of them *are* fashion models, returning from photo shoots on the luxury yachts that now pack Bodrum harbour or from partying with the local glitterati in the town that Turkey likes to boast is its own St Tropez. There was the usual mix of London-based Turks returning home to Green Lanes, London's 'Little Turkey', along with a handful of out-of-season British holidaymakers wearing their faint winter suntan like a badge. But Will and I, craning forward together, could not see the Russian pastry-maker who had taken over our lives.

And then a woman veered out of the stream towards us.

She was tall and slim, with the body of a dancer and hair the colour of bitter chocolate. She had a clever face with heavy Slav features and she was wearing a green dress that would have matched Will's olive T-shirt perfectly, had he chosen to wear it.

As I watched, she folded herself into Will's arms and he kissed her with all the hungry ardour of our first night together. And there they went—my husband of ten years with his arm around his lover's shoulders, heading for the exit and their two-week-long holiday together.

Leaving me gazing after them, my *hijab* soaked in tears.

I started after them. I had planned to disrobe now, to enjoy the shock on her face and the horror on his as he realised that the silent, robed woman at his shoulder, who had been witness to this scene of passion, was not some anonymous shadow—she was the woman with whom he had shared more than a decade of life.

But when it came to it, I stayed still, robed, silent. I didn't want them to know that I was audience to their love scene. I didn't want my husband's thief to see the damage she had caused me, to see eyes swollen to cochineal slits or the hurt that I knew was scribbled all over my face. And I didn't want Will to know that I knew. Not yet, anyway.

I decided instead that what I needed now was a very un-Islamic glass of red wine, before I headed back down the M25. A glass of wine and a quick debrief with Rachel.

The barman looked at me oddly when he took my order and, to provoke him further, I decided to strip myself of the *hijab*. I reached up and lifted it off my head, grabbing the entire bar's attention, and, when I pulled out my mobile and dialled Rachel's number, I felt all eyes focused on me.

'Well, it worked,' I said without preamble when she answered. 'He didn't have any idea I was there.'

'Christ,' said Rachel. 'I was convinced it would all go wrong and he'd recognise you somehow.'

'Nope. Not a flicker.'

'So what happened? And where are you? You're not still at the airport?'

'I'm in the bar. Decided I needed a stiff drink.'

As I put the phone on speaker while I applied crimson lipstick, someone dropped something behind me and for a second everyone in the bar swung to stare at them, then they swung back to listen to me. 'He's such a bastard, he really is. Two weeks after he swore he'd finished their affair and wanted to make our marriage work, he's meeting her for a holiday.'

'Where is he claiming to be now?'

'He told me that he had a gig at a music festival in Norway this week, remember? It makes me wonder about all his other "gigs" this year.'

Rachel made a sympathetic noise. It was the wrong thing to do. My fragile self-control gave way and I began to weep again, the tears dribbling miserably into the wine and threatening to dilute it.

'Are you going to be okay?' she asked.

'*In sha' Allah*,' I answered and hung up. I thought I could hear someone in the bar choking.

Immediately I texted Will: 'U r a bstrd'.

Right away came a reply. 'Thank u v much. I was hoping u wld wish me luck wth the gig.'

I wasn't really surprised. Will was nothing if not an accomplished, even a pathological, liar. Part of him was probably genuinely offended that I hadn't wished him luck for this non-existent gig. I put the text into the 'save' folder. It would serve as ammunition at a later date.

Three months ago, when the first clues that Will might be seeing someone else began their poisonous drip-feed into my consciousness, I had considered hiring a private detective. But I decided not to; it would denote such a huge destruction of trust that you could really only take that route when you knew your relationship was all but over.

Now I knew that our marriage was almost certainly fatally wounded, but I still saw no reason to hire a private detective. After all, why pay someone else when you can do the job so much better yourself?

⁕

Back home in my little oast house in Kent, which I had bought years before Will and I married and where we now lived most of the time, I looked in the old silver mirror I had once found in a Paris junk shop and my mother gazed back at me from out of the cracked pane. For the first time I recognised the desolation I had sometimes glimpsed in her eyes and wondered now if the similarities we shared included betrayal. Gazing at this face that had aged so much between the putting on and the taking off of the veil, I wondered what the hell I was going to do.

Thirty-six hours later, I was doing it. And as I lay back in the chair in Lucy's tiny pied-a-terre in Chelsea, while she put the Botox into the syringe I took the opportunity to recount to her my airport adventure.

'Men are such bastards,' Lucy observed automatically. 'Now, smile! That's it.' She then put the needle into the creases at the corner of my right eye—once, twice, three times—and moved to the other side. 'How did you know she was coming to England anyway?'

'I rang her,' I replied, almost smiling.

'You did what!? And she told you?'

'Well, she didn't know it was me, of course.' As I then told Lucy, I didn't suspect Will's lover was coming to England—I had actually planned to go to Turkey to confront her, to tell her to stay away from him. But I needed to make sure she would be on the peninsula when I arrived, so on Monday I rang her at work. I knew she catered for private parties so I pretended that I wanted to commission her for a housewarming. I gave her a false name, of course, when I told her that I would be in Gümüşlük this week and asked if we could meet. She said that was impossible because on Tuesday she was flying to England for a holiday. That was when I realised she was planning to come over to be with my husband.

My sense of triumph at my little bit of detective work had a sour taste to it, but I ignored it. Knowledge, I reminded myself, was power and, if Will refused to have any kind of relationship with the truth, I had no alternative.

'You realise you haven't yet called her by name?' Lucy pointed out. 'Do you know what it is?'

'She's a Russian,' I said. 'I call her Slutski.'

Lucy laughed so hard the needle jerked, making me whimper with pain. 'Sorry, darling,' she said, and injected the first bit of Restylane into the ageing lines running down from my nose to my mouth. No wonder Will had fallen for a woman seven years younger than me, who didn't have rail-tracks on her forehead and Arctic crevices down each side of her mouth.

'She might be a little trollop,' I said, 'but she's still the right side of thirty-five and I've passed the forty peak. What can I do?'

Lucy had the obvious reply, but that would cost another £1500 and I had spent enough for one day.

I spent the rest of the morning ringing Will's mobile. He didn't answer, of course. The mobile was switched off, the automated voice from French Telecom told me each time I rang.

So they had gone to France. But where? I didn't really have to ask.

At our own beginning, like most new lovers in England, we had chosen Paris for our first weekend away. Then, after that first clichéd trip, we had returned regularly, until we made the little hotel in le Marais ours; until the next-door cafe, with its homemade tartines, knew us by sight; until the jewellery store just behind La Place de la Bastille knew as soon as we walked in that we would be looking for another piece of amber.

I had introduced Will to Paris, at least to my Paris. I had taken him to my favourite little Impressionists' gallery beside the Louvre, to Rodin's house, to the tiny street just below Sacre Coeur, where I had once lived as an impoverished young poet abroad.

But I knew Will, and I knew that he would re-live that time of ours with his new love and return to the places I thought belonged to us, so he could scrub out my scent and replace it with hers. Knowing Will, he would probably claim Sacre Coeur as his, too, in the same way that he had stolen so much of my life and repackaged it in his identity.

On the morning that Will Jamieson first strode into my office, wanting to buy a house I had for sale in Hampstead, an air of adventure had followed him through the door. It was like the breeze that springs up over the bay in the late afternoon and fills your flaccid sails with hope. Tall and carelessly elegant, blond hair as light as an ice storm and eyes the colour of the Pacific, he cast his charm at me with the skill of a marlin fisherman and reeled me in effortlessly.

Over champagne that evening he spun an enticing web of anecdotes about his peripatetic life with his bass guitar— the band he played with, the gigs they travelled Europe for, the famous friends, the parties.

The second time we had dinner together, I told him how my early plans to be a great poet had died on the pyre of poverty that I didn't have the talent to extinguish. After being evicted from one too many flats, I had finally given in to my despairing parents' blandishments and got myself a Proper Job as an estate agent and property manager, which I loathed. I had turned to property as a career of last resort because even in my nomadic life I had always loved redecorating the various homes I lived in. I thought, naively, that it would be fun to work in property and that it might give me time to work on my poetry on the side. My first few months of commissions bought me my pretty little oast house which, more than a hundred years ago was used for drying hops for the local beer industry but which had long since been converted into a cottage, like so many others scattered around Kent. I'd always loved the look of oast houses, with their conical roofs and (I imagined, wrongly as it turned out) lingering scent of hops and mine immediately became my sanctuary. But the constant, petty demands of clients and tenants drained me of creativity and my poetry eventually drifted off into my past. When I told Will that every time I sold a house a little bit more of my soul died, he boasted that his band was so successful that he didn't really need to keep his own Proper Job as an investment banker and in fact was considering resigning so he could concentrate on music, his real love.

It had taken me a while to comprehend that the band Will played in had ceased to be in the charts more than a decade earlier and that the famous friends existed more in his imagination than at his dinner parties. But by the time I stopped listening to the stories of his prefabricated life, we'd been married for six years; his bosses at the investment bank had decided that it was they who no longer needed his services, rather than the other way around; and I had taken over the payment of his mortgage as well as my own.

But if my early adoration had blurred and faded into disillusion, it was easily replaced by that of others willing to believe he really was a good friend of Sting's and a mucker of Liam Gallagher's, and not just the bass guitarist for a band that couldn't get a recording contract anymore.

When Will ran out of his own stories, he would borrow mine. Once, after a film producer client of mine invited us to dinner and asked for my help in finding a location house for his movie, I was surprised to hear Will on the phone the next day telling a friend that the producer had asked him to collaborate on a film script. After my third London Marathon he told friends that he'd managed a personal best in the race, although the last time he'd put on running shoes was decades ago, at school.

Then there was the Ritter Roya bass guitar that I'd bought him on our second anniversary. For years I'd listened as Will dreamed aloud of this handmade guitar, of which only about sixty were created each year, and whose music was as beautiful as its black maple finish. On our anniversary I got all my credit cards together to come up with the thousands of pounds needed to buy one for him. The cost made me wake up shuddering in the night, but it was worth it to see the utter joy that illuminated Will when he saw the Ritter leaning casually against his music stand in Hampstead.

But only the next week, at the launch of a book he would never read, I heard him boasting to a person he would never see again that he'd bought the guitar with that year's munificent bonus. The next time I heard him mention it, he'd bought it with the proceeds of an especially successful gig. A year later he told someone that Jens Ritter, the guitar's designer, had come to a gig and been so impressed with his playing that he had insisted on crafting a guitar for Will himself.

When I asked him why he didn't tell people that his wife loved him so much she'd put herself in debt buying the Roya for our anniversary present, he'd shrugged. 'That's just boring,' he said.

Against the dull truth of real life, Will much preferred the different personas he presented. His aim was always to be more exciting than anyone else in the room—and far more interesting than the person he really was.

I needed to know for sure that Will had gone to Paris for his latest reinvention. So I cancelled all my appointments for the day and rang Suzanna, who shared an office with Will. Located just off Hampstead High Street, she had three large rooms, from which she ran her interior design company, and a smaller back room, from where Will now worked as a financial consultant to pay for what he believed was his true vocation as a musician.

'Please, please, please,' I prayed as I dialled. 'Be in the office.'

The phone picked up.

'Hi, Suzanna,' I said brightly. 'It's Lili. Can I ask a huge favour? Will has just called me from Norway. He's left some details about the gigs in his computer and he needs me to go into the system to retrieve them.'

Suzanna sighed, with exaggerated exasperation. She preferred not to be disturbed when she was working, even if it was just to open the door to Will's wife.

'I'm really sorry,' I apologised. 'But you know Will: memory, sieve.'

'I'll be here for an hour, that's all,' she answered. 'And only if you bring coffee. Mine's a latte.'

I was there in fifteen minutes. Suzanna buzzed me up, I gave her a hug and placed her latte on her desk before taking my own double espresso and retreating into Will's little cubby-hole, jam-packed with files and secrets. The computer came alive as soon as I flicked the 'on' button. No code to be entered, no password. Thank god. He obviously hadn't dreamed that I would resort to these tactics.

As I reached over to move my bag I glanced up at the photograph of us standing laughing on the boat we took once from Bodrum up the Dalyan River to the Lycian tombs, loggerhead turtles just visible in the water behind us as they played in the boat's wake. Together we'd hung the picture on the wall opposite his desk so he could, as he told me, always be reminded of that first, happy week we spent on the Aegean peninsula. It hung slightly askew now and the dust was so thick on the glass my face was almost obscured, while the jewel-bright sea appeared no more than a clouded memory.

Sadness overtook me and I let my eyes drift downward; otherwise I would have missed the Post-it note stuck on the outside of his top drawer. 'Eurostar,' it said. 'Jan 17. 08.25 a.m.' Today's date. With some numbers that were obviously the ticket code. So they were in Paris, probably already making wild love in our *pension* in le Marais.

If I had stopped then, turned off his computer and left, how would my life have turned out, I wonder? Would I have lost more? Won more?

At the time, all I knew was that simply knowing that Will and Slutski were in Paris was not enough. I needed to know how much danger our marriage was really in. What else is she planning to steal from me, I asked myself as I opened his emails, not realising just how prescient that question would soon become.

The inbox proffered nothing interesting so I moved to the archive drop-down, where a file titled Fin caught my eye. Curious, I opened it and read an email dated nine months ago. 'Hi darling,' it said. 'GOD I'm unhappy. I don't know why I'm here anymore.' A recognition flickered.

'We've got people coming over for lunch tomorrow but he refused to mow the lawn because his latest thing is that as an "artiste" he shouldn't have to do manual work. So I ended up mowing it by moonlight otherwise our friends would have thought they'd strayed into a Rousseau painting.'

The flickering recognition crystallised into certainty. This was an email from me, to my sister Zara in Australia.

I kept reading, my heart stammering.

Another, to my other sister, Eve, in Shanghai. 'I'm very lonely. He makes every excuse he can to go back to Turkey, I'm beginning to think he prefers it there.'

I opened another, and then another, the certainty growing. But there was no time to continue, to see just how many of my secret thoughts he had uncovered. More time for that later. I moved on.

I could see nothing else that suggested the Russian. Apart from Fin there was only one other file that couldn't be explained: Nat. The name made no sense, but with nothing else in the drop-down it was my only hope. So I opened it—and there they were.

While my emails to my sisters described a relationship in its terminal phases, the emails between Will and his lover would narrate an affair at its exciting birth.

I opened one at random. It was devastating in its ordinariness. 'Darling,' it said and in that one, simple word, I knew I had lost. 'Darling, my boiler has gone. Can you send one of your men to fix it?'

No lust, no intimacy and its very banality made it clear that they had moved far on from that first stage of rampant sex—the stage you can kill off if you catch it early enough—to the comfortable, settled relationship of committed lovers.

When people begin an affair, they give each other flattering, intimate, explicit honorifics. They use the language of multiple orgasms to describe each other because they know that the relationship is still only as strong as their last moments of lovemaking, and they need to remind each other how good that was.

'Darling' is different. It is the word lovers use once they are sure of each other, when they've stopped swopping stories about their separate lives, and begun to share the one life. And that is also when they start talking about broken boilers instead of silken knickers.

Suzanna came in, warning me she would be leaving the office soon, so I forwarded everything in the Nat folder to my email address, then everything in the Fin folder went the same way. I deleted them from the 'send' folder and then deleted them from the 'delete' folder. Then I went into the IMAP settings, and hit the button 'Delete messages forever'.

Leave no footprints. The technological equivalent of brushing over your trail in the sand.

Before I said goodbye to Suzanna I went to the loo, because I knew that in the cupboard in the tiny bathroom she kept a spare key. As the loo flushed I opened the cupboard and slipped the key into my pocket. I didn't want to have to depend on her goodwill again.

Back in her office I promised that the three of us would have dinner soon, and retreated into the damp mid-winter crowds.

Three months earlier

I turned my neck slightly so I could—just—see over Will's shoulder to the alarm clock on the table under the window. It said 1.13 a.m. Sleep! All I wanted was sleep. I tilted my pelvis slightly in the vaguely desperate hope that it looked as if I was joining in this loveless lovemaking.

But Will was away somewhere without me, coming in his mind with someone else.

'Hurry up, oh hurry up,' I prayed silently.

One of Gerard Depardieu's better movies, before he sold out to Hollywood, is called *Trop Belle Pour Toi*, a film in which he plays a man whose business and marriage is failing. Overweight and losing his confidence, he is married to a woman who is charming, successful and utterly beautiful. Too beautiful for him. So he has an affair with his frumpy, middle-aged and very grateful cleaner.

I'd never forgotten the terrible sadness of the opening scene: the beautiful wife lying coldly, passionlessly, as Depardieu made a frantic kind of love to her, and ordering him as if she was urging on a reluctant horse, 'Hurry up, hurry up!'

Will and I could never reach such an emotional disconnect, I had thought at the time. But after more than ten years together, that scene was being replayed in our cream bedroom: Will desperately scratching his itch, and I was desperate, too—desperate for him to roll over and start snoring so I could sink into forgiving oblivion.

But at least I was keeping my 'hurry ups' to myself.

Without warning, my body seized control. The thermonuclear heat started just under my lungs and then, increasing in intensity, it spread like lava across my chest, my upper arms, up through the neck and finally to my face, opening up my sweat glands as it went, until rivulets of water poured from my skin. The outbreak had the desired—if unintended—effect. Once Will and I would have delighted in our lingering lovemaking and when we had finished he would have stayed in me, on me, kissing my neck, holding me. But this time he rolled away from me in disgust, avoiding my touch. 'Christ, you're sweating' was all he said before he started snoring.

Oh well, I thought to myself. *Touché*, I suppose. And I slid out of bed to get a towel and dry my poor traitor of a body.

The wild bees that lived in the chimney had just begun to stir when the beeping of Will's mobile woke me. I opened an eye and looked at the clock, even as he slipped out of bed and crept to the window to read the text by the light of the street lamp outside. Five a.m. Who would be texting him at this time?

He tiptoed from the room and, as soon as I heard the bathroom door close, I, too, crept down the hall, trying to avoid the creaking floorboards of my 150-year-old oast house. I pressed my ear against the door, but could hear almost nothing. 'Love,' I thought I heard, and 'miss' but nothing else. I was back in bed before the door opened again, and I stayed very still as he crept under the sheets and turned his back to me.

Wide awake, I stared at the wall, half-focusing on the painting we had hung only yesterday, of the stone house in Turkey we had just finished restoring after four years of painstaking hard work. The painting gave me no answers and eventually I slipped into a damp, restless, uncomprehendingly sad sleep.

An hour and a half later I was standing in front of the bathroom mirror naked, critically regarding my body. Had it changed so much in a decade?

Years of relentless running, aerobics and yoga had given me toned muscles and a flat stomach, but exercise had proved no weapon against that ghastly, sweaty proof-of-age that had descended on me ten years earlier than it was supposed to. The medical dictionary definition ran again through my mind: 'Night sweats and hot flushes will increase the body's temperature by at least three degrees . . . some women might find it impacts on their day-to-day life . . .'

I remembered the 46-year-old man I'd slept with when I was nineteen. A Sydney radio producer, his only attraction for me was that he could get me into the premiere of a film I wanted to see. After paying my debt, I'd looked with some disgust at his naked body as he slept, and told myself disparagingly, 'Old person's flesh.' Then I'd grabbed my clothes and slipped out the door before he could wake up and demand an extra payment.

I imagined a nineteen-year-old boy gazing on me now or, worse still, witnessing one of my thermo-nuclear outbreaks; I shuddered in sympathy. It was, I supposed, quite lucky that Will took so little notice of me these days that he hadn't realised what was really happening last night. I comforted myself, as I stepped into the shower, with the thought that, as long as no one else did either, I could keep on pretending. Until it began to impact on my day-to-day life.

Wrapped in a towel, I slipped into the study, where Will was sitting at his computer. His study door was, as was habitual these days, three-quarters closed and, as I opened it, I saw him quickly minimise what looked like an email.

'What are you doing?' I asked curiously.

'Just checking on bookings for the villa,' he said. 'Look, we've got it booked out for next March and April already.'

I had fallen in love with Bodrum years earlier when I was living in Istanbul and had chartered a yacht with friends to sail around the Aegean. We had picked the boat up in what was then still a sleepy port; at that point the plague of tourists sweeping through southern Europe had not yet reached this Turkish peninsula, although the first outriders were beginning to arrive. To a young colonial girl in love with the past, I was immediately seduced by Bodrum's origin as the city of Halicarnassus and the birthplace of

Herodotus, the father of history, but I also loved the winding back streets crammed with shops selling leather and carpet, the chaos of the bazaar and the view out to sea from the English Tower of St Peter's castle. By the time I returned with Will, shortly before our wedding, the little port was a bustling tourist resort, with opulent hotels and flashy nightclubs filled with peroxided Russian girls. But we'd caught a dolmus to Gümüşlük, once the ancient city of Myndos but now a small fishing village a few kilometres further up the peninsula from Bodrum. and there we found a vestige of the peace I had first discovered all those years earlier as I sailed up this part of the coastline.

We visited regularly after that, our arrival usually timed to coincide with the annual classical music festival held in Gümüşlük, in which Will harboured a forlorn ambition to play; and in 2002, shortly after our fifth wedding anniversary, we bought this old ruin above the town in the shadow of the Karakaya hills, paying the £18,000 asking price on a credit card.

When I bought my oast house, I had sworn to myself that I would never allow anyone else to have their name on its lease. After years of financial and emotional insecurity as men came, saw, and disappointed, I considered my house my only safety net and I refused to let it be compromised, even after Will and I married and he moved into the cottage with me. We rented out his Hampstead house, living in it only between tenants, and it was never anything more than a London bolthole. But as we began restoration work on the Gümüşlük house, we were certain that it would be the shared home that would provide us with our future.

We were sure of our lives then. In the wake of 9/11, the rest of the world was threatening to dissolve into financial and fundamentalist terror; but we felt untouched, untouchable. Will was convinced that he was indispensable to the investment bank he worked for and I was convinced that I was indispensable to him.

We were both to be proved wrong, but Will's reality check came before mine. The first sign appeared months after we bought the ruin, when his bonus—which we planned to spend on the rebuild—was slashed from the million he had expected to mere thousands.

He hadn't recovered from that shock before he was asked to fill a box with items from his desk and to give back his security pass. It transpired that he had made one too many unwise investments with the bank's money and it could no longer afford his high-risk manoeuvres.

Others would have been humbled by such an outcome, but not Will. Convinced that another job lay just behind the next soon-to-open door, he spent most of his payout on restoring the house and persuaded me to throw my income at furnishing it lavishly.

The rest of his money he 'invested' in projects that were just as unwise as those on which he had wasted his company's finances—the building development in Suffolk that turned out to have Roman ruins beneath it, the greywater filtration system that was too many years before its time, not to mention the racehorse that went lame after just one race.

Despite my increasing despair at his fecklessness, I was, for too long, seduced by the refrain he sang of greater things; I trailed in his wake, like a tender tied to a yacht, bouncing around in the waves he created. Even when our joint account started evaporating I clung on, desperate to believe in his tomorrow, and tomorrow, and tomorrow.

Before my belief in him was completely drained, the money had gone and I had agreed to pay the mortgage and upkeep of the Hampstead house. He promised that, in return, he would add my name to the title deeds, although we both knew his promises were as empty of substance as wind chimes.

But at least the Turkish ruin had been rebuilt into the stone beauty that we both hoped would bring us a new kind of reality cheque. And the first step was to get it onto the holiday market as soon as possible, with the help of Stella, one of the handful of English realtors who had set up business in Bodrum.

Even so, it seemed a shame that we could not enjoy it a little longer—making love in the hand-painted four-poster beds I had discovered at the back of a builder's shed; swimming in our infinity pool overlooking Rabbit Island; or planning the citrus grove we wanted to plant on the slopes behind us.

'Why check on your emails so early in the morning?' I asked Will as he remained sitting in front of the now-blank screen of his computer.

I saw his eyes flicker but he answered immediately. 'Stella texted me this morning saying someone out there was interested in taking it for the last week in May, so I was just making sure it was free.'

So that was the text this morning. It made sense: 5 a.m. our time was 7 a.m. in Turkey, and the locals got up early to start work before the heat of the day sapped their energy.

But then why the creeping around the house? Why the whispered conversation in the bathroom? Why the word 'love'?

Kent

After leaving Will's office that morning, I didn't go straight home to the cottage. First I went to the gym; I needed something to dull the pain and I knew the opiate of exercise would restore at least a semblance of calm.

After the first couple of miles on the treadmill, the pounding of my heart became steadier and my mind started to clear. As the sweat began to pour, I felt that familiar sense of relief, of separation from the world that hard exercise gave me.

I showered slowly, dressed and went upstairs for coffee. But as I stood at the counter waiting for the teenaged cafe staff to stop gossiping and serve me, I knew I couldn't delay any longer. Time to face the fall.

I hurried home then, staying in the motorway's overtaking lane all the way back to Kent, tapping the steering wheel impatiently when slower cars threatened to delay me. Even so, it took me nearly two hours to get back to my village and, as I entered the cottage, I stopped only to turn up the heating before going into my study and opening my laptop.

The emails seemed to take an age to download, but finally they were all there.

First Fin. I opened one randomly and started from the bottom. 'Hi darling,' it began, as my emails to Zara in Australia always did. 'I don't think I can carry on in this life much longer. I love Will but he doesn't seem to have any real commitment to me anymore. We fight all the time. What to do? Lots love xxxx'

Next came Zara's reply. 'Maybe it's just a down period. You're under so much strain with the Turkish house; you need to get away somewhere completely different and have a real break. xxxx'

And me again. 'Maybe . . . anyway, I have to make things work until M & D's visit next month. They'd be devastated if they thought something was wrong. Lots love xxx'

I stared at the emails. They dated back to my parents' last visit to the UK from their Sydney home, almost a year ago. We had moved to Sydney from Toronto when I was fifteen but I never felt I belonged there and after university I became restless and left again—first for Istanbul, then Paris and finally to London where, for the first time in my life, I felt at home. Dirty, overcrowded, dysfunctional, the city nevertheless drew me close and it took me less than a year to know that I could never leave.

My parents, both romantics, understood my need to keep moving and never asked me to come back. Instead, they would make frequent trips to Britain, using my cottage or the Hampstead house as their own jumping-off point to explore the rest of Europe.

I remembered now that, during their last trip to England, Will had removed himself, pleading urgent work on the Gümüşlük villa that needed his presence. Was it because he'd read these emails? Because he had got into my computer and read the secrets that I'd shared with Zara and Eve as my disappointments mounted?

As I wondered how long he'd been spying on my narration of a relationship deteriorating into dust, I started to laugh hysterically. Just when I thought that I was the clever one, learning his secret life through his online imprint, I was discovering that it was he who had been accessing my hidden life for all these months.

I had been so innocent that time when his computer crashed—I had given him my internet password so he could use my laptop to check his own emails, trusting him not to delve into my online communications. Yet all that time he had been spying on me.

We're as bad as each other, I thought bitterly. What had happened to us? Why was it that the only way we could share our lives now was by creeping into each other's private conversations with other people?

The Nat file was surprisingly short. Only five emails in it, apart from the one I'd already read, and two of them were just as dull in their detail and just as devastating for that very fact. The latest was sent last week.

Slutski to Will: 'Darling I can hardly wait til next week. What shall I bring? The naughty lingerie you bought me?'

W to S: 'Why bother, darling? I'll only have to rip it off you as soon as I see you.'

Feeling slightly ill, I opened another one. This was dated nine months ago. I checked the date again. April 18. The day after Will and I had returned from a week in Gümüşlük—a week which had been, I thought, a rare oasis of happiness.

We had hiked up the hills to the windmills scattered on the ridge and strolled hand-in-hand through the tangerine groves, the way we had the first time we spied the ruins of what would become our house. We'd shopped for Turkish teapots at the Wednesday market and spices in the Thursday bazaar and lingered for hours over raki at our favourite fish restaurant on the bay in old Gümüşlük. We had actually been happy together . . . or so I thought.

But here was this email, sent less than twenty-four hours after we had walked back in the door of my cottage. It was from Will to Slutski: 'Hello, you. It's been three days since I've seen you and that's four days too long.'

So he had seen her during 'our' week together—had slipped away, somehow, to be with her. But how could he have managed that, when we were hardly apart? I thought back. Of course. Every day we were apart for a couple of hours, when Will went for an early morning progress check on the house and I ploughed up and down the bay.

The previous time we'd come to Turkey, a couple of months earlier, he'd tried to persuade me to abandon my aquatic exercise and join him on these dawn excursions up the roads lined with whitewashed houses and bougainvillea to the home that was beginning to emerge from its chrysalis of rubble.

But this time he didn't seem to mind at all. In fact, I remembered now, on one particular morning he'd appeared irritated when I said I thought I might come with him to the house. 'But you love swimming. It sets you up for the day,' he'd said.

I'd argued that I would rather check on the house with him, after which we could go to the Pasticceria Mamochka, our favourite cafe, for coffee and almond cake. That seemed to enrage him.

'We don't have time to go to the bloody *pasticceria*!' he'd said, his voice rising in anger.

I couldn't understand why the mention of the *pasticceria* should send him into such a rage, but he was becoming increasingly short-tempered. I joked with my sisters that the only time he called me 'darling' anymore was when it was preceded by 'for fuck's sake'. So when he slammed out, I'd tried to shrug it off and ran down to the water.

But he was away for much longer than usual that morning. Now that I was forced to think about it, his morning trips this time around were all longer than they used to be, but he always had so much to say about the house when he came back that I hadn't noticed anything out of the ordinary.

There was one day, I now recalled, when he had disappeared for an especially long time. Slightly worried—the Turks drove like madmen, and there were always accidents on the road to our house above the town—I rang his mobile, but it was switched off. Odd. So I had texted him to say I was going to the *pasticceria* for coffee and to ring me when he was on the way back.

Pasticceria Mamochka had been closed, inexplicably, so I'd wandered around the harbour until he showed up, another hour later, with a complicated story about how the rental car had broken down and he'd had to walk to the garage to get someone to fix it.

Now I got it. He wasn't walking along a sun-parched road to the garage that morning; he was with Slutski instead. So this must have been, more or less, when it began.

The next email, sent in May, was less surprising. 'Darling,' he wrote, 'I've FINALLY seen *Burnt by the Sun*; they showed it at a Russian film festival in Hampstead this week. You're right, it's a fabulous movie, although it was no fun seeing it on my own. You should have been with me. But never mind, I've bought the DVD so we can watch it together when I'm next over.'

I recalled that he'd rung me one afternoon in May, insisting I leave work early and go to see *Burnt by the Sun* with him that evening. I'd been surprised—years earlier, when I had first seen this wonderful Russian movie which had moved me so powerfully with its depiction of the 1930s purges, I had tried to persuade Will to see it too. But he wasn't interested in films with subtitles. 'I don't go to the movies to read,' he had complained the only time I had been successful in getting him into a 'foreign' film, and I had long got used to going to European movies on my own. That time, as we sat in the dark cinema, I thought— hoped—that maybe, just once, he was actually trying to take an interest in something I loved. I was disappointed. He'd dismissed the movie with his customary contempt, but when I'd argued with him, he insisted I buy the DVD, so he could watch it again at home. 'Maybe I'll prefer it the second time around,' he had suggested.

I couldn't remember what had happened to the DVD— he'd resisted all attempts to watch it and I had consigned it to the growing collection of films I used to watch when he wasn't around. Now I ran to the living room and searched the old Victorian bookcase by the bay window. The bottom shelf was filled with a mixture of books about the cinema and DVDs of those films, but the *Burnt by the Sun* DVD had gone. And now I knew where.

The last email was dated November. Two months ago. Sent the day after a strange phone call Will received during dinner at our local Italian restaurant—the call which first alerted me that something was definitely going on with someone, somewhere.

Slutski to Will: 'Darling, I'm in pain. Do you know how hard it was for me when you hung up like that? And to know that you were in a restaurant with her?'

Will to Slutski: 'You mustn't fret. There's no relationship here, we were just talking business. And all the time I was thinking of you.'

And Slutski again: 'I think about you, too, every minute. You haven't forgotten you promised to put that £1500 into my account this week? Of course I'll repay you.'

I remembered then that, before going to dinner the night of the phone call, Will had put on his humble mask and asked me to pay £1500 for the villa garden's new watering system.

'It's just I'm a bit short this month,' he had said.

I paid because Gümüşlük was our future and, besides, our marriage had become punctuated with similar demands for financial 'loans' that Will never repaid.

Now I wondered how much of the money I'd handed to him over the past year had gone the Russian's way, and I wondered whether she was playing him the way he was clearly playing me.

It was well into the night by the time I had finished reading the emails and analysing the consequences. But I felt the need to contact my sisters before I could call it a day. Zara and Eve were the only people who had remained a constant throughout my adulthood of careless partnerships and unwise affairs, and whenever my life threatened to spiral into disarray I would turn to them first.

I always felt guilty that I had lost so much contact with Lori, our fourth sister. Like me, she too had fled our suburban life soon after university but while I had escaped to what I told myself would be a more cosmopolitan existence in Europe, Lori had gone to the other extreme, running into the arms of a rather strange religious group. Older and more reserved than us three, she had always seemed slightly disapproving of our lives, even in our teenage years, so we were less surprised than shocked when she announced that her future lay with God and she was turning her back on the world. When, a decade of silence later, she declared that relationship over and left the group, Zara, Eve and I joked to each other that she was as bad at relationships as we were; but we would never make that joke to Lori. She might have come back to the world but she never really returned to us. She moved to a small country town in New South Wales where she worked with a religious organisation and, although she kept in vague touch with Mum and Dad, she remained remote from her sisters. By then, of course, I was living in London and our contact was reduced to cards and emails at Christmas and birthdays. Zara and Eve tried harder to draw her back into the family, mainly for the sake of our parents, who felt as if they had lost a daughter. But after being repeatedly, if politely, rebuffed, they gave up. We loved Lori, but she would never be part of our own little sisterhood of three. And that sisterhood had been the rock that steadied us all through the turbulence of our lives. Of the three of us, Zara had remained longest with one man, although her marriage to Sergei, a wildly charismatic Russian, went through its own tempests. Eve's marriage was more of an enigma; behind the sunnily anarchic humour that defined her, there were greyer shades that suggested her husband Henry was not always kind and I often wondered what really lay behind the façade they presented to the world.

Now I emailed Eve, camouflaging my pain by turning the scene at Heathrow into a comedy made for laughter. I imagined her wiping away her tears as she replied, 'Outstanding, darling', but the brevity of her actual response was unusual. I wondered what her silence was hiding and resolved to call her in the next few days.

I was still wide awake, my mind churning, at 12.27 a.m. when my mobile vibrated beside me. I moved only to stretch out my left arm and hold the phone above my face so I could read the text.

'V v sorry I hurt you,' it said. 'Please forgive me. I love you. xx'

I put the phone down and returned to staring at the ceiling. I was remembering that late-night phone call eight weeks ago. And the premonitory dream that hadn't stopped haunting me since.

Two months earlier

We were walking towards the sea, past the market where we always bought our vegetables, when Will suddenly veered right at the olive stall and steered me toward Pasticceria Mamochka.

As we walked into the cool interior and approached the tall, slim, dark-haired woman stirring a pot of spiced chocolate on the stove behind the counter, Will turned to me.

'I want you to meet the woman I really love,' he told me.

I was still crying when I woke up from my dream and found him watching me warily—like a hyena waiting for the gazelle to leave the safety of the herd.

The previous night he and I had gone to the Italian restaurant in the middle of the village for a late supper. It had been after 9.30 p.m. by the time I'd got back from the office, but the restaurant owner greeted us with delight, as she always did, and brought us the smoked mozzarella and wild garlic antipasto, the dish in which her restaurant specialised. She poured us each a glass of Macon Blanc and we began to relax.

We were, for once, enjoying the evening. There had been too many rows lately and we were both on our best behaviour, trying to get back some of our old, easy love.

Will had his hand over mine, the way he always used to sit when we ate together, and for the first time in months I felt almost happy. He had just suggested that I take a long weekend and come out to Turkey, to put the finishing touches to the house interiors, when his phone rang. It often rang at night—clients asking for out-of-hours advice, musician pals calling to discuss fresh gigs. So I thought nothing of it until he spoke.

'Oh, hello,' he said coldly.

I heard a woman's voice say, 'Bad time?'

'It is, actually,' he said. And hung up.

I felt cold, sick with foreboding. 'Who was that?' I asked.

'Oh,' he said, looking awkward. 'Wrong number.'

I stared at him, aghast. 'The wrong number? When does the wrong number ask you if they're calling at a bad time?'

He began to stutter. 'Look, it was just nobody, all right? Nobody at all.'

And that's when I knew that it was.

Belgravia

At 8.30 a.m., as I emerged from the Blackwall Tunnel, my mobile vibrated again.

'I love u v much,' he said this time. 'Plse forgive me and let's try again.'

Steering with one hand, I texted back angrily, 'If you loved me you wldn't be in Paris with the lover you said you'd left.'

I knew that would get him. He would be wondering how on earth I'd found out about Paris. Then I wondered if I'd let him know too much. Damn.

The phone vibrated again. 'I do love you and I want to be with you. I'm just very confused right now.'

'Well, yes, he would be,' said Justine when she called me later, as I was draped over the ice-cream freezer in the local supermarket trying to stave off another hot flush. 'You run two women and lie to both of them, of course you're confused. Look, why don't you stay here tonight? We can drink too much Grey Goose and decide what to do. Rick's away on one of his do-gooders and I'll divert the kids with a couple of DVDs so we won't be disturbed.'

Justine's marriage was, like that of many of my friends, well past its use-by-date. She had married Rick at twenty-four, leaving her first husband for the young lawyer. Husband Number One had been a dedicated doctor, and she had adored him, until the day he came home and said he'd resigned from his job and was going to pursue his true love, art. Justine, whose knowledge of art began and ended with Van Gogh's *Sunflowers*, was furious with him for making such a ridiculous and marriage-threatening decision.

Garret living wasn't for her so, when she met Rick at a work dinner, she abandoned her doctor-cum-artist and moved in with him. They were married within a year and Rick's ambition ensured they got the house in Belgravia, private schools for the children and as many Louboutins as Justine could buy.

Even when he switched from corporate law to human rights law, Justine wasn't unduly worried. After all, at the innumerable law society dinners they were invited to, the human rights lawyers were just as glossy as Rick, their wives as sleek as she was. But then, to Justine's horror, Rick started getting idealistic, talking endlessly about Afghan asylum-seekers, Iranian dissidents, Chinese detainees.

To pour Himalayan sea salt into the wound, it was just about now, twelve years after she had left him, that Husband Number One won an international art prize with one of his sculptures and began to be talked about in serious circles.

Justine comforted herself with the fact that he might now be famous but he was still relatively poor. And she comforted herself with lovers. The week after HNO was shortlisted for the Turner Prize, she took a young, tongue-tied tree surgeon to bed. When she tired of the dirt under his fingernails, she swopped him for another, equally young but with better conversational skills and a cleaner collar line.

'Sex with much younger men just does something to your skin,' she insisted when people complimented her on her new glow.

But toyboys weren't the real secret. Rick's money bought her youth, in the form of Botox, laser treatment and buttock implants, and that was what kept her inside the marriage. Without Rick's fat bank account, there would be no more visits to Dr Kash and, without his little miracles, there would no more toyboys. She would become her very own portrait in the attic, and the thought of that terrified her.

The problem was that Rick, who had adopted her knife-style after admiring her suddenly smooth forehead and plumped cheeks, had also regained his youthful good looks. Worse, young and unforgivably beautiful women were taking him aside at law functions, pretending an interest in the plight of Afghani women in Taliban-held areas so they could brush their breast implants against his arm and flutter their eyelash extensions at him.

Justine had gradually become enraged at the risk to which this exposed her. It was fine for her to have affairs. After all, younger men never threatened the marital bed. She hated to admit it but, if they were going to discover commitment, it was unlikely to be with a woman fifteen years their senior. But if one of Rick's dalliances took a more serious turn, it could be fatal for the financial security that she'd worked so hard to achieve. So she'd made sure that she was ahead of him at every turn.

I watched Justine fill a third of each glass with Grey Goose before she added the tonic. Then she poured in another splash of vodka. 'Vodka sandwich,' she called this speciality of hers. She'd learned the technique from her sister-in-law—a dreadful old alcoholic, of course—but still, it was a good tip.

We clinked glasses and sat side by side on the big Turkish rug in front of the fireplace, our backs against the sofa. It was how we always sat when it was just us two—sprawled on the floor, sharing our lightest and murkiest thoughts.

'Men are permanently confused,' Justine said, brushing a strand of ash-blonde hair out of her eye before taking a slug of her drink. 'Face it, they don't know what fidelity is. They think they want it, but what they really want is security. That's what we provide them with, along with children and a well-run home life.

'But once they've got the security thing tied down, they begin fantasising about being single again—and that's when they start to look elsewhere. They want it all—the safe house they call home, plus the excitement and passion of the eternally new romance.'

I agreed, but as I gazed at the empty fireplace I reminded her, 'But I haven't exactly been there for him over the last couple of years. By the time I get home from work, I'm too tired to do anything but have a row and go to bed.'

'So what are you going to do about this? Are you going to take him back?' asked Justine.

'I don't know. I shouldn't but . . . oh god. It's been so many years, I can't just walk away.'

'Why not?' asked Justine. 'You don't have any kids. You don't have anything really to tie you together.'

'We've had more than ten years together. Most marriages don't last that long anymore. And,' I pointed out, 'there's Luke.'

Luke was Will's son, aged, as he would describe it, twelve-years-nine-months—nearly-thirteen. He may not have been mine, but I loved him with a visceral power that surprised me at times. We had known each other since he was three, and we had fallen in love almost from the first day.

Once, not all that long ago, Luke reduced me to tears as he recounted what he'd learned from me—how to snorkel in the Aegean, what to feed the fox cubs at the end of my garden, why God had invented washing machines solely so that small boys could jump out of trees and into puddles.

I knew that, if I left Will, I'd probably never be allowed to see Luke again. It would break my heart almost more than ending our marriage would. After all, step-parents don't get access to the children.

'Well then,' said Justine. 'We had better get out the big guns.'

I started to protest. I didn't want lawyers involved, or private detectives.

But Justine was talking about an entirely different weapon of choice.

Last month

Will had met Jeremy on one of his increasingly solo trips to Gümüşlük and they quickly became friends. They were both in a bar one night during the music festival and, drinking too much red wine under the walnut tree that gave the bar its name and, swopping notes about the projects that had brought them here—our restoration and the house that Jeremy was building up in nearby Yalıkavak—they found they shared the same builder, whom they both suspected of cheating them.

Shared anger and shared hangovers were a powerful bond, and the two men became inseparable, often travelling together to Turkey to work on the houses and play in the bars. Now, on a day with snow at its edges, Will and I were on our way to the fisherman's cottage in Devon which Jeremy shared with his new partner, Claire.

Our fury with each other, on the night of the restaurant phone call, had within days been blunted by the mundane necessities of ordinary life. It was easier to shunt the suspicions and the unhappiness into a back cupboard, even if we both could hear the tectonic plates grinding away beneath our sheets.

Christmas had been strained, and we'd filled it with friends so we wouldn't have to face each other. Now we were evading ourselves again in those deflated days between Christmas and New Year with this visit to Salcombe.

I took an immediate liking to Jeremy and Claire. A horse trainer, he was lean and greying, with a slightly vulpine air and a voice that knew how to persuade others to his will. Claire, a lawyer-turned-artists'-agent, had cropped curly black hair, a disarming giggle and a falcon that she took hunting on winter weekends.

Over a dinner of local crab on Salcombe Harbour, Will regaled them with tales from what I had come to call his 'Walter Mitty life', impressing them with an anecdote that involved drinking into the early hours with Ricky Gervais and Jude Law. The reality was that, while Gervais and Law frequented the same pub in Primrose Hill that we sometimes did, they had never spoken to us, because they had no idea who we were. But these new friends were taken in, as new friends invariably were, by Will's tales of secondary fame and, as always, my well-developed sense of loyalty prevented me from exposing them as lies.

How could such intelligent people believe his fantasia, I wondered the next morning as I wandered about the cottage while Will and Jeremy prepared Sunday lunch. Claire was out with her falcon and I was bored. I decided to go for a run across the cliffs and was changing shoes in the guest room when I spotted Will's phone lying on the side table.

I crept down the hallway and heard him in full flow. Jeremy was lapping up the story of Will's dinner with Michael Douglas and Catherine Zeta-Jones a few days earlier (he and his band had actually been playing at a birthday party three farms away from the Douglas/Zeta-Jones dinner, but in Will's Mitty-world, there was almost no difference between the two events).

Back in the guest room, I turned on Will's phone, flicking down the menu to the call history. The list of calls was innocently boring. My name was there, his brother George's, Jeremy, me again. Then I saw it. Two letters: *La*. I checked the date and the time, knowing even before I looked that this was the mysterious 'wrong number' phone call the night we were in the Italian restaurant.

The number began with the area code 90252. Which meant it was from the Bodrum peninsula. She was there, La, whoever she was.

I opened the message inbox. The first from La was very short. 'I wish you were inside me now,' it said.

Starting to shake, I scrolled down to the next La. 'Why are you there and not here with me? We could be making love by your pool.'

It was sent two days before the phone call, just before Will suggested we go away to Gümüşlük for a weekend.

Then I thought back to that 5 a.m. text in September that had given me the first warning my security was at threat; it wasn't sent by the woman managing our house at all but from La, as she was getting up and missing his warmth in her bed.

Now I was trembling uncontrollably, shivering like a dying leaf. There were more from La, but I moved to the 'sent' folder to find three messages to her. These were much longer than hers. 'I can see you rising naked,' one started, 'your wonderful breasts . . .' I couldn't read any more of that one. I felt like a voyeur.

So I opened another. 'It will be hell being stuck in Devon with her,' he had written. 'But at least we'll be sleeping in different parts of the house and I can pretend you're on my pillow, my darling.'

I didn't need to check the date to know he'd sent the message yesterday morning, before we left for these few days together.

His last message read simply, 'You are the only good thing in my life.'

My legs gave way.

When Will came into the room, I was curled up on the floor, the duvet pulled over me, shivering still.

'What on earth are you doing?' he asked, amused, until he noticed his phone missing from the table.

'Lili?'

I could hear the fear in his voice, but I was shuttling away from him until I was crouched against the wall. I held his phone up for him, opened at his last message.

'Oh Lili,' he said. 'What have you done?'

I threw the mobile at him as I stood up and pushed past, grabbing a coat that was by the door before running down the driveway. At the road I slowed and started walking away from the village, towards the line of trees at the top of the hill.

As I began climbing the slope, I pulled out my phone and called Zara in Sydney. It was late in the evening in Australia, but I knew that if she saw my name flash up, my sister would answer. We'd always been there for each other, the three sisters, ever since we were growing up together in Canada and even now, separated by unhelpful time zones and disparate lives, we always knew where to go when trouble loomed.

'Get in the car and drive back to London now,' she commanded, once she'd worked out what I was telling her through rising sobs and hiccups. 'Get away from him, go home and change the locks. The bastard!'

Her loyal fury only made me weep harder, so she suggested, 'Why don't you just dump everything and come over here? We'd love to have you.'

I pictured her standing in her courtyard overlooking the harbour, the possums running along the wall to snatch the slices of apple that Sergei always left for them. I longed to do as she suggested, to leave Devon and go straight to Gatwick. I told myself I could be in Sydney, watching the fireworks on the harbour on New Year's Eve. But I also knew that I would not go. I would have to face the drums.

Trudging on towards the treeline, I tentatively probed the wound I had just opened up. I wasn't really surprised to find that, although excruciatingly raw around the edges, the centre was totally without feeling, like dead flesh. After months of watching our once all-consuming love contort, and wondering what, or who, was behind this new ugliness, it was almost a relief to discover the truth.

It was like being diagnosed with a serious illness after being plagued with vague symptoms; there would be pain, and all-consuming fear, but at least you'd know what you're up against. Then you faced a stark choice: letting the disease take hold, or fighting it off.

I may not have been physically ill but infidelity is another type of disease and my choice, too, was stark.

As I gazed over the wild gorse at the tumbling grey sea wondering whether I would die or fight, I heard my name and turned around. He was striding towards me and he looked as bleak as I did.

'Lili,' he said when he reached me. 'Why did you have to go into my phone?'

As if all this was of my doing.

I glared at him. 'Who is she?'

'No one,' he answered.

I laughed, a laugh that sounded the way bile tastes. He began to stutter, as he always did when he knew there were no more lies to fall back on. 'It's just a silly thing,' he said. 'It doesn't change anything for us.'

'It changes everything,' I said and started walking away from him.

'Look,' he said, grabbing my arm. 'Don't make such a thing of it.'

I swung around and he flinched. 'Who is she?' I asked again. 'And don't say no one. Don't insult me.'

'She's just someone who works in the *pasticceria*,' he said. 'She's just a little empty-headed cake maker. Honestly, it doesn't mean anything.'

He giggled—a high-pitched, unpleasant whinnying sound I'd never heard him make before. 'I've made a mistake, that's all. I've been a silly boy.'

I looked at him, stunned. He'd said it with such a transparently fake shame that did nothing to disguise his secret pride at the act. Like the schoolboy who has just been caught fucking behind the bike sheds and has to pretend regret for the teacher, but wants all his mates to know he's got off with the school tart. I was so insulted I nearly laughed.

The rest of the day passed in a surreal blur as, somehow, we kept up a pretence of amity. No one seemed to notice that I said almost nothing throughout lunch, ignoring my food and digging the nails of my left hand into the back of my right, trying to make the superficial pain cancel out the internal agony.

As the others chatted about our houses, the iniquity of the building manager we had now sacked, how we could maximise our villas' rental income, all I saw was a big demolition ball swinging at my life. The Gümüşlük house—each stone carved lovingly by hand, surrounded by mandarin and lemon trees—which was going to provide Will and me with our future . . . I watched the big black ball smashing into it and reducing it all to a volcano of dust.

We drove in silence back to London, where we'd planned to spend New Year. Once inside the Hampstead house, he tried to hold me but I pushed him away.

'It doesn't mean anything,' he said again.

'So ring her and tell her that,' I demanded. I held out the phone to him. 'Go on, ring her now. Tell her you won't be seeing her anymore.'

'I . . . I can't do that.'

'Why not?'

His voice was cold, emotionless. 'There is nothing to end,' he said.

———❊❊———

I got to my office in Primrose Hill early the next morning. The property market died over the Christmas break and even the most troublesome tenants took a break from complaining unless frozen pipes or leaky roofs threatened to ruin their festivities. So I knew the office would be empty and I wouldn't be disturbed. I rang my friend Kate, who had bought a house just down the hill from us in the village, and who was attempting to make a living out of bed and breakfast for holidaymakers in the summer and ornithologists in the winter months.

'Hi, darling,' said Kate in delight. 'Pleeeease tell me you've just arrived. I'm so lonely here. Why on earth did I agree to move?'

'I'm at work, I can't really talk,' I said. 'Just tell me quickly—do you know anyone in the *pasticceria* whose name begins with "La"?'

'Larissa?' said Kate immediately. 'She's that Russian cake maker, the one everyone uses for their housewarming parties. Why? What's wrong? What has she done?'

I forced myself to make my voice sound light. 'Oh, nothing really. I just think that she and Will might have become a little too close.'

'You're joking,' said Kate. 'An affair? Never. She's not Will's type. Or more to the point, he's not hers. She's a classical musician, you know, a cellist; she only bakes pastries because the quartet she plays with doesn't make any money. She regards all of us as philistines—she loathes rock music and would never look at any man who couldn't tell his Bach from his Beethoven. And no offence, Lili, but Will is hardly Nigel Kennedy.'

'No,' I agreed. 'But he does haunt the annual music festival; in fact, I bet that's where they met. And he lies so pathologically that he has probably convinced the both of them that he is really a viola player with the London Symphony Orchestra.'

That would do it for her,' agreed Kate. 'Do you want me to ask around?'

'No,' I said. 'No, don't repeat this to anyone. I'll have to sort things out my own way.'

I hung up, slowly, locking a door on all the texts, secrets, lies and excuses of the last twenty-four hours. I wouldn't let them out until later, when I was safely on my own.

Belgravia

We were halfway through the second vodka sandwich when Justine took me into her study to show me her safety net against a Rick divorce.

She switched on her computer while I added tonic to our glasses in a vain attempt to instil a bit more sobriety into the proceedings. Then she opened her inbox and clicked on the file marked 'Bitches'. (Justine didn't believe in obfuscation.) She scrolled down through hundreds of emails between Rick and an impressive array of women—students, legal clerks, secretaries. Women who had just one thing in common: her husband.

Our eyes met over the rims of our glasses.

'Welcome to the spying game,' said Justine, swallowing the remains of her vodka.

I was puzzled. How had she managed to collect all these emails without Rick knowing? Didn't he keep the emails hidden behind a password?

'Of course,' she replied. 'He has done everything in his power to stop me finding out about all of this.'

Well, then?

'I said "in his power", not in my power.' She leaned over and clinked her glass to mine. 'And I have something he doesn't have—spy software.'

Justine revealed that she'd bought the software after it was recommended by a young Danish lover who'd told her, as casually as if he was describing how he marinated herring, that he used it to keep an eye on his girlfriend.

'All you have to do is to buy the software off the net and download it onto his computer,' she explained. 'It only takes a couple of hours and, once it's installed, every keystroke he hits is copied onto your computer. He has nowhere to run, nowhere to hide . . .' She laughed evilly, although she looked unbearably sad.

'Of an evening,' she continued, 'we sit in our individual studies next door to each other, pretending to work. And while he's emailing his lovers, I'm reading his messages even before his girlies do.'

I stared at her. 'How long have you been doing this?'

'Two years,' she answered. 'For two years I've read every bloody detail of every bloody affair. I've seen them start, I've seen them finish. And I get all the sex in between. I never knew how much he likes to do action replays via his modem. It's quite addictive, really, in a toxic kind of way.'

'But why didn't you tell me?' I asked.

Justine gave me one of her looks, rolling her eyes up under her eyelids like an ultra-glamorous zombie. 'What would I have said? "Oh guess what, I'm spying on my husband"? You would have been shocked.'

I opened my mouth, but she held up her glass like a stop sign.

'No, Lili,' she went on, 'you would have been appalled. Everyone condemns people who spy on their partners until they've gone through what you're suffering right now, and what I've had to deal with for the last few years.'

I stayed at Justine's that night, hiding in the spare room the next morning while the children got ready, noisily, for school. Then, when the front door had slammed for the last time, I slid into the kitchen where she was huddled over a big cup of black coffee.

She got up and made a fresh cafetière, and as she handed me a cup she warned, 'Once you do this, there's no going back. You've admitted that there's nothing left between you but distrust and betrayal.'

'Putting on the *hijab* burnt that particular bridge,' I pointed out.

'The thing is, it's incredibly damaging, having their lust for someone else laid out before you. It might be addictive, but only in the way that self-harm is. Nothing good comes out of it, you know—just a lot of blood.'

'But I need to know, Justine. He won't just leave my house. I have to stockpile my ammunition.'

Justine sighed. 'Okay,' she said. 'This is what you do.'

Kent

I was just reaching the turn-off from the M25 to my village when the phone rang. It was Luke's mother. I stared at the phone. Why would Bronwyn be ringing me on a Friday afternoon? Surely Will had remembered to cancel this weekend with Luke, so he could go to the music-festival-that-wasn't in Norway?

But, no, probably not. He was almost certainly too excited about his Paris dalliance to remember that this was our weekend for the son he claimed meant everything to him.

By the time I'd worked all this out, Bronwyn had hung up. I dialled into voicemail and listened to her frustrated rant. Will hadn't picked up Luke from school, hadn't even bothered to call to say he was late and, when she rang him, his phone had a French telecom message on it. 'What the hell is going on?!'

I pulled in opposite the village green and watched the footballers waltzing through the dusk shadows for a while before I rang her. I wasn't going to tell her that Will had run off to Paris with a Russian lover—I didn't want to give her that pleasure. But neither was I going to make excuses for him.

'Bronwyn, I can't believe Will didn't bother to tell you he had a gig this weekend,' I said as soon as she picked up the phone. 'He's so unreliable, and I'm so sorry.'

Before she could draw breath, I went on. 'I can still have Luke. You could drop him down in the morning if you like, or we could meet halfway.'

The next day I pulled up alongside Bronwyn at the halfway point outside the Black Horse pub and Luke skipped into my car. Luke had his father's glacier-blond colouring and although Will's good looks were muted in his stocky, bespectacled son, they shared the same magnetism that drew people into their sphere. But while Will's charm was calculated to hide cold shadows, his son had a natural warmth that was as enticing as sunlight. A weekend alone with him would help soothe me after the week's fury.

We drove home with his favourite radio station playing at full volume and singing along in an out-of-tune duet. In between songs, Luke spoke seriously about why he couldn't decide whether he loved Beyoncé or J-Lo more.

Later, after our usual rainy afternoon fare of a movie, which we then re-enacted in the Chinese restaurant across the road from the cinema to the delight of the children at the next table, I put Luke in front of an *X-Men* DVD and, once he was safely ensconced, I shut the door to the study and switched on Will's computer.

It took me just over an hour to download the software. While I was waiting I went downstairs to see how Luke was. He was sitting on the floor engrossed in the movie, but he turned and grinned at me as I entered, shoving his Harry Potter specs back up his nose. I sat on the chair behind him, and he shuffled back and leaned against my legs with a little sigh of contentment.

Luke had just turned two when I found out about his existence, after an unusually forthright Will sat me down to tell me about the little boy he had fathered in error. I was so in love at the time that I made myself believe his tired lie: that his girlfriend had left him for another man nearly three years ago but, a few weeks later, she had lured him to her apartment and seduced him, specifically to become pregnant. 'To trap me,' he had said bitterly, adding, 'I've always wondered if Luke is really mine.'

Six months later, Bronwyn called me to accuse me of breaking up her family and I found out she was not an ex-girlfriend but a recently created ex-wife. And that Luke had been the son for whom they had both longed for eight years, even going through three difficult bouts of IVF which had put their marriage under intolerable strain.

I swore to her that I hadn't known Will was still married when I met him. I repeated to her his awful lie—that she'd left him for another man and he suspected Luke wasn't even his. She became garrulous with anger at this, until she admitted that when she first met Will he was living with another woman, a journalist about whom she knew nothing until the woman rang her in a rage.

'He's more than a serial adulterer,' Bronwyn had said. 'He lives by James Goldsmith's creed: that marrying your mistress only creates a vacancy. You just wait. He will do to you what he did to me. He'll break your heart, too.'

When I returned to the study, Will's computer told me that the download had been successful. I typed some sentences and checked my laptop. There they were, in perfect duplicate, in my inbox.

While I thought about it, I quickly changed all the passwords on my email system and on my laptop. No point in snooping on my husband if he could still spy on me.

Now I just needed to make sure Suzanna was going to be out of her office for a couple of hours, so I could put the same software on his computer there. Then I would be ready and waiting for his return. Moroccan lamb to the slow cooker, I thought as I switched off the light and went downstairs to send Luke to bed.

When I dropped Luke back at his mother's house the next day, he hugged me harder than usual. Adults always underestimate how perceptive children are and I knew that Luke sensed something was badly wrong.

I didn't say anything to him about it, of course. I just told him I was sorry I'd been boring all weekend and promised that next time he was down we would have more fun. He didn't reply but, as he was about to open the door, he stopped, turned around and looked hard at me.

'Are you and Dad splitting up?' he asked.

'Gosh, darling, why do you think that?' I prompted cautiously.

'He never rang you this weekend, and I heard you crying last night,' he said. 'And last time I stayed, all you did was row.'

As I digested this, he added, 'Mum told me that she split up with Dad because they couldn't stop fighting. She said that after a while you get tired of the rows and it's easier to walk away.'

He leaned into me and hugged me hard.

'If I do leave your Dad, will you be okay?' I asked.

He looked suddenly very old and very sad. 'Oh yes,' he said, his face turned from me. 'Remember—I've done this before.'

Then he jumped out and ran across the road and into his front door.

I was still thinking about Luke as I drove to Will's office, where Suzanna was working late. I sat outside until I saw the lights go off and she'd come out of the little red door, got onto her Harley and roared down the hill out of sight.

Then I let myself into the office and, in the dark, turned on Will's computer.

Two hours later I was on my way home again, starting my journey into the unknown.

Or, at least, into the known unknown, as Donald Rumsfeld would have said.

Two weeks earlier

After that weekend at Jeremy and Claire's, I remained in Kent while Will stayed in the Hampstead house, which, fortunately for the sanity of both of us, was between tenants.

He had suggested half-heartedly that I stay in Hampstead so we could 'talk things through' but I needed to be alone in the sanctuary of my cottage.

As I built up my income from the property business, I had turned the humble little oast house into my version of the quintessential English country cottage that I used to read about as a child in the suburbs of Toronto. It was still humble compared with my friends' chic London homes but I loved my old Victorian fireplace, the Aga in the kitchen and the wisteria that climbed around the door. The house had drawn me in from the first day I viewed it and the longer I lived here the more I felt that it had become almost an extension of me. It was, I had realised years before, the only place where I felt completely safe and at times I resented Will when he, too, called it 'home'.

But even as I sheltered behind its thick walls, Will and I still spoke every night. Or, to be more accurate, I would ring him and cry down the phone and he would sigh and tell me not to upset myself. Every night I would ask him if he'd ended it with Slutski, and every night he would say, 'There is nothing to end.'

On New Year's Day I gave up and called my friend Charlotte. 'Can I come and play on your boat?' I asked.

Charlotte shouted something to her husband, Sam, and I heard him laugh. 'We've got a new main, and Sam wants to head across the Channel to Honfleur for a shake-down sail,' she said. 'We're leaving tonight. If you can get down here immediately, you're welcome.'

I whooped to myself as I grabbed my sail bag and threw in my oilies, my boots and a few fleeces. It was going to be bloody cold, but it would be worth it—a couple of days on the water were just what I needed. Then I sped down the A3 to Hamble, a yachties' village inhabited by hundreds of serious sailors, just across the Solent from the Isle of Wight, where Charlotte and Sam kept their boat.

The moon was already high as we left the river on the tide, cutting through the Solent on a beam reach. We drew straws for our watches as we huddled in the cockpit and drank pumpkin soup. I cheered as I drew the dawn watch. We all loved this watch—or at least the way it ended, with the alchemist sun scattering pink diamonds over the waves as it chased away the dark.

I stumbled out of my bunk at 3 a.m. My watch-mate was Daniel, Sam's recently divorced friend who'd been at a loose end over New Year and also tagged along. Standing at the helm in the dark, with the boat slicing its way effortlessly towards France, I felt the unfamiliar tug of happiness. This was where I felt truly myself—at the helm of a boat, where nothing really mattered except for the pull of the sea and the wind's whims.

In the darkness it is easy to swop confidences—Charlotte, Sam and I had met fourteen years ago during Cowes Week, when England's sailors converge on the Isle of Wight for a week of racing and partying—and, over the years, we had spent many nights on watch together, getting to know each other far more intimately than we ever could in the cold light of land. Here, too, it seemed natural to tell Daniel about Will and Slutski. But he only grunted occasionally as I spoke and I thought I must have bored him with my trivial little tale of infidelity.

Eventually he took his turn at the helm and I made us a cup of coffee to keep the pre-dawn chill at bay. As I sipped mine, he said suddenly, 'When I suspected my wife was being unfaithful, I put a tracking device under her car, which allowed me to see exactly where she went each day. I found out that not only was she having an affair with the electrician, as I'd suspected, she was also sleeping with half the tradesmen in London.' He laughed, bitterly. 'I suppose she must have liked more than just a bit of rough.'

I stared at him, impressed. 'What did you do about them?'

'Actually, events ran away with me before I could confront her. She took the SUV to be serviced and, when the garage put the car on the ramp, they spotted a suspicious object underneath it. You know how paranoid everyone is since the IRA and 9/11, and they called the bomb squad. The cops tried to reach my wife, but she was shagging a Polish plumber at the time. So they blew up the car in a controlled explosion.'

I laughed so hard the coffee came pouring back through my nose, scalding my nostrils.

The next day, as the four of us ate mussels and frites and drank Muscadet under hanging baskets filled with geraniums on Honfleur harbour, Daniel tried to talk me into putting the same device onto Will's car.

'Go on,' agreed Charlotte. 'You need to know everything.'

I pointed out that Will's affair wasn't in Britain, where I could track him, but a few thousand miles away, where I could not.

'But there will be others,' said Daniel. 'There always are.'

It rained all the way back across the Channel. It was that fine English rain, as cold as ice shards and as dismal as a funeral, but my new-found happiness didn't fade until I pulled into my driveway and saw Will's car crouching malevolently, waiting.

I slid in through the back door, unsure of what I would see. He had thrown his bag down carelessly in the hallway, the way he always did and, as I looked at the bag, I realised I was looking at a homecoming. I didn't feel happy. I didn't feel anything. I walked into the study and he was sitting at his computer, just as he had been three months earlier on the morning of the first Turkish text.

He turned around. 'Oh hello,' he said coldly, and turned away again. 'I've ended it with Larissa. I'm not going to talk about it, but I've ended it.'

I hit his shoulder in fury but he didn't turn his head. 'Have you any idea how much you've hurt me?' I demanded.

He gazed out the window. 'I'm sorry you've been hurt,' he said, carefully removing himself from the equation. 'But it's your fault. If you hadn't gone into my phone, we could have continued the way we always have.'

He turned and looked at me. Or, rather, his head was turned to me but his eyes were gazing at something else, something that wasn't in the room with us.

'I-love-you-very-much-and-I-want-to-make-our-marriage-work,' he said, running the words together to get rid of them quickly. 'But you nearly ruined everything with your snooping.'

An overwhelming feeling of exhaustion came over me. I understood that in his mind he had already rewritten our history, had absolved himself of all blame and passed it on to me. The version he would tell himself would be stripped of guilt and, without remorse to hold him back, nothing was going to change.

So why didn't I end it then? Why didn't I slam the gate shut on us and throw the iron bar across, so the marriage vows could never get back in?

I still can't answer that. I can't tell you if it was because I loved him still, or because I was too cowardly to change the status quo.

I used to wonder at women who stayed within violent marriages, who took the black eyes and the cracked ribs in silent suffering, thus giving their tormentors mute permission to continue the cruelty by their failure to flee. But men don't have to be physically violent to violate women; Will battered me emotionally and just as brutally as a vicious drunk who breaks his wife's body. Yet— just like those other women—I remained, my continued presence giving him all the excuse he needed to hammer me into submission.

When I first found out about Bronwyn and Luke's existence, I emailed my sisters. Zara had emailed back immediately. 'Leave now. Go. This is a warning.' Eve had written, with exceptional acumen, 'You and I always end up with men who won't make commitments to us. Perhaps it's because it's we who can't commit, so we choose men like this, because they give us the excuse to stay free in our souls. And when they leave us, we can blame them for the ruin, not ourselves.'

It suddenly occurred to me that they'd both been unusually silent recently. After my sobbing, near-hysterical call to Zara as I climbed up the hill in Salcombe, I hadn't called her and, more unusually, she had not called or emailed to ask how I was. I wondered if I should be worried and I determined to email them both during the week.

In the morning I reminded Will that Luke was coming next weekend, and that's when he told me about his 'gig' in Norway.

And that was, really, the start of everything. And, also, the end.

Kent

After putting the spy software on Will's computer, I had nothing to do but wait until he returned from his Paris tryst. I tried to concentrate on work; I'd ignored my clients over the last week and a number of them were getting more than a little irritated by my neglect. One particularly troublesome tenant from Florida had left a message to say he was withholding rent until he got a fridge with an ice-maker in the door like the one he owned in America. His landlord was away so I knew it was up to me to placate him.

I flicked through the New Year sales ads in the paper to find said fridge, but I had no enthusiasm for the task. Besides, Daniel's words in Honfleur kept coming back to me: 'There will be others. There always are.' I also remembered Bronwyn's description: 'He's more than a serial adulterer.'

On Wednesday morning I rang Daniel. 'About that spy box you put on your wife's car . . .' I said.

Within twenty-four hours Daniel and I were standing beside Will's car, which he'd left outside the Hampstead house while he was in France. I'd bought the most expensive GPS tracker from the Spy Shop off Oxford Street and they'd shown me how to trace the car's movements via a small map on my smart phone. Even better, they showed me how to get the tracker to text me when the car started moving and how to get the exact address of wherever the car was by just touching any pin on the map—just as you do with the GPS tracker on your phone.

Daniel helped me attach the tracker to the bottom of Will's car. 'Just don't let him get the car serviced,' he joked later as we toasted my spying game over a not-very-good red wine at a local cafe bar.

A week later I was leaning back on my chair, arguing with a tenant who could not understand why I couldn't go around and change the light bulb in his living room for him. 'But my fingers are too fat,' he was wailing plaintively. Then my phone beeped three times. I frowned at it. The tri-tone indicated that the GPS tracker had gone off, but I knew this was impossible. Will wasn't due back until the weekend. Perhaps someone was stealing his car?

I got rid of Fat Fingers as diplomatically as I could and opened my new spook link. And there was his car, in Downshire Hill, going past the Freemasons Arms. He turned right into Hampstead High Street and then parked across the road from Flask Walk, metres from his office.

I was confused. Had they come back early? Had he abandoned Slutski in Paris? What was going on?

I would know within half an hour, when the first key strokes began appearing in my inbox.

'My darling,' he wrote, and I knew immediately the message wasn't intended for me. 'I'm so sorry we had to cut our wonderful time short. I miss you so much already but as I told you, she was threatening suicide if I didn't come back and I need to talk her down. After what I went through when my friend Jim killed himself, I couldn't survive another such death.'

The email didn't make any sense. I had threatened nothing. After that first text, when I gave the game away by revealing I knew he was in Paris, I hadn't contacted him. Jim—who was *my* friend, not his—was alive and very well, living on a small apple orchard in Normandy, where he and his girlfriend made cider and sold it at the weekend market. Had I somehow got a crossed email line? I checked. No, it was Will's email address and he signed it xWx the way he used to in his early emails to me.

I made myself a cup of coconut and mango oolong tea to help me think and, as the kettle boiled, realisation hit me. Of course; he was lying to her, too, needing an excuse to get away from her so he could come back to England.

And once more he was stealing my life to furnish his excuse. Two years earlier, I had fallen apart when my best friend, Poppy, leapt from the top of a carpark building in self-loathing because of the casual affair which she'd indulged in out of boredom, but which had ended her marriage. As I grieved for her life cut short, Will had coolly stood aside from my anguish and detachedly observed it, and me; he had examined my writhing pain, the tortured silences and sudden hysteria with an almost forensic interest.

I knew that one evening in Turkey, as he and Larissa looked out into the thick Ottoman night, he would have dressed himself in my mourning clothes, daubed his face with my tears and become, for those few hours, a grieving me. And her heart would have melted, because he would have persuaded her that she was the only person with whom he could entrust his sorrow.

But why was he using me as his excuse to return? Was he about to come home, to attempt a reconciliation?

I disappointed myself when I felt my heart skip a couple of beats as my inbox lit up again on my dozing computer screen. 'I'm on my way,' said the message. 'So sorry I went away but will explain everything when I see you. xWx'

So he was on his way back to our life—the xWx, his old signature of love, was the clue.

I leaned back in my chair and sipped my now-cold tea. What would I say to him? What would I do? Should I go home? Or stay here, where I would be safe from his guile?

As I wondered, my phone beeped again. He was off, out of the office. I turned on the little map and watched him drive up Hampstead High Street. But, instead of turning right up Heath Street towards the A40, which would eventually take him to the M11 and on to Kent, he turned left, towards Swiss Cottage and Regents Park. Perhaps he was going to visit Luke before he came home, I thought.

However, as I watched, he drove relentlessly past Luke's street in St John's Wood before cutting through Maida Vale and continuing on to Little Venice. Where he stopped. I touched the little pin and up came the street: Warwick Avenue. And a street number.

I stared at the map for half an hour, but the car didn't move. Another two hours went past and still my phone didn't beep its alert. Shaking myself out of what had become a quasi-trance, I suddenly realised that xWx may not have been meant for me. I hadn't bothered to look at the email addressee, so sure was I that my name would be there. Amateur! I scolded myself.

Clicking on the addressee details, I saw an unfamiliar address: AK47@gmail.com. I clicked again, but the computer wouldn't tell me who the address was registered to. How could I find out?

I reached for the phone and rang Drew, my closest male friend and the investigations editor on a national broadsheet. Back then, in 2007, phone and computer hacking was rife among journalists, particularly those on the tabloids, but Drew scorned the hacks who depended on these methods to get their stories. He tracked people down by more traditional means, including electoral rolls, or reverse directories, which could give you the names of the people who lived at a particular street address.

'You only ring me when you want something,' he complained as soon as he picked up. 'Have you left the bastard yet?'

Drew made a point of cordially loathing every man his female friends dated or married; he liked to think that he was indispensable to us all, and in a way he was.

'Getting there,' I said. 'Do you still have those reverse directories?'

'Will you buy me a beer?'

'Of course.'

'Give me the address.'

I gave it to him and twenty minutes later he rang back. 'Amanda Kirby,' he said. 'Thanks to my fantastic investigative powers I can also tell you that she is thirty-six, divorced and a lawyer. Is the bastard having an affair with her?'

'Not sure,' I said. 'It's a bit complicated.'

'Well, come out for a beer now. You can stay in my spare room, as long as you don't smash a glass of red wine all over the living room the way you did last time.'

'No—thanks, Drew, but not tonight,' I said. My voice sounded very small to me.

'Have you got a better offer?'

'Kind of,' I said. 'But only if I can borrow your car. You can have mine for the night.'

He laughed. 'You're not going to doorstep him? I've taught you well, haven't I? But he'll know it's you if he looks through the car window.'

'No, he won't,' I said, and pulled the *hijab* out of my desk drawer. 'Trust me.'

———✳———

Two hours later I pulled up in Drew's car in Warwick Avenue, not quite opposite the white stucco-fronted period building that once contained three large apartments but which, the name by the doorbell told me, now belonged entirely to just one person—Amanda Kirby, 36, divorced. Correction: Amanda Kirby, 36, Very Rich Divorcee—she had clearly divorced well if she could afford this entire building in this extremely wealthy part of London. Will's car was still outside and I could see slivers of light whispering through the shutters that the Very Rich Divorcee had closed over the windows.

I had stopped a few streets away to put the *hijab* on, and now I put the back of my seat down so I could see VRD's door without being too visible to passersby. I positioned the rearview mirror so I could also keep an eye on what was happening behind me, in case the pair had gone out for a post-prandial drink or dinner.

Then I waited. It was very boring. How did tabloid hacks manage to do this, I wondered. Doing nothing but stare at a front door for hour after hour. No wonder they'd started hacking phones instead. Much faster, and probably more fun.

Shadows passed by me—people pouring out of the tube station on their way home from work, couples going to the Red Pepper restaurant or the Prince Alfred pub. I was suddenly certain that I would find Will at the Prince Alfred, famous for the private little 'snugs' which had allowed unfaithful gentlemen of the late nineteenth century to entertain their mistresses unseen by polite society or suspicious wives. When I first took Will to the pub and told him its history, he'd pretended indifference, but I knew he would enjoy taking a mistress there and referencing his faithless predecessors.

I locked the car and started up Formosa Street. But, as I got to the Red Pepper, Will came around the corner, holding the hand of a small, quite dumpy blonde with a chemically enhanced mouth painted bright scarlet and oscillating hips that would have been seductive if she had been about three stone lighter.

He would hate that, I thought. Will hated garish makeup and overt sexual promise; he preferred catching tantalising glimpses of a woman's sensuality, like slivers of light from behind the shutters.

They brushed past me. Will offered a glance of negligible curiosity, the woman no glance at all—she was too busy shaping her mouth into a perfect bow.

I stood in the doorway of a shop selling country furniture and watched them go into VRD's house. I knew I would have to stay until Will left, or at least for several hours more, to prove to myself that this was more than just a passing visit.

As I slid back down in my car seat, my phone went off, twice. Two messages.

The first was from Will. 'Back home tomorrow,' it read. 'So sorry I hurt you. Can we talk?'

So he would be staying the night with VRD. I didn't text back.

The second message was from Claire. This surprised me. We had swopped phone numbers, but out of courtesy rather than any real interest in staying in touch. However, what I read sent a shockwave through me so hard I could feel my entire body start to shake.

'Sorry to disturb,' she had written. 'Do you happen to know a woman called Amanda Kirby? She's a friend of Will's, I think.'

I texted back, carefully. 'I've heard of her,' I said. 'Why?'

'Because I think she's having an affair with Jeremy.'

I stared at the phone. What on earth was going on? I glanced up and saw the lights go off behind the shutters. I knew what I had to do, and I was going to have to act fast.

Quickly I texted Will. 'Don't come home,' I wrote. 'Let's meet somewhere neutral, near our offices.' I needed time and space to put things into place.

Then I texted Claire—'Why do you think that?'—and drove to my office. I was going to have to sleep there tonight.

Claire came right back. 'Classic mistake of the unfaithful husband. He sent me a message on Facebook that was meant for her. Very soppy. Grrr.'

'How do you know who it was meant for?' I asked.

' "Amanda, my love" was a small clue.'

'And he has only one Facebook friend called Amanda?'

'Correct.'

I wondered whether I should tell Claire that I had just left Amanda's house and it was Will who was in there, not Jeremy. But for the moment I wanted to keep this information to myself. 'Call you tomorrow,' I texted and turned my phone off.

At 9 a.m. I was back at the Spy Shop, holding an innocent-looking powerboard as the man behind the counter described how the GSM SIM inside acted as a listening device. All I had to do was ring the SIM number and I would be able to hear everything going on in the room. After he assured me it would start working as soon as I plugged it in, and that it doubled as an ordinary powerboard to allay suspicion, I paid and drove home fast, slowing only for the speed cameras whose locations I knew by heart along the route.

It had hit me, as I waited outside the Very Rich Divorcee's house, that spy software and a car scanner weren't enough to find out what Will was up to. He was umbilically attached to his phone, rivalling my most garrulous girlfriends for the amount of time he wasted on it. It was time to bug my own house.

Bugging device safely installed in Will's study, I was back in London by mid-afternoon, sunk into a chair at the back of a cafe on Belsize Park Road. Will had texted, saying he would be there by 3.30, so I arrived at three. I wanted to watch him as he arrived, see the unadorned man before he cloaked himself in contrition for the sake of me, his audience.

Eventually my phone beeped its alert that he was on the move and I watched the virtual car drive down Rosslyn Hill and park outside the cafe.

Then we were in real time and I was watching as he weaved through the pavement tables, his face sullen, brooding. It was the face Luke and I dreaded—the face Luke had dubbed 'Dad's anti-Santa face', because it invariably meant a weekend of extra homework for him and arguments with me.

But as he came through the door, I saw him pull on his mask, so the peevish mouth was shaped into a conciliatory smile. As he saw me he bowed his head, eyes gazing upward, in Princess Diana's infamously subservient mien. We had actually seen her in a restaurant once; Will would go on to embellish our non-encounter by telling people he'd had lunch with her, and it was certainly true that he'd ignored me throughout the meal, watching her closely instead as she used the pose to beguile her lunch companion. Now I saw why he'd paid such close attention as he attempted to replicate her technique for my benefit, which he no doubt did for the benefit of many other women beside me. I could have laughed, but that would have ruined the cloak of sadness with which I had decided to camouflage my own fury and bitterness.

'Darling,' he said as he sat down, heavily, 'I'm so sorry.'

'How was Paris?' I asked coldly. I couldn't resist adding, 'Did she like our *pension*? Did you buy her amber earrings?'

He gazed at the table. 'Don't,' he said. 'It was all a terrible mistake, and I've told her it's over.'

To my horror, I felt a part of me longing to believe him, but I quickly shut that feeling down before it could rise up and swallow me whole.

He kept going. 'I came home early, because I couldn't do it any longer. I told her that I was being dishonest to her, because I love you.'

I gazed at him. 'When did you tell her this?'

'At the Gare du Nord,' he said. 'Before I got on the train back home. Then I think she flew straight back to Bodrum.'

'Was she upset?'

'She thanked me for being honest,' he lied. He reached out and took my hand, which stayed limp in his. 'Darling, it's you I love,' he lied again. 'Can we put this behind us and try again?'

I said nothing for a minute and when he kept his head lowered, I asked him, 'Do you really want our marriage?'

He lifted his gaze and, finally, looked me in the eyes. 'Yes,' he insisted. 'I miss you. I miss us. I was just very lonely.'

For the first time I glimpsed a spark of honesty behind the mask and I almost forgave him, despite everything. I knew that I'd allowed my work to take control of my life, my fear of the breadline keeping me in the office and away from our marriage. I knew I was also at fault; I knew that infidelity was not a solo act, and I also knew that it did not always have to break a union.

And then I remembered the Very Rich Divorcee.

Whatever he was doing with her had to be for a purpose. Will never did anything for no reason—he pretended to be impulsive, but every move was calculated to make life better, or easier, or more lucrative, for him.

I had to know what he was playing at. While I couldn't do that without letting him back into my life, into the spy-trap I had set for him, I needed to keep my own guard raised.

'We can try again,' I lied too. 'But everything needs to change.'

He nodded, humbly. 'I'll do anything to keep us together,' he said. 'Now, let's just go home.'

On the drive, I let Will chat away as if we really were finding our way back into our marriage. I could scent his relief, could almost hear him congratulating himself for getting away with it.

Suddenly I wanted to jolt him out of this smug confidence, to shock him into the confused world in which I had become trapped. I had the perfect weapon.

As he eased onto the M25, I said casually, 'By the way, do you know someone called Amanda Kirby?'

To give him credit, only a tightening around his eyes and an edge in his voice gave anything away. Consummate actor, I thought.

'Name rings a bell,' he said. 'Why?'

'Claire texted,' I said. 'Jeremy's having an affair. With Amanda Kirby.'

'Jesus!' I added as the car swerved from side to side, narrowly missing an Audi whose driver hit his brakes, horn blaring. 'What the fuck?'

Will was gripping the steering wheel so tightly the veins in the back of his hands were buckling. 'Sorry,' he muttered. 'Thought there was a rabbit on the road.'

After fifteen minutes of absolute silence, I ventured, 'You seem upset. Are you okay?'

'Just surprised. I always thought of Jeremy as the uxorious sort.'

I resisted the temptation to say, 'Unlike you.'

I kept very quiet for the next forty or so miles. I didn't particularly want the ignominy of dying in a road crash on the dullest of all England's motorways. I wondered how the evening would go. I didn't for a minute expect that Will would offer to change his ways; as I had seen in the week before he had flown to Paris, he had a psychopath's inability to feel remorse. The only slight modification, I thought, would be that for the next week or so he would play at home rather than away.

Even so, I was surprised that he went straight to the study when we got home, muttering that he had a lot of work to catch up on.

'I've got work to do, too,' I called after him as I went downstairs and took the laptop he had just brought back in his carry-on case. I pulled out my mobile as I started to load the spy software onto his third computer. Keeping a close eye on the screen, I quickly dialled the SIM in the powerboard which was now placed under Will's desk.

The voice came through clearly, although he was speaking in a near-whisper. I had missed the first part of the call, but not by much. '. . . about you and Amanda,' I heard. 'She texted Lili.'

There was a pause while Jeremy answered, then Will spoke again, coldly and with breathtaking hypocrisy. 'Don't shit in your own backyard, mate. We just need her to sort our paperwork out, we can't risk complications.'

A silence while Jeremy said something and Will laughed nastily. 'Yeah, and that. I've already got her to "lend" me £1200 to "pay something off my credit card". What? Oh, yes, I told Lili it's all over with Larissa. I'm going to have to play at being the faithful husband until I've got all my ducks in a row.'

I hung up as Will did and gazed out over the lavender bushes that edged the patio and, even in the cinereal depths of winter, brought the scent of my long-dead grandmother whispering in on the wind.

What exactly were they playing at? Dumpy, wealthy

Amanda was obviously a means to an end, but how would the end unfurl?

Will and Jeremy, I thought, were two of a kind—cruel men who tap the generosity of others, feeding off it like blood to increase their own strength, until their victims were left lifeless husks.

Will had drawn off my blood often enough, 'borrowing' money to pay off mortgages and bills the same way he persuaded Amanda to 'lend' him money for his credit cards. He would have assured her, as he had me, that he would repay her. He would have told her, 'You *know* you'll get it back,' so that, if she dared hesitate or question him, it would appear as if it was she who was undeserving of trust.

If manipulation was an art, then Will was a master, hiding his deceit beneath layers of verdigris.

I remembered his fury once, after I had confronted him over one of the many 'loans' he had never repaid. 'Are you calling me a thief?' he had shouted at me. It was around the time that *The Kite Runner* was at the top of the best-seller lists and I had repeated to him the line that I loved most from that book, that theft was the only real sin, with all other sins variations of it: 'When you kill a man, you steal a life . . . When you lie, you steal someone's right to the truth. When you cheat, you steal the right to fairness.' I could have added: if you are unfaithful, you steal a person's trust. But I hadn't known then that Will's own particular version of theft would include infidelity.

I had been trying to tell him that it wasn't just the unpaid loans that made me feel robbed. His fantasy world, the experiences of mine that he appropriated for his own stories, the lies and semi-truths that punctuated our marriage, were also a form of theft, depriving me of any sense of security or trust.

He'd hesitated when I told him this and, for a minute, I thought the truth of it had sunk in. But then he had returned to rage, shouting me into silence, so I never mentioned the book again.

Now I thought I'd try again to make him understand how he had robbed me of faith, but when I wandered to the bookcase, *The Kite Runner* had gone. Note to self, I thought—stop lending your books out. I shrugged. Tonight probably wasn't the right time to lecture him about truth anyway.

The spy software had installed while I was searching for the book so I closed his laptop down and opened my own. Clicking on my emails I saw that, even as he had been speaking to Jeremy, Will had been busy emailing Larissa.

'I know it's not fair,' he had written. 'But it's not for long and it will be worth it once we've got the house to ourselves. In the meantime I'll put the money for your rent into your account this week. £1200 will cover two months, won't it?'

I wondered what Amanda would think if she knew where her £1200 had really gone. More importantly, though, what did he mean by them having the house to themselves? I was losing the thread of what was happening.

I shivered suddenly. I hadn't put on the heating when we came in and my draughty little cottage was icy cold. Where the hell are the hot flushes when you need them? As I got up to switch the boiler on, Will walked in. His eyes immediately went to my laptop and mine followed, just in time to see the screensaver flash up, sheltering my spying behind the photograph I took last year of Dubrovnik from the sea.

He was wearing his mask and I didn't try to look behind it—it cloaked him as effectively as my *hijab* did me. 'Let's go for a drink in the village,' he said, as if we still dropped down to the Golden Hynde the way we used to. I couldn't remember the last time we'd been there, but I agreed, in the spirit of this new game I found myself playing.

I crashed my computer, so he couldn't try to unlock it, and, as I got my coat out of the closet, I quickly texted Claire. 'We shld talk,' I said. Then I deleted our message trail.

He tried to take my hand as we walked into the village, but I avoided his touch by wrapping my arms around myself. 'I'm freezing,' I explained to his irritated sigh.

He bought us large Bombay gin and tonics, and we sat on the battered leather sofas on either side of the inglenook fireplace, eyeing each other warily.

Eventually, after what looked like an internal tussle, Will spoke. 'Why don't we go to Gümüşlük next week? It's the only way you're going to trust me again and we can get the house ready for holiday tenants. We still need to get sheets and towels, crockery and god knows what else. You're better at things like that than me.'

I was torn. In Turkey I couldn't keep such a close spy-eye on him—but on the other hand I might see Will and Larissa together at firsthand, rather than through my home-styled looking glass.

I nodded slowly, although I knew that his plea for me to stock up with sheets and towels and crockery meant that once more it would be my bank balance that was denuded rather than his. Another cup of blood to replenish his supplies. Then I remembered. 'I thought we were having Luke next week.'

He hardly paused. 'I called Bronwyn earlier and suggested we take him to Gümüşlük. I said he could bring that new best friend, Harry. I knew you wouldn't mind.'

He knew nothing of the sort, although he did know that I couldn't bear to disappoint Luke and would comply for my stepson's sake, if not for his. But I also recognised his naked ploy: far from wanting to spend a week alone with me mending our marriage, he had ensured that I was kept busy with the boys so he would be free to see Larissa. I was there to provide child-care and finance, nothing more.

———————◦≍≍◦———————

Early the next morning Will announced that he was going to drive into the village to get the newspapers. The village shop was only a quarter of a mile away, a gentle stroll at most, but I knew he would need to get far from our neighbours so he could speak to his lover in peace, and without fear of being recognised by passersby.

I dialled Claire's number as, on my computer screen, I watched his car turn left at the church and drive on through the morning mist until it stopped up on the North Downs.

'Curiouser and curiouser,' said Claire as she picked up the phone. 'Jeremy claims that Amanda Kirby is having an affair with Will.'

'All I know is that she's rich, they seem to be taking her money and I have a nasty feeling that you and I are going to be the losers in all of this,' I replied.

Claire said nothing. I realised that I knew very little about her relationship. She and Jeremy seemed happy enough; but then so, on the surface, did we. Unhappy couples are skilled at deceit; they smile through vicious rows, paper over deepening cracks. The stigma of divorce may be long dead, but no one wants to be the first among friends to admit their happy-ever-after is heading for an entirely different ending.

As I waited for Claire to answer I saw Will's car turn around and start driving slowly, reluctantly back home. 'I can't stay on the phone too long,' I said. 'Will's gone out for the papers, but he's just turned back home,' I added, forgetting that she knew nothing about my new skills. (Should I add them to my LinkedIn profile, I wondered. Lili Jamieson has added new skills—snooping, lying, spying.)

'I think Jeremy needs the money for a gambling habit,' Claire said. 'He's lost most of our money and I've told him I'm going to leave if he doesn't stop.' Then she added, 'How do you know that he's turned back?'

I thought for a moment, then decided to trust her. 'How much do you want to know about what Jeremy is up to?'

'I need to know,' she answered and I recognised the desperation in her voice. So, just as Justine had to me, I outlined to Claire what she needed to do. And just as Justine had, I warned her that reading all her husband's emails to someone he might be in love with was as poisonous as swallowing mercury.

'Lili, I need to know,' she repeated and I understood exactly the journey she was embarking on, and where it would take her.

Gümüşlük

I climbed onto the roof of the house, turned my back on the solar panels and began my yoga in the amber dawn. The citrus groves that lined the hills filled the morning with the sharp scent of tangerines and the day's first *muezzin* rippled across the flat roofs laid out like a prayer mat between our house and the Aegean. Usually this was my hour of peace; it was shared, I knew, with hundreds of Turks in the villages around me, on their knees to Mecca before their breakfast of bread, yogurt and thick black, sweet coffee.

But there was no peace for me today. As the last notes of the *muezzin* faded, so did my enthusiasm for the downward dog. Instead I sat on my mat and began plotting, while I watched the sun force the fading moon from the sky.

On the plane to Bodrum, Will had announced grandly that he'd booked a glass-bottomed boat trip for the boys and me at lunchtime today, while he would tackle the dull practicalities of our troublesome electrical supply. It took the rest of the flight for me to work out how to out-fox him on this plan; then a quick (and secret) phone call rescheduled the trip as an early morning one and another to Kate organised for the boys to spend the rest of the morning in her heated pool. So I was soon back on track.

Kate was waiting as the boat tied up in front of the harbour cafes, her gold hair burnished in the Turkish sun and her breasts straining so willingly out of her top that both boys instantly fell in lust with her. Luke didn't even bother to ask me where I was going. Kate was the MILF of all MILFs, and I knew the boys would spend most of their time in her pool, trying to hide their little erections from her.

Then it was a brisk walk around the harbour to the narrow side street where Slutski lived. Our hire car was already lurking outside and, as I stood in the shadows of the shoe shop opposite, I saw her hurrying down the road from the *pasticceria*, which I could see from where I stood. I rang the *pasticceria* to double-check, and the woman who answered told me that Larissa had gone home for a couple of hours because she had a plumber coming in.

I imagined her ecstatic reunion with Will, but resisted the temptation to intrude. Instead I walked up to Pasticceria Mamochka and sat at a pavement table with a clear view of her door. Two hours and four coffees had passed before I saw them emerge and start down the street towards me. I retreated inside and waited until they were standing just outside the shop next door, his arms around her, she kissing him, before I walked out and leaned against the door jamb like any casual passerby, observing them.

Will saw me first, and pushed her sharply away from him, as though she were a grenade whose pin I'd just pulled. I heard him start to stutter excuses but I was more interested in Larissa, whose face seemed to collapse inward when she saw me. I smiled at her.

'Hello, Slutski,' I said pleasantly.

Her voice, when she answered, was small and tearful. This wasn't what I expected. 'I'm not a slut,' she said.

'Yes, you are,' I replied. 'Women who sleep with other women's husbands are sluts. Ergo, you're a slut.' She looked as if she would faint.

'You told me you'd left her,' she whispered at Will and ran inside. The tears that I had concealed at Heathrow were now pouring down her face.

I felt almost sorry for her but I quickly locked that unwelcome emotion into a cupboard and turned to Will, who was already stalking back to the car.

'You've ruined everything,' he cried as I quickly caught up and jumped into the car with him.

'Really? You continue your dirty little affair and *I've* ruined everything?'

Lili

Then the lies started tumbling out—a recycling of those awful untruths he'd provided her with only days earlier. 'She kept ringing me, emailing me, begging me to come back,' he said. 'She was threatening suicide and, after my friend Jim . . .'

'*My* friend Jim?' I corrected him, eyes wide, innocent. 'Are you saying he's committed suicide?'

'Yes . . . no . . . look, that's not the point,' he said, caught in his own web of lies and half-truths. 'I was just talking her down, all right?'

'Talking her down? You were kissing her passionately in front of me a couple of minutes ago.'

'No, I wasn't,' he said.

'Will, you were. I saw you.'

'No, you didn't,' he said.

My head began to spin, as if I was falling into some kind of vortex.

'You told her you'd left me,' I pressed on.

'No, I didn't,' he said, flatly.

He began driving.

'Have you fucked Slutski in our house here?'

He looked at me coldly. 'When did it become our house? It's my name on the deeds.'

My breath stopped, trapped in my throat by fear of what he was telling me. 'We both own it,' I finally gasped. 'I'm on the deeds. You showed me the paperwork.'

His expression didn't change. 'No, I didn't.'

'But you did. You presented the papers to me tied with a red ribbon.'

'No, I didn't.'

'Will, you did.' I hated the desperation in my voice as I remembered, suddenly, that the ownership papers he'd

173

flashed in front of me, on the day after my payment for the house had gone through, were all written in Turkish.

As understanding dawned I could hear myself begging. 'Will, I have spent thousands on that house. All the furniture I've bought . . . the antiques . . . the garden . . .'

His eyes were as cold as coal. 'Prove it,' he said.

And it hit me—I couldn't. I'd paid cash for everything, as you did in these villages, and any receipts we did have Will kept locked away with the deeds in a carved wooden chest for which only he had a key. I had no proof of all I'd contributed. If Will wanted to take everything from me, he could. I had nothing to fight him with.

I slumped in my seat. 'Has Slutski put you up to this?'

'Up to what? I don't know what you're talking about,' he said, staring at the road.

'Or has Amanda Kirby?' I pressed on.

'Look,' he said, his voice rising again. 'Make your mind up for fuck's sake, darling. Who am I having an affair with? Larissa or Amanda?'

Then his voice sank back again, almost to a whine. 'Please don't do this, not when I'm trying so hard to make things work for us,' he wheedled. 'It's very debilitating.'

There was a beat of silence while we both wondered what was coming next. He got in first.

'Actually, I think you need help,' he said, speaking the way you do to comfort a child who has just fallen over. 'All this suspicion over nothing. It's abnormal—you know that, don't you? It was my idea to come to Turkey, so you would start to trust me again, but you're obsessed with proving something that doesn't exist. You ought to see someone about it.'

I stared at him and suddenly everything in my vision shifted slightly, distorting my view. I shook my head a little, but nothing changed. It was as if I was looking at someone else's world through a cracked pane of glass. I didn't know it then, but that would be my line of sight from now on—everything that made up my life shattered into a thousand fragments that would never fit properly together again.

—————— ❧❧ ——————

Back at the house, while Will (very bad-temperedly) was picking up the boys from Kate's, I threw a few clothes into a bag. As I passed through the kitchen, the old bronze mortar and pestle, which I'd bought from Feridun the Bodrum antiques dealer, caught my eye and I slipped it into my little backpack. I had a feeling that it would be all I'd be able to salvage from this house and the life I'd planned to have in it.

I had dumped my backpack by the heavy wooden front door and was turning to get the rest of my belongings when the boys got back. They were giggling as they got out of the car, but Luke's laughter shut down when he saw my backpack. He froze and his eyes searched for mine, but I couldn't look at him.

'Are you leaving?' he whispered.

'Only for a day or so, darling,' I lied to him.

'That's what Dad said when he left Mum and me,' he told me.

'Luke,' I said. 'I'm not Dad.'

'No, but . . .' He came over and put his arms around my waist. 'It's Dad that's making you go.'

I knew that if I cried I would stay, so I closed my heart down and wrapped my arms around him. What do you say to a not-quite-child at a time like this? They see through the lies before you've finished the words. And when they've

175

been through it before, as Luke had, they know how the story ends better than you do.

I decided on a half-truth. 'If Dad starts being honest with me, then I'll come back,' I said.

He turned to look at his father, who was standing in the doorway, working his mouth into a silent rage.

'Then you won't be back,' Luke said and loosened his hold on me. He brushed past his father and went out into the garden, pausing only to tell me, 'Love you more than chocolate.' It was the phrase we'd made up for each other a lifetime ago, when he was six and we both thought that we would be together forever and hearing it again now, like this, completely broke my heart.

I would have done anything then to have been able to stay, to promise him that I would fix everything and make us all happy again. But I knew that was out of my power now, and my wise stepson knew it, too.

Without speaking to Will and before I could change my mind, I quickly collected the rest of my things and walked out into the street. As I passed through the door I allowed myself one glance back at the garden and was relieved to see that Luke was already dive-bombing Harry in the pool, his sadness sloughed off like a snake's skin. I remembered what he had told me only weeks ago, when I asked him if he would be okay if I left: 'Remember, I've done this before.'

The hotel I checked into was once the grand house of the village head, or *muhtar*, but it looked more like an old colonial mansion, with its wide verandahs covered in bougainvillea, brass fans that pushed the still air around in lazy eddies and the sweeping staircase that took you up to a landing filled with bookshelves. At the harbour side of the landing was a huge, floor-to-ceiling window through which you could see as far as the Greek island of Kos on the horizon and at dawn and dusk the glass was stained a thousand colours by the reflections of sun and sea.

The hotel had been faded by the years and its faithless clients had long abandoned it for the more voluptuous attractions of Bodrum but I was fond of the way it still clung stubbornly to its crumbled grandeur, like an impoverished dowager who still dressed for dinner and poured wine out of crystal decanters even when there was no one there to share it with.

Each of the rooms on the seaward side had little balconies with blue painted balustrades, and when Will and I had stayed here early in our romance with Gümüşlük, we would breakfast on our balcony each morning, watching the wooden *gulet*s put out to sea as we devoured coffee and warmed croissants.

Now here I was back on one of the balconies, watching a storm fling itself on the town, the rising moon devoured by thunder clouds. Clinging to the balustrade as the wind battered me, I thought how easy it would be to fling myself into the raging waters below. I wondered why I'd come to Turkey. What had I expected to achieve? What the hell was I going to do?

For a twisted moment, as I walked down to the village, I had let myself wonder if Will was telling the truth—that he really had met Larissa to tell her their affair was over, that I was abnormally jealous, that I did need help.

Those doubts returned in the darkness, with the vengeance that night brings. I wondered if perhaps there was something wrong with me. How sick did you have to be to spy on your husband as closely as I had spied on mine? Was I so wounded by his affair that I would never let it go, clinging to it as a weapon that I could eternally turn both on him and myself?

The seedling of doubt he'd planted was threatening to take root when a pinging from the bedside table dragged me back to the now. I glanced at the clock as I picked up my phone. It was only 11.30 p.m., but I already felt as exhausted as if I'd been struggling with sleep all night.

'He says you followed him to Gümüşlük,' the message said. 'He says you can't accept your marriage is over, that you threatened suicide. Just leave us alone.'

I threw the phone down on the bed, but seconds later I picked it up again. 'He said YOU threatened suicide,' I wrote. 'He said HE told YOU to leave him alone.'

She didn't respond, but at least I knew now what I had to do. I just hoped Kate's B&B wasn't going to keep her busy in the morning.

Kate was already serving breakfast when I rang at 7 a.m. but, ever loyal, she handed over post-breakfast duties to her housekeeper and was sitting down, as arranged, at the harbour cafe by 10.30 a.m. when I arrived. I sat at the next-door cafe facing the sea, my back to the crowds.

A yellow balloon bounced over the restless waves and, as I turned to see which small child had let it go, I saw a slim, nervous figure enter the cafe where Kate sat and wave tentatively at her.

I waited until they had ordered coffee and Kate's mandatory baklava before I slid into the cane chair opposite Larissa. She was gazing into her Turkish coffee as she spoke to Kate and took a second to realise who had joined them. She reared back when she recognised me and I noticed that she looked less startled than venomous—like a cobra about to strike.

I put my hand out to ward her off and Kate spoke quickly. 'Sorry to deceive you, Larissa,' she said. 'But you need to hear what Lili has to say.'

Larissa was on her feet now, hissing with anger, so I stood, too. 'If you go now, you will always wonder what I was going to tell you,' I said.

She remained standing, but at least she remained.

I was brief—I knew I didn't have much time. I told her about Will's after-midnight text from Paris telling me he loved me, about his tearful promises to make our marriage work again. I didn't tell her about Amanda Kirby, but I told her that Jim was my friend and that he was still alive and very unsuicidal . . . and that the woman who really had committed suicide was also my friend, not Will's. Gradually I saw the fangs retract.

'But he is always so honest,' she said at last.

I smiled encouragingly.

She added, 'He said that if you lie you are stealing . . .'

'. . . someone's right to the truth,' I finished for her. 'Yes, I know. I taught him that quote—from *The Kite Runner*, which, by the way, he has never read.'

I could see that she was starting to slip into the vortex of doubt that had become my habitat.

A thought suddenly struck me. 'Has he told you about Luke?' I asked.

She looked puzzled. 'Who is Luke?'

'His son. We're a family. He's here with us in Gümüşlük. Look!' I pulled out a photo of Will and Luke and me, taken on the underwater causeway to Rabbit Island by a passing American tourist as we stood laughing, arms flung around each other, on the sunken walls of the ancient city.

She gasped. 'When was this taken?' she asked.

It had been snapped two years earlier, on a pre-Larissa trip to our house, when there was still some vestigial happiness in our marriage. But I decided to be a little economical with the *actualité*, as Alan Clark would have said.

'Oh, a couple of months ago,' I said airily, and added another wee fib. 'In fact, Will has suggested we renew our wedding vows on the causeway.'

She drew in a breath, as you do when you feel a sharp pain. I dipped the tip of my stiletto into one more poisonous little lie, feeling no guilt as I did so. After all, Myndos was where Brutus and Cassius had plotted Caesar's murder (according to Shakespeare, anyway) and, like them, I knew that if I showed any mercy now, it would be my undoing. 'By the way, if you think you've got your claws into a rich man, you'll have to think again. I own the villa here, and everything inside it. You're not going to get anywhere near it.'

She shook her head violently. 'This is lies,' she said. She started to stalk out of the cafe, but checked herself and returned.

This time it was she who was clasping the stiletto. 'I don't care about this villa,' she said. 'When Will marries me, I get visa for England. And he has beautiful house in Kent that we are going to live in.'

She reached for her bag and pulled out a photograph of my oast house.

Now I was gasping for breath. 'I own this house,' I said. 'Will has no claim on it.'

She smiled at me, kindly. 'He has good lawyer,' she said and swept out, her long skirt flouncing along behind her.

'So what did that achieve?' asked Kate. 'Do you really want him back after all this?'

I caught a glimpse of myself in the window's reflection as I turned to her. My face, closed and cruel, was that of someone I didn't recognise and would not want to know.

'Of course not,' I said. 'I just wanted to find out what's going on. And now I know.'

⸎

The sun was thinking about setting when I went out onto the balcony with a glass of wine and my laptop. Will had rung and was surprisingly conciliatory. 'There's no point in wasting your money on a hotel,' he had said. 'Come home. The boys miss you. I miss you.'

I'd asked him what he was plotting and he'd again taken on the voice for the bruised child. 'Darling,' he said, 'you've really got to stop all this suspicion.'

The shattered glass had begun to interrupt my vision again, so I hung up on him and now I was opening my emails, unsure of what I would find.

My inbox was filled with messages between Will and Amanda Kirby. Right at the end were a couple to Larissa. I opened the last one first, wondering why he was on his laptop rather than the phone to her, with me out of the way.

'My darling,' the first one read. 'My phone battery has died so I can't ring but I know you'll get this. Thank you for a beautiful night. It washed away the madness.'

He added, 'I've made sure she won't be back tonight—it means I can slip out again to spend the night with you. The boys sleep in so late they'll never notice I'm not there.'

I could feel rage building—how could he leave Luke alone at night? How dare he put his tawdry sex life before his son's safety? But I smothered my fury and opened the previous email.

It was clear that Larissa had asked him about Luke, so she'd obviously told him about our encounter. (I could imagine his fear that his plans were about to be discovered.) Now she had written, 'I didn't think he could be yours, I couldn't believe you would not tell me about someone so important as a son.'

His reply shimmered with sincerity. 'No, of course not. He's hers, as I told you. But I do everything for him, I even pay his school fees, so he has come to think of me as his dad. It's very sad that she would disown him to you like that, but it shows you how unstable she is.'

Indeed I felt my sanity begin to loosen its moorings, and I wondered about my mental safety if I read further. But I had come so far that all the doors to go back—the doors of stability—had been bolted behind me.

I opened the first email to Amanda Kirby and was immediately gripped in its terrible thrall. His emails to her were scattered with love words, but these were as relevant as dust now. It was her emails that held me, as they spelled out what Larissa had already hinted at in the cafe.

'Stay with her for the moment,' Amanda advised. 'Effect a reconciliation if you have to, but don't move out of the house until you've wound down your known income enough to persuade a divorce court that she has to support you.'

He had queried the need to stay with me for a minute longer, pretending an urgent need to tie his future with hers, but she cautioned him against it. 'You have to display as broke,' she said. 'This will take time.'

Then I read the killer paragraph. 'Just be patient, we're nearly there, now. Thanks to a few expensive dinners I'm very good friends with that real estate agent in your village. When Lili is forced to sell the house to support you, he will sell it to my ex—for less than it's worth, of course. My ex will pass it on to me as the last part of our divorce settlement and I, my darling, will sign it to you.'

So this is what Larissa had meant when she had said, 'He has good lawyer.' But was he really planning a future with Amanda? Or simply using her to effect a life with Larissa?

I didn't know. I didn't care.

All I knew was that they were plotting to steal my house in Kent—my beloved home that had seen me through so much in my life and which I had always sworn I would never sell. It was the only thing I truly owned and now here he was, planning to rip it from me.

The glass was falling around me like dying moths.

Years earlier my mother had fought a long battle with cancer, Zara and Dad supporting her through the ghastly bouts of chemo and Lori arriving to accompany her during her slow recovery. The chemo left her sick and too exhausted to leave the house and after Lori had left, with my father at work all day and her closest friends on the other side of the world, our gregarious mama was forced reluctantly into a solitary existence. One day, when Zara called to ask how she was, she had replied, 'Sometimes I'm so lonely I want to go into the middle of the road and scream.' Now, I wanted to join her, to stand in the empty road by the sea, screaming into the wind.

I went downstairs and joined the crowds fleeing the evening chill to the harbour cafes, moving blindly through them until I found one that was half-empty. Determined to drink this pain away, I ordered a bottle of wine, but was only halfway through the first glass when the young Turkish hyenas arrived. Idly, I watched them work their way through the bars, targeting middle-aged, single women who could be flattered into paying them for sex.

The waiter, his indigo eyes blinking arrogantly at me, wondered why such-a-beautiful-woman-was-sitting-here-on-her-own and told me he would finish work at 10 p.m. In reply I suggested, not unpleasantly, that he fuck off and, grabbing the bottle, returned to my hotel.

Back on the balcony I dug my phone out of my bag and saw a missed call from Zara. I realised I hadn't emailed her or Eve as I'd meant to, but I knew she would understand why when I explained the events of the last weeks.

She tried to sound calm when she picked up, but I could hear her voice trembling. 'I'm with Mum and Dad at hospital,' she said. 'Lori is in intensive care. She was hit by a car when she was crossing the road.'

She put Mum on but all I heard was the sound of her weeping until Dad took the phone from her. 'I'm sorry, darling,' was all he could say, over and over. 'I'm sorry, I'm sorry,' as if it was all his fault.

Sydney

Should I feel guilty that, rather than sobbing my way from Turkey to Australia, I spent most of the flight to Sydney plotting how to save myself? I don't think I should. I knew Mum and my sisters would be the first to advise me that, however great my grief, I would achieve nothing but an unattractively swollen face if I wept my way from the northern to the southern hemisphere.

'Use your time properly,' Mum would say. So here I

was, utilising my thirty-six hours properly—the flights for plotting, and my time on the ground for putting my plans into action.

I had taken the short flight from Bodrum to Istanbul for a Turkish Airlines flight to Sydney and during the transit in Dubai I called Zara. She sounded anxious and tearful, and handed the phone to Eve, who had flown in from Shanghai.

Eve sounded strained, too, and her voice was granite hard; in times of trouble she erected a barrier to deflect sympathy as well as pain, because she couldn't afford an empathetic arrow finding her vulnerable spot. 'She's in an induced coma,' she told me. 'But at least she's still alive.'

'What are the doctors like?' I asked.

'Not hot,' answered Eve and for the first time in days I laughed out loud. Only Eve would make a crack about hot doctors while at our sister's hospital bed, but I also knew that the joke was just the barbed wire on top of her barrier, a sign that she wanted all emotion to be kept safely at bay. I knew, too, that like me, Eve and Zara would be riven with guilt that we had let Lori remain at a distance for all these years, that we hadn't tried harder to let her into our world. And now here she was in a coma, hovering on the edge of death without ever sharing our friendship or our lives and I knew we would not forgive ourselves if she died before we could start to know her.

The girls had told me that Lori had come to Sydney to stay with Mum and Dad and, unusually for her, had taken them to lunch at a spot overlooking the ocean. After lunch she had dashed across the road to get her wallet from the car and as she waited to cross the road back to the restaurant, a vehicle had appeared from nowhere, crushing her before racing off again. Mum had travelled with her in the ambulance to hospital and had not left her bedside since. 'She's hardly stopped crying since it happened, either,' said Eve sadly.

I ended the call and gave in, briefly, to tears before plugging in my laptop to retrieve the emails from both Amanda and Larissa. They both subscribed to gmail, which was going to make my work easier, and I had both their home addresses for the subscription details.

I tackled Larissa's new identity first. Her email address was lari887@gmail.com. It was easy to set up a new account for her as lari8887@gmail.com. At first sight you wouldn't notice the extra 8.

Amanda's email address was AK47@gmail.com— I didn't waste time thinking about what Freud would have said about that. I wasn't sure how I could change it imperceptibly, but eventually I decided on AK_47@gmail.com—I never noticed the underscore in people's email addresses and I hoped that she would be similarly unobservant.

Then I ordered a double espresso and logged into Larissa's new email account. I hit compose and typed in Amanda's real email address. In the subject, I wrote simply, 'Will'.

I had decided to keep these first emails short. All I needed to do at this stage was to make each aware of the other's presence in Will's life.

'Stay away from Will,' I wrote without preamble, on Larissa's behalf. 'I am his girlfriend. He is in love with me and we are planning to marry. He says you mean nothing to him.'

Then it was time for Amanda to contact Larissa. From Amanda's new email account, I sent almost exactly the same words to Larissa's real address. 'I don't know who you are but stay away from Will. I am his fiancée. He says you are a nothing.'

As my flight to Sydney was called, I pressed the send button. They would receive the emails while I was in the air and I was sure that, by the time I disembarked, both women would be in frantic contact with each other. Except, really, with me.

En route from the airport to hospital, Zara and Eve filled me in on Lori's condition. She was still in a coma but they were sure she was aware of their presence. At times when they made desperate little jokes to her about Dad's notorious ineptitude in the kitchen, a strange sound would erupt from her throat. 'She's trying to laugh,' a nurse had told them.

The intensive care unit broke their two-person rule just this once and let us all sit at her bedside, stroking her hair, holding her withered hands, talking to her brightly of her beloved garden, which we told her she would soon be tending again. We used a damp cottonwool bud to soothe her dry lips and we arranged the blanket delicately over her shattered limbs. Our unhappiness filled the room, and we took it in turns to go back into the corridor and sob out our heartbreak.

As Sydney's brief sunset gave way to night, Eve and Mum stayed with Lori until Dad arrived, while Zara dropped me back at our parents' house. She was quiet as we got into the car but in the dark, staring straight ahead, she said suddenly, 'I think Sergei and I are in danger.'

I gasped. 'Not Caitt?'

Zara had been suspicious of Caitt for months, wary of the way she had targeted Sergei with overt flirting, and dinner invitations whenever Zara was away. She had often worried aloud to Eve and me about the possessiveness Caitt had started to show towards the handsome, gregarious Russian who had been part of our family for so many years.

I understood her concern. When Sergei and I had gone to the gym during a previous, happier visit to Sydney early last year, Caitt had walked in and, even before we were introduced, I had recoiled from the air of malevolence that surrounded her like a cloud of overly pungent perfume.

Now Zara could only nod miserably. 'He says he wants to experience passion again,' she said. 'And he says he won't experience it with me.'

I was stunned by the cruelty of his words, the harshness with which he was spurning my sister, whose fragile beauty had once been such a powerful draw for him. The song is wrong, I thought sadly as she dropped me off with a hug. It's not love that's all around, it's betrayal and madness.

Back at my parents' house I chopped up some apple for the lorikeets as Mum did faithfully every day and opened my rivals' emails. Both were obviously in shock.

Amanda had emailed 'Larissa'. 'Who on earth are you? Where did you get my email address? Will couldn't possibly have another girlfriend, he's completely faithful.'

Larissa was more emotional. 'I don't believe you. Will loves me completely, we will be together as soon as he can divorce his horrible wife. Who are you, anyway?'

Eve texted to say that she was on her way home with Mum and Dad and would pick up Thai takeaway. I asked for a tofu stir-fry and turned back to my computer.

First I responded to Amanda. 'I want to say that I am Will's only love,' Larissa's cypher wrote. 'He told me that infidelity was a sin because you steal your lover's trust. But now I get this email from you. I wonder if his wife was right—that he is unfaithful to everyone.'

I copied the same email into Amanda's answer to Larissa. It wouldn't hurt for them both to receive the same message, or to believe that the other was in contact with me.

I shut down the laptop as the others came in. Mum was stooped with pain and fear, and Dad's eyes were hollow. As we picked our way through the food, Eve and I tried to reassure our parents that Lori, their first born, was still young and strong, that it wasn't her time to leave us yet.

But we couldn't fool them. They have seen too many of their friends die; they know too well the savage vulnerability of our physical selves, regardless of our spirits' strength. 'We need a miracle,' Dad said hopelessly as they went to bed.

Eve and I poured ourselves a glass of wine and sat out on the deck. Zara had told her about Sergei and Caitt and we cursed the woman who had inveigled her way into our sister's life, only to try to destroy it. I told her briefly about Slutski and we wondered at the strange parallel of nationality—that my husband was having an affair with a Russian while Zara's Russian husband was also breaking her heart. Was there something in the psyche of the Steppes that put passion above fidelity?

We decided in the end it was nothing more than a coincidence of fate. We loved Sergei, who was like a brother to us and, despite everything, we didn't want to taint him by comparing him with Larissa. Besides, Eve pointed out, her own husband had been unfaithful with another Australian woman and that hadn't made us query the Aussie psyche.

Eve had only recently discovered Henry's affairs but even as we compared our scars, I saw something in her eyes slam shut, like shutters closing against the coming storm.

<hr>

It was midnight by the time we went to bed, 1 p.m. in London, 3 p.m. in Gümüşlük. I checked my emails to see if the girls had got theirs. They had responded immediately and in more detail than their first, shocked correspondence to each other.

Amanda wrote, 'He said something similar to me about lying being a sin. He said it was from his favourite book, *The Kite Runner*. It's part of what made me love him—his love of books and art and European cinema instead of that Hollywood rubbish.

'I'm not just his fiancée but his lawyer, and I'm handling his divorce. We will get his wife's house once she's forced to sell it.

'Will says you don't mean anything to him, he toyed with you in Turkey when he was bored and lonely but he wishes you would leave him alone. I'm not saying I believe him, I'm not sure what I believe any more. By the way, he calls you Natasha. Is that your real name?'

I laughed when I read this last sentence. Once, we had fallen into conversation with a young waiter from Northern Cyprus who was genially contemptuous of a table of Russian women at the far end of the restaurant, telling us they were 'nasty little Natashas'. When we asked him what he meant, he explained that 'Natasha' was the Cypriot nickname for the Russian prostitutes who swarmed around the casinos and nightclubs of Kyrenia, taken from the alias they invariably chose for themselves. So that was what Will had meant when he named the file of Larissa's emails 'Nat' on his office computer.

Despite myself, I felt an uncomfortable pang of sympathy; the name showed the depth of his contempt for her, and indicated that there might still be time to expel her from our lives and try to put the fragments of our marriage back together again. But it had all gone too far to be mended. And anyway, I reminded myself, at heart Will held all women in contempt—otherwise he would not be such a skilled seducer.

I opened Larissa's email. 'I'm shocked at your email but I'm not really surprised,' she wrote to Amanda. 'I want to believe Will loves me but after he told me he'd left his wife, she came to Gümüşlük with him. I met her. She said that she taught him that line about trust and theft and that he had never read *The Kite Runner*. I fell in love with him because he loved all the same things I did . . . art, Russian movies, he even loves my little canary. He said he wanted a canary of his own but his wife refused to have one. Now I don't know what is true. Maybe he isn't really divorcing Lili? Maybe he isn't supporting Luke, her son?'

Clever girl, I thought. You're beginning to catch on.

I wanted to email both women and tell them, yes, yes, he is lying to you about everything—about movies, about canaries, about trust and infidelity. And, most importantly, about Luke.

I wanted to tell them—Will hates European cinema, and books don't even figure in his life. He confided in me that he got away with reading nothing by memorising book reviews in the *Sunday Times* and regurgitating snippets at salient moments during dinner parties. 'Life's too short to read,' he had shocked me once by saying.

Yet here he was, convincing these women he was an art connoisseur, a voracious reader and, most hilarious of all, a bird lover. Once again Will was deceiving all around him, dressing himself in my clothes to reel them in. I wondered what they would do if they realised that, rather than falling in love with the real Will, they had fallen in love with a version of the wife they both so loathed.

I decided that the women's own emails were more powerful than anything I could write, so I simply cut and pasted Larissa's email into her cypher's address and sent it to Amanda, then did the same with Amanda's message.

The girls were beginning to do my work for me.

———✖✖———

Eve and I got up at 5.30 and ran together down the beach to the lighthouse on the hill. There was a mobile coffee bar opening as we ran back past the incoming tide and we grabbed one each, sitting on the sand to catch our breath as we watched the surfers riding the waves like apocalyptic horsemen.

'I think Lori is going to live,' said Eve suddenly. 'I think she will live and we will all get through this. There has to be a reason that we are all having our hearts broken at the same time as Lori's had her body shattered, but we will all survive it.'

Eve, Zara and I spent the rest of the day at hospital, taking it in turns to join Mum at Lori's bedside, brushing her steel-grey hair, applying makeup to bring some colour to her faded cheeks, chatting to her of the inconsequentialities we would once never have bothered her with. She had come out of the coma the night before and seemed gently overwhelmed to see us all sitting around her, realising that Eve and I must have flown in from our distant lives because of her. The knowledge that it was love that brought us here lent her a softness that we had never seen before and, as she gripped each of our hands in turn and brought them to her cheek, we all hoped that, dreadful though the accident had been, it would be the catalyst to bring her back to us.

But our joy at her return to consciousness was tempered. At least the coma had kept her oblivious to the awful injuries she had suffered and now she was facing weeks of pain and crushing humiliation as catheter changes and intimate bed baths became her daily routine.

So, while the doctors worked to mend her body, we worked on saving her dignity. Why is it that, as soon as someone is put into hospital, it is just accepted that their self-respect should be locked away in their bedside cupboard, along with their dentures, spectacles and wash-bag? Every time an orderly came into Lori's little cubicle, her eyes would fall and the despair in them would trickle down her cheeks like tears. So, when they hoisted her onto a trolley to be wheeled away for blood tests and scans, we would make sure her night-gown was not rucked up around her thighs and the blankets were arranged to shield her from those she would pass in the corridor.

*

That evening, as Dad took over at our sister's bedside, I went back to my emails and found a whole trove as the women began to unlock their Pandora's boxes.

First their emails to each other.

Amanda: 'She told him that quote from *The Kite Runner*? It makes sense in a way: it was the only thing he seemed to remember from the book although he showed me a copy that he said he carried everywhere. (Aha! So that was where my book had gone.)

'This is very confusing,' she had continued. 'I wonder if the stuff he came up with about European movies and art also came from her . . . Maybe he's lying to us both, the way he has been lying to Lili for all this time. But I can assure you he's divorcing her. I should know. I'm his lawyer.'

She had added, 'Who's Luke?'

Larissa wrote in her email, 'I don't believe he calls me Natasha. That is a Cypriot word for prostitutes. He would not be so cruel. He told me he only slept with you because it was cheaper than legal fees and he needed you to get the house in England for us.'

Once more, I decided that their emails stood on their own . . . with just a little tweak.

In Amanda's reply to Larissa, I added the true line that, 'Will hates canaries! He once told me that the only good thing about cats was that they ate canaries.'

To Larissa's missive, I added a very untrue line: 'But I'm beginning to think that of the three of us, the only one he really loves is his wife.'

Then I opened the other emails the spy software had sent from Will's computer, in which the women had demanded answers from the man betraying them. Amanda was full of rage at the deception of which she was now certain she had been a victim. Larissa was sadder, more pliable, willing herself to believe his denials.

His emails to them both were carbon copies of the rebuttals with which he had showered me when I first found out about

Larissa. To each he described the other as a nothing, a silly aberration caused only by loneliness. He repeated his mantra of making a 'silly mistake', and swore that he loved them and them alone. 'Let's try to make it work again,' he had wheedled them both, just as he was still wheedling me.

I checked the timeline on his emails; he had sent them only minutes ago and I knew that they would soon be winging their way back to my inbox, sent by the women to each other.

That night we had one of the wild Australian tempests that I missed in the English winter's prison yard of grey. Sheet and forked lightning took over the sky, vying for prominence like fighting cocks.

I went out to the living room so I could see the sky's whole panoply while I worked on my own storm. As I had expected, Larissa and Amanda forwarded Will's emails to each other as proof of the other's non-status; dutifully I passed them on.

I kept a close eye on Will's emails then, waiting for the women's fury to be unleashed but . . . nothing. So I called the SIM card in the powerboard back in the Kent study and his voice came over as if he was in the same room.

For a minute I thought he was talking to me, so familiar were his words. '. . . All this obsessiveness over something that isn't true,' he was saying, in that viciously kind voice. I wondered which mistress had called him first. 'Why are you like this? It's not normal and it's very debilitating,' he added and I knew what was coming next. 'You may need help.'

I was amazed at his ability to keep lying, even when faced with proof of his deception. I listened as he talked Larissa down, persuading her that he really did love her, that Luke really was my child and that her unhappiness was her own fault for believing a lie he insisted Amanda was perpetuating. Eventually he hung up.

But almost immediately the phone rang again, with an obviously enraged Amanda on the line. This time his increasingly tired lines—'You need help' and 'I-love-you-let's-make-it-work'—fell on closed ears, so he played his ace card.

'Anyway,' he said coldly, 'going on about fidelity doesn't come too well from someone who is screwing my best friend.'

There was a silence, and I wondered what she was saying. Was she playing his game of say-it-wasn't-me? But then I heard Will say 'Hello? Hello?' and I knew she'd hung up on him.

Thank you, Will, I thought. You've just slashed her tendon. If I'm quick, I can finish her off. And you.

By now it was 1.20 a.m. in Sydney and early afternoon in London.

I worded my email to Amanda carefully. 'Larissa Slovo has told me that you are planning to take possession, illegally, of my house in Kent in order to pass it to my husband. She has also forwarded me your email detailing how both the local estate agent and your husband will help you do this. I am about to pass the email to the Law Society.'

I knew this would get her. She would be overtaken with the fear of being found out by the legal profession's regulatory body, of being debarred, ruined. I doubted she would question whether Larissa had really gotten into Will's computer and found their emails, or if the two of us were now in cahoots.

But I couldn't help adding, just for good measure, 'I know a lot more than you think I do. Do you remember that £1200 you lent Will for his credit card? He used it to pay Larissa's rent.'

The return

When my grandparents died, my aunt told me that she and my father had been adopted after their own father committed suicide. Papa and she had promised never to tell their own children that the grandparents we adored were not ours by blood, but now she felt we had the right to know. I became obsessed with finding out who my biological grandparents were and, in a flurry of teenage rejection, even changed my name to that of my father's birth name. I opened a bank account and obtained a passport and credit card in that name and, while my enthusiasm for my blood family eventually wore off and I reverted to 'our' family name, I kept the bank account and the passport. I told no one, not even my sisters, about their existence; I always believed that, if I ever needed to disappear for any reason, they would be my . . . well, my passport to a new life.

Now, sitting at Lori's bedside, I went onto the website that advertised our villa as a holiday stay.

The previous night I had made a quick phone call to Charlotte, Sam and Justine, then retrieved the passport for my other life and the debit card that had the same name. Now I booked the villa for a week, for three people, in that name. The money would leave the bank account within days and then I would cancel both the account and card. They wouldn't be needed again.

Amanda had responded aggressively to my email, denying everything (had she taught Will this trick or had he taught her?). So I'd sent her own plotting email back to her, repeating my plan to forward it to the Law Society—and adding that I would also post it on Facebook, and warn the estate agent that I knew he was in cahoots with her.

She started pleading then, insisting that she had never really planned to help Will . . . things had got out of control . . . he had been exploiting her love for him. She was clearly just as terrified that I would dynamite her career as Will was that his carefully laid plans were about to be blown sky high.

Will called just as Zara, Eve and I were feeding the lorikeets that had gathered in the dusk. Perfunctorily he asked after Lori before repeating his tired plea, imploring me to forgive him, to come home and try again. I could hear the fear grating in his throat, but I hardly listened to the words. Last night, he had made the same appeal to Amanda, but she had remained silent.

I suddenly heard Will's tone change from a whine to a more assertive note. I listened hard, but I only caught 'your mortgage'.

'What?' I said, startled.

'I said my legacy from Aunt Mae has finally come through, and I'm willing to help pay off your mortgage on the Kent house.'

'What?' I said again. The stink of rat was all around, like the stench of death in an earthquake zone. His aunt, a wealthy spinster, had died two years earlier, but he'd been fighting with his siblings over her will ever since— each determined to grab a larger slice of her legacy than the others. Now it was settled, so he said, but an offer like this came with alarm bells screeching around it.

So this was Plan B. I knew exactly what his condition would be and waited in silence when he added, 'I want to do this to prove my commitment to you.'

I counted down the pause. Five, four, three, two—and then it came: 'As long as you sign over half the house to me.'

Although I had been expecting it, I could not help gasping. It meant that he was not yet ready to give up, and it convinced me that my own actions over the next week would either assure my future or leave it in ruins.

Three days later I held Lori's hands as I farewelled her, promising that I would be back in a few weeks. 'Before you know it,' I said and kissed her on each cheek, my eyes closed so she couldn't see the tears.

———⋯⋯✦✦⋯⋯———

My heart always lifted when I rounded the last bend before Gümüşlük and saw the town glinting like a promise below. But this time my heart stayed still, wary of what would happen to it on this final visit.

Charlotte and Sam had picked me up at Bodrum's little airport and, as we drove, we discussed our preparations. We had all done our bit: I had organised the container, Sam had cleared the paperwork with Customs, and Charlotte had hired a truck—and persuaded the housekeeper and gardener to take a few days off.

We drove straight to the villa and, with the bolt cutters that Sam had bought, we broke open the heavy iron padlock on the chest in which Will had locked away the deed that he had once flashed in front of me as proof of his love. It still had its red ribbon tied around it and we swept it into a bag, along with the receipts for all that I had bought to furnish our Turkish life.

It took us until noon the next day to clear the villa. Not entirely—only of the hand-painted beds, the carved wooden armoires, the ancient olive pots and all the other pieces of furniture that I had lovingly collected. We left the rugs that had appeared between my trips to Gümüşlük and which, no doubt, he had bought with Larissa. We left the print of a whirling dervish that she had clearly persuaded him to buy, and the rather tacky table covered with shells. I had no desire for possessions that spelled out a life loved with someone else.

Before driving back to Bodrum, we had one brief stop to make. Larissa's eyes were dull when she raised them from the pot of spiced chocolate she was stirring as I entered the *pasticceria*. I recognised the cochineal tint around her eyes as the same that had coloured mine only a few weeks ago at Heathrow; I knew that she would have spent her nights weeping in despair. But sympathy was by now a foreign country.

I was brief. 'He's all yours,' I said.

She kept her eyes low. 'It was you all along, wasn't it?' she said.

I thought she meant it was me behind the emails from Amanda and I opened my mouth to deny it, but she added, '*The Kite Runner*, the Russian films, the art, all the interests I thought I shared with him. It was really you, wasn't it?'

I nodded.

'And I suppose you really do have a canary?' she asked hopelessly.

'No,' I answered. 'I love canaries, but I don't believe in caging free spirits.'

While Sam supervised the transfer of my furniture to a container ship at Bodrum port, I strolled into the old town and down the side street to Feridun's antique shop. He greeted me with delight and sent his nine-year-old son Abdullah out to bring us both Turkish coffees. I ordered mine *orta*—medium sweet—and after Abdullah had returned with the coffees in hand-painted cups, along with two glasses of water, I handed Feridun the deed. He untied the red ribbon and read it closely, his glasses slipping onto his nose.

At last he raised his head and took a sip of coffee. 'Your name is not on this deed,' he confirmed. 'But I think this is a good thing.' He pointed to the last paragraph.

'This says that Will is legal owner of the land and of the house. But it also denies permission to rebuild the ruin. No reason is given, but you know how tight the building restrictions are in Gümüşlük.'

'What does that mean? Is the house illegal?' I asked, images of all we had put into it flashing across my mind like a movie on rewind.

'Yes. And they are very strict about this. If they find out, they will tear the house down and charge him a big fine. But,' he added with a grin, 'you know what we Turks are like with foreigners. They're not going to go checking on the house; they won't do anything unless someone informs on Will and forces them to take action. He will probably just get away with it.'

We sat there for a long time, gazing into the gloom of his Aladdin's cave as we talked. Then Feridun sent Abdullah out for another coffee.

⋯⊷✠⊶⋯

We waited until we'd landed back at Heathrow before Charlotte emailed Stella, the property manager, and explained that an emergency had required our instant departure from Turkey. Stella would call Will as soon as she arrived at the house and I wanted to be in England when he was told.

I met Justine and her tradesman down at the Golden Hynde, and we drank lemonade in the beer garden overlooking the only road out of the village while we waited. I knew that Will would be on the first plane to Bodrum after speaking to Stella. He would be hoping that if he got there quickly enough he could stop the furniture from leaving port. He couldn't know, of course, that the container ship had sailed twenty-four hours before he landed.

It wasn't long before we saw his car barrelling down the road en route to Heathrow, not even slowing for the speed camera that we had campaigned to have erected by the school.

As the locksmith moved from front to back door, from the garage to the gate over the driveway, making the changes necessary to bar Will from my life, Justine and I took our time packing my soon-to-be-ex-husband's belongings.

I was in the middle of settling with the locksmith when Justine picked up Will's beloved Ritter Roya and looked at me, questioning. That bass guitar had cost us so much over the years but in better times, before the monster took him in its claw, he used to play it quietly to me.

I shook my head at Justine. We would leave all Will's other possessions at Hampstead, but I had a better plan for the Ritter Roya.

Three years before, when Will's spending was reaching dangerous proportions, I considered selling the Roya to keep our heads above the ever-rising waters. I knew he would refuse to give it up, so I had paid a guitar maker to produce a copy. To a purist it neither looked nor sounded like the real thing, but it was good enough to hold off Will's rage until our finances were sorted out. In the end I couldn't bring myself to sell the Roya, so the copy had stayed locked in Charlotte and Sam's basement. Until now.

In Hampstead I opened the Dom Perignon Will had bought to celebrate the hostile takeover of my property. While I poured the champagne, Justine rummaged through the wine rack and pulled out a bottle of Petrus that must have set him back a couple of thousand pounds. Silly boy, I scolded him as I pulled the cork to let it breathe; you don't have the money to buy wine like this.

We drank the champagne fast and were already tipsy when I outlined my last plans to Justine.

While she lay on the floor giggling and spilling the Dom all over the carpet, I untied the red ribbon from the Turkish villa's deed and tied it around the fake Ritter. I leant the guitar against the music stand, as I had eight years ago when happiness was still ours. In the winter light Will wouldn't be able to tell the difference between the fake and the real thing. His heart, as bitter as Cypriot lemons by now, would soften and he would think that this was a message to tell him we still had hope.

Until he opened the envelope that I tucked under the ribbon.

'You deserve all this . . .' Amanda had written.

We had talked rather a lot, Amanda and I, and I shouldn't have been surprised that we got on as well as we did—after all, like many women who find they are in love with the same man, we had more in common than we thought. Certainly we had more in common with each other than either of us did with Will.

Amanda told me that she'd fallen in love with my husband before realising he was still married, but that he'd sworn, as men like him do, that we lived separate lives. 'By the time I found out the truth, it was too late,' she said, and I suspect that Larissa, too, had found out the truth only when the time to escape love's grip had passed.

Once Amanda understood that Will's love for her had been as false as his love of European cinema and that she was only being exploited as a conduit to his life with Larissa, it didn't take much to get her to agree to help me.

I was surprised that Will had given her Power of Attorney over his finances, although it made sense—it meant she could hide his assets from me without an obvious paper trail. When I pointed out that Will didn't actually have any assets, she explained that the failed investments that had punctuated our marriage had concealed others that were far more successful and whose profits he had been hiding offshore for years.

I wasted little time being hurt by the new cognisance that, even back then, when I thought we were planning our joint future, he was stockpiling for a life without me. At least it meant he couldn't plead poverty when I divorced him.

In her letter, Amanda told Will that she had used her Power of Attorney to sign the Hampstead house over to me and had removed his name from the deeds.

'Please consider this letter your eviction notice,' she wrote.

I turned the dimmer switch to low and left Will's parting gift displayed in the muted light, then went to find Justine, who was in the bedroom pulling his clothes out of the bags we'd brought from Kent. As she dumped them in a pile on the floor, my phone rang. It was Will, hysterical with rage. 'We've been burgled!' he cried.

'No, we haven't,' I replied tonelessly.

'Lili, I'm in Gümüşlük. Everything's gone.'

'No, it hasn't,' I said.

I thought I could hear his heart drumming in panic.

'Lili! Believe me, we've been cleaned out!'

'No, we haven't,' I repeated. 'You've been cleaned out. There is no we anymore.'

I turned my phone off and picked up the bottle of Petrus. I had planned to tip it ceremonially over the clothes—over the linen trousers I had bought him in Rome last year, over the faded lavender and blue striped Provençal shirt, over the Ralph Lauren loafers that I never knew he owned.

But I decided against it. There is revenge, and then there is the waste of a good wine.

So, instead, I left one last letter on Will's pillow.

It was written in Turkish, although Feridun had thoughtfully provided a translation alongside it. It was a photocopy of a letter to the planning department of the Gümüşlük Beliyidersi—or town council—informing them that a big house had been built illegally on the site of an old ruin above the town. It gave the address of the house and the name of its owner, William Jamieson.

Feridun and I had debated the fate of the house throughout that afternoon. Should I rip it from Will's grasp, the way he had tried to tear my home from me? Did I really hate him that much? Yes, I thought I did. I was gripped by a white-hot desire for revenge and I wished with all my heart for his undoing.

But then my mind turned to Luke. I remembered his giggles as he dive-bombed Harry in the pool and my despair that this would be my last glimpse of him. Luke loved that house almost as much as I did and, if I swung my demolition ball at it, Will would not be the only person to crumble.

There was something else, too. I wanted to stop the destruction. My obsession with spying on Will, of finding out his every move, of having every keystroke of his life copied onto my memory stick, was becoming a madness. Will's infidelity had not only destroyed my trust; it was also in danger of killing the goodness in me. I didn't want to be one of those vengeful, bitter women who are defined by their rage. I was afraid of what I was becoming and I needed to find my way back to the person I used to be.

I had taken back what was mine; that was enough.

So I had scribbled a note at the bottom of Feridun's translation. I told Will that the letter had not been sent to the planning department, but was sitting in a safety deposit box in London. My demands were few and relatively modest.

I would get half the rental income from the Gümüşlük house. He wouldn't try to wrench the Hampstead house back; I would sell it and split the profit with him, after subtracting from his half all the money I had poured into it.

And Luke and I would get to spend our summers together in our house on the Aegean for as long as Luke wanted.

'This is my insurance against you,' I wrote.

＊＊＊

I called Mum from Gatwick and she held the phone to Lori's ear while I told her that I was on my way back to Sydney. She was still too weak to talk, but Mama told me she was smiling her new, sweet smile for the first time that day.

In the airport lounge I poured a glass of champagne and

opened my laptop. I left Will's correspondence unopened; it wasn't important to me now.

Claire had emailed, briefly. 'I'm leaving Jeremy. The thing with Amanda seems to have petered out, but now he's in contact with some Russian in Gümüşlük. I think her name's Natasha.'

I was about to shut the laptop down when I saw that a Facebook message had been pushed to my inbox. Opening it, I recognised the face of a man whom I had loved many years ago in Quebec but whom I hadn't tried hard enough to keep.

'I have been looking for you,' he wrote on my timeline. 'I live in Australia now. If you're ever in Sydney, I'd love to see you again.'

I sipped at the champagne as I considered how to respond. It had been a very long time ago and all the world's oceans had passed under that particular bridge.

But . . . there is always a but.

Slowly, cautiously, I pressed 'Like'.

Eve

I stand naked in the hotel room, the adjustable leg-spreader forcing my legs two feet apart and the six-inch heels starting to take their toll. It is cold and I'm shivering, but not because of the cold. My nipples are hard as steel, I am wet inside and blood is pounding through my veins. It's late and I'm waiting, waiting for him to come into the room. It is his plan. He makes me wait.

The door opens with a creak and all of a sudden he's in the room, his young body dressed but I can imagine what's beneath those clothes. His face is masked, but the deep green colour of his eyes is obvious through the slits. My heart is pumping and I swallow because my throat has gone dry.

He walks behind me and moves in close, so close I can feel his breath on my neck. I'm in agony and he knows it. He is nibbling my ear and I am bursting inside. He entwines his fingers through mine and this movement makes me take a few steps forward and start to turn around. He kisses my shoulder and forces me to shuffle back into place, so my arse can just feel his hard cock through his jeans.

He moves his hands up around my wrists and pulls them behind me so they rest on the top of my buttocks, where he handcuffs them. I can feel his eyes on my body and I want him, but for that pleasure I know I will have to wait and be a good girl.

He helps me to kneel now and then stands before me. My eye line is on his crotch and I'm breathing hard. He reaches behind my head and pulls my long thick auburn hair away from my face and twists it to form a ponytail down my back. He steps behind me and reaches forward to place a red ball gag in my mouth before buckling it hard against the back of my head.

He circles me twice, before stopping and crouching in front. His eyes are on the same level as mine. He leans forward slowly to bite my left nipple while staring up and into my eyes. I flinch as his teeth increase their pressure. I know not to make a sound, but my slight movement has him on his feet.

He walks behind me, picks up a cane and strikes me on my arse, twice. I groan with pleasure. He walks back and reaches into his pocket for the nipple clamps and watches me closely as he crouches and clips one clamp to my left nipple. I tense as the pressure takes hold and he smiles, hard, at hearing me whimper. He clips the other to my right nipple, knowing that I'm going to take the pain for him.

He stands in front of me, undressing slowly and deliberately, and I am wet with desire. His cock is so hard it stands against his belly. He likes watching the pain I am enduring because I cannot reach out to him.

He moves forward and pulls my head towards him. With one deft movement the gag is unbuckled from my mouth and I am sucking him, licking him, wanting to fuck him. His upper leg muscles tighten and I know he is liking this. My mouth is tight around his cock as it moves up and down, slightly faster, then slightly slower. Then he pulls out and his cock is glistening with my saliva mixed with his pre-cum.

He pulls me to my feet and is kissing my neck. I am shaking. He asks me if I have been a good girl today. When I don't respond, he pulls the nipple chain down until I shake my head. I have been naughty and need to be punished.

He leaves the room and I know I'll have to wait for my punishment, my pleasure.

Six weeks earlier

In the garden amongst the white gardenias and huge deep green ferns, I was reading *Be Fluent in Mandarin in Twenty Days*. Encouraging as the title was, twenty years was more likely the timeframe for me.

I took a break and looked up to admire the tiny waterfall I had created the year before. It attracted all sorts of butterflies and their graceful, albeit erratic, flight provided colour to the movement of the water behind them. I stood up, placed my book on the chair and walked over to break off a dead frond from one of the ferns. There were ants all over the tip of it and I threw it over the low box hedge into the compost behind.

My husband Henry and I had moved from Sydney to Shanghai two years earlier because his textile company was proving a success and expanding at a great pace into Asia, particularly China. We had met in the mid-1990s in a cafe beneath the Brisbane office where I was working for three months on a film set. He had just formed his company and was using the cafe as a makeshift office at the time.

In that time I learned that Henry was younger than me by four years, was passionate about textiles—especially silk—was a regular gym junkie, and had never been married. Once my contract was complete I returned to Sydney and we had continued long-distance relationship over two more years before Henry made the move into my apartment in Sydney.

As film design wasn't an easy profession to get into in China, I decided to study Mandarin part-time at Jiao Tong University. The students in my class came from all over the world and I delighted in the way we all learnt a little of each other's native words while we were trying to get a handle on the official language of China.

My Mandarin teacher said it was very auspicious to have a colourful water feature in the garden, as it would help the chi flow and create a hatching place to attract butterflies. I had read that some of the ancient cultures believed butterflies symbolised a rebirth of life after being cocooned for a period of time. I looked at the butterfly character I had painted on the miniature old Chinese *hutong* door we'd bought at the Russian markets in Beijing, where we'd holidayed in the first month of our move to Shanghai. It was, I suppose, another way of attracting butterflies into my sanctuary.

Moving to Shanghai had a secret meaning for me. I had adopted out my son Ezra when I was eighteen years old and all I knew was that his adoptive parents had moved to Asia. Somewhere.

The agency had linked us together by telephone when he was a teenager, but he'd showed a total lack of interest in my first two questions. The questions to be expected from a mother who had given her son away: What's your name now and where do you live? He never answered me.

Whenever I thought about him I was reminded of Hemingway's six words that spoke an entire story: 'For sale: baby shoes, never worn.' I hadn't bought the shoes because I had known from the beginning that I wouldn't keep my child. And I had never been able to tell Ezra's father Tomas about his existence, before Tomas died.

My mobile started to vibrate on the garden table and I quickly touched 'answer' before the ringtone disturbed the peace.

Henry had just opened an office in Thailand and the new sales manager had not appeared at work for the past two days, so Henry had booked a flight to Bangkok and left home early this morning. It was part of the reason for his success, I thought, as he kept a close eye on every aspect of his business. Henry was the type of person who didn't accept failure easily.

His distinctively deep voice sounded even deeper on the phone. I could hear airport noise in the background as he asked me to email a presentation that was on his other laptop at home. I could tell he was stressed—he added that it was critical and needed to be done immediately.

I sighed, said a silent goodbye to the peaceful surrounds and walked inside, stopping midway up the stairs to admire the view up the Huangpu River through the glass wall on my left. A mechanical crane was sitting on the edge of the river across on the Puxi side, shifting iron pipes on the riverbank; long low boats were moving up and down the river's edge, carrying various supplies to designated building sites as far as I could see. A few minutes passed before I dragged my attention away to focus on my task at hand.

Going to Henry's home office, I turned on his laptop and while I waited impatiently for Windows to perform its various functions, I decided a fresh pot of coffee would be a good idea. I walked back down the stairs, picking up a dead butterfly on the floor outside the kitchen.

Taking the rubbish outside I thought about my sister Zara in Sydney, who would have been horrified about throwing bottles, plastic and food refuse into a single bin. Apparently, recycling didn't translate into Mandarin.

Returning to the office, I found the email application had opened automatically without requesting a password; an irony I would contemplate later. Minimising that window I then proceeded to open the presentation and divide the sixty slides into two documents.

While gmail was sending the presentation, the computer's email application window popped up again, willing me to read unread emails. There were none. However, in the left pane, a folder named 'Chrystal' caught my eye and my hands went cold.

Chrystal had been Henry's PA for three years in Brisbane, but she had moved to Italy with her husband and son the year before we moved to China. Henry was always much more animated whenever he was in her company and I wondered whether he may have been even more animated when I wasn't there. She had once confided to me before she was married that Henry had paid a lease for an apartment closer to the office so she wouldn't have to make the 45 minute trip from the coast each day. I suspected that this gesture was him playing 'hero', to facilitate a conquest on another level, namely horizontal, but I wasn't sure and had never confronted him about it.

Chrystal had visited Shanghai last year on her way to Sydney for a brief holiday which at the time I thought rather odd as it wasn't a normal stopover destination from Milano. I had met her for coffee and had taken a friend of mine, Ben, with me and his words echoed with me now— 'There's something sly about Chrystal.' Strangely, both she and Henry had caught the same flight out to Hong Kong that evening.

Henry and I had only recently bumped into her husband, Justin, when we travelled to Hong Kong on one of Henry's business trips. The men knew each other through business ventures and seemed to get on well, but then I never really knew how Henry felt about fellow colleagues, especially if they were male. When we were checking in at our hotel, Justin was behind us in the queue, so we arranged to meet him at the bar in the foyer half an hour later. In the meantime I asked him about Chrystal and he looked down before telling us that he was going through a nasty divorce with her. I remember glimpsing the concentration on Henry's face.

Justin was waiting at the bar when we got there. He ordered drinks and launched into his story before we had a chance to breathe. 'I never got the right of reply. I arrived home one day after a two-week business trip and there was an envelope on the dining table. Inside were divorce papers, awaiting my signature. You know Chrystal now lives back in Australia with my son? He is the only reason I go there now. The only reason.'

He looked sad and I heard the determination in his voice, yet I asked him for Chrystal's mobile number, to lend her some support, somehow. I didn't know why I felt that way, but I knew there was always another side to every person's story. I texted her a brief message to say I would call her soon.

But for some reason, since then I had not texted again, nor spoken to her.

I moved the mouse over the email folder, hesitating before clicking it. I saw three email headers to the right. Judging by the date stamps, I figured they were written not long before she had visited Shanghai last year.

I double-clicked the first message and started to read the latest thread.

'I will be there for the 4th. We are partnering with a small German company to open our opportunities into Europe. I'll call you at home in the next couple of days to confirm. Henry'

'Not sure if I can take the time off work because as you know I may be getting a promotion. It would be great tho' if you're over here on the 4th of next month for my birthday. I will wear the red set you bought for me! Chrystal x'

'I said, I want to take you back to Spain. You are in my head every waking moment, I wish you were in my bed instead. Your voice on the phone the other night was making me crazy. I miss your lips, your eyes and your sexy legs. Henry'

I stopped reading and closed the email application.

The phone rang and I let it go to the answering service. Somewhere in the background I could hear Henry's message being recorded—he was saying something about his old boss. I wasn't listening; I was immobilised.

Their dark secret was in front of me, on Henry's laptop, in our home.

I woke from a wretched sleep, switched on the lamp and stole a glance at the old Chinese clock beside the bed, willing it to be night-time, so my pain would be blanketed in darkness. It read 1.31 a.m., four hours before dawn.

Having no energy I felt a dire need of water as the tears had sapped all the fluids from my body. I sat up slowly, planted my feet on the floor and pushed my body up from the bed. Walking unsteadily to the bedroom door I grabbed and turned the door handle—not only to open it, but also for support.

A piercing light suddenly filled the room, making me flinch. I leaned against the door jamb, to make sense of the scene, and glanced back at the clock, which still read 1.31 a.m. The clock had stopped, I realised, and now the harsh daylight had my full attention.

I reached for my sunglasses from the coffee table and squinted at the digital time on the iPod crib. It was Friday noon and the heat of the day was making me sweat. I fell sideways into the leather chair. A red light was blinking on the telephone. I pressed play and heard Henry's voice saying that Mark—his old boss and a friend of us both—was in town and had invited us to the Face Bar in the old French Concession on the other side of the river tonight. Henry would go directly from the airport and I would meet them at 6.30 p.m.

Back in his office I stared without expression at the computer screen. I opened the file manager and found the entire email application database file, which included all Henry's emails, calendar meetings and contacts. I copied it onto the new memory stick that had been lying innocently in the desk drawer, and then put it amongst my other memory sticks in a black velvet bag in my satchel. I was a stickler for keeping copies of everything digital, in case I lost everything.

It seemed like only minutes had passed, but my watch told me otherwise. It was now 6 p.m., and in the intervening time I had somehow managed to make up my face and fashion my body into the green silk dress we had bought in Tahiti five years before. I accessorised it with a long Swarovski crystal necklace, worn back-to-front to emphasise the low back of the dress, which was cut to the base of my spine.

The doorbell chimed. A taxi had arrived to take me to Shanghai French Concession Building Four on Ruijin Er Lu, across the river in Luwan. I slipped into a pair of high-heeled cream Jimmy Choo shoes, picked up the house keys and casually brushed Henry's favourite Ming vase backwards from the high wall shelf in the foyer to the marble floor below, shattering it into a million pieces.

My anger had just begun.

It was raining hard as I stepped from the taxi, narrowly missing a cyclist who had swerved to avoid the open car door and me. I looked down at my cream shoes, which were fast becoming a muddy brown from the water gushing up over the gutter and splashing onto an uneven footpath.

I ran to take cover under a huge plane tree and took off my shoes to tip out the water that was squelching under foot. The beauty of some of the original French residences of the early 1900s in this district, with their mansard roofs and shutters, always took my breath away, no matter how many times I visited.

Between the umbrellas passing in front of me, I got an occasional glimpse of the old red building opposite, where I was heading. But, attempting to cross the street amidst the cars, bikes and occasional dog—in bare feet—I began to wonder whether this was a mad suicide attempt to escape my impending soirée.

Finally reaching the other side, I walked into the gardens and savoured the ever-changing scene before me. Lots of different people from many places, casting shadows in the candlelight in front of the backdrop of old and new Shanghai. The whole scene softened by the changing autumn colours of the leaves on the plane trees.

Slipping into my shoes, I faltered. I didn't want to go further but, before I could escape, I saw Henry sitting on a chair inside the bar with Mark, who was waving and directing me over to them. I felt sick, and very tired, and I made my way across the garden towards the old red building.

Henry was wearing the Canali suit I had bought him for Christmas and his athletic physique was visible when he stood up as I approached; my smile froze as he kissed me on the cheek. I pulled my wet hair back from my face as I leaned over to kiss Mark before sitting on the pink chaise longue beside Henry. I ordered a pinot gris and listened to them talk about their past employ while I began to prepare for combat.

Henry was trying to encourage me to talk about life in Shanghai, but I was too angry to speak. I was in a very dark place and answered in cold monosyllabic answers. Suddenly Mark's attention switched to me and he asked, 'Whatever happened to Chrystal? Do you still keep in touch? Where is she now?'

Mark had just fired the first bullet and smashed my darkness into a vicious white. Turning to Henry I could hear the strain in my voice as I replied, 'Why don't you answer that, Henry? After all, you're the one who's been screwing her for . . . how many years now?'

An old myth states that sudden silences mean it is twenty-past or twenty-to the hour, and that an angel is flying above. I glanced at the antique French clock in the corner, which read 7.20 p.m., and I smiled, because there were no angels in this place.

The look on Mark's face was one of shock; he quickly stood up and suggested he should leave. He kissed me on the cheek and shook Henry's hand, and then quickly walked away, actually half-ran out of the building and across the grass.

Henry was smiling with a strange almost lunatic look in his eyes. Despite the fact that I could feel his fury, I asked him how long he had been sleeping with Chrystal and whether there were other women in his hoard.

His wineglass exploded against the mirror behind me and its contents splattered the left side of my back. Before I could react, he had exited the bar and left me in a soaking mess.

Ignoring the intense scrutiny of the other patrons, I walked with a white face to the bathroom and looked into the mirror. My embarrassment and anger had heated the tips of my ears to a fiery red. There was a trickle of blood on the back of my left arm, where a splinter of glass had struck. I washed away the blood, smiled at my reflection and said out loud the end of one of my favourite quotes:

'. . . it is, perhaps, the end of the beginning.'

I applied bronze powder to my cheeks and a neutral gloss to my lips before walking out of the bar, through the gardens and into a thick fog.

It was nearly 10.30 p.m. before I was able to find a vacancy in a tiny boutique hotel down on The Bund, the old financial district of the 1920s that had been converted over time into a street of six-star hotels and restaurants, exclusive bars and designer shops. Sitting in my room at last, on a large cane chair piled with cushions to the side of a kind of windowed alcove, I watched the river below, reflecting the colours that divide the east and west of modern Shanghai.

Suddenly I felt tired. I stood up and drew the curtains on the scene before me. I always looked forward to the solace of sleep, as a sort of prolonged pause in events and as a time of remembrance. Tonight I returned to the very beginning of my adult life.

Tomas

You were kneeling on the floor at the end of the bed and playing with my toes in your mouth. I was giggling, as I always did when we were together.

You painted the story of us with your words; how we would always be connected by an invisible thread of love and that nothing would ever break such a strong union. To prove it, you had given me a silver ring earlier in the day and, when I asked which finger I should put it on, you had replied, 'Whichever one it fits. Your choice—entirely up to you.'

I placed it on your lips instead, forcing you to make the choice. You slid your mouth down the fourth finger on my left hand, expertly placing it before moving your lips to mine.

It was the early 1980s—the end of our final year of school and our worlds were about to separate. While I was still figuring out which course I was going to take, you had already been selected for yours.

You climbed onto the bed, licking my calf muscles and reaching for my upper thighs, your fingers massaging the inner muscles and making me writhe. You reached my stomach and licked my belly button, watching me closely the entire time. I was shivering with lust and tried to reach for you, but you took my wrists and held them down above my head on the bed.

You knew I loved that, Tomas, and you smiled into my eyes and watched my helplessness.

And then you stopped.

This was our game. That you stopped there without going further, for a little while.

◦━━━━━≠·≠━━━━━◦

I woke at dawn and lay flat on my back and stared at the ceiling. It was obvious I had to leave Henry and move away from our blatant lie of love. In retrospect, I began to see that our relationship had started to slide when Chrystal started working for Henry. His late-night meetings had become more frequent as had his business trips interstate, always with Chrystal in tow. I eventually got up and showered, letting the warm water soothe my sadness while I stood motionless, angry and very much alone.

In the foyer downstairs I placed my black Amex on the counter, to test whether Henry had cut it off yet. The sweet smile on the clerk's face proved otherwise and, as I signed the docket and waited for the receipt, I smiled, too, but for a different reason.

I was thinking about the Christian Lacroix dress in one of the Hilton shops I had seen a few weeks ago. Ha, that could be a departing gift, a goodbye to my history with Henry. I knew if my sister Lili were here, she would have encouraged me to spend the $3000 by telling me I was worth every cent of it. It was tempting, but I decided that what might ensue would be bittersweet.

I wasn't ready to go home. It also was too early to go to my favourite teahouse in the Old Town, so I caught a taxi to Fuxing Park to lose myself in the extraordinary theatre played out by the older residents of this district.

I sat and watched in awe as an orchestra played Beethoven in perfect rhythm, as red sashes swirled around ballet dancers, as a single man displayed impressive strength with slow controlled yoga poses and hundreds of people performed their tai chi. Chairman Mao believed this form of martial arts was crucial for the health of his people and they still continued to practise it here, long after the end of his regime. I knew that tai chi was essentially a defence discipline, performed in slow motion, and realised that I was practising my own version, in my head.

My bag vibrated and I saw a notification from Facebook on my mobile phone. There was a private message from my closest girlfriend, Emma. I noted her updated avatar showing her newly acquired cottage on a beach near Byron Bay, near the border between New South Wales and Queensland. I felt such a strong longing to be able to dive into the surf in the photo and swim with all my heart.

'What's news Evie? Can't reach you on your mobile and your landline answers with that droll voice of what's his name—zzzzzzzzzz. Message me when you get this. Miss you.'

I inboxed back with, 'Do you want to chat on Skype tonight?'

Her reply was instant and we agreed on a 6 p.m., China time, link-up.

I wondered if I should I go back to Australia. Or even back to Canada, our family's original home. Perhaps I should take a flight over to Lili and finally see the old village house in southern Turkey that she had painstakingly brought back to life; she'd sent me a photo showing the wonderful ruins she'd fallen in love with its walled garden of fruit and olive trees.

I tapped to update my Facebook profile and changed my 'relationship' to single, while thinking cynically that I should be able to change my 'place of residence' to 'it's complicated!'

It was more than complicated and I knew I was just further delaying going home. I thought gym would be a great way to start and exorcise Henry from my mind. Remembering I had left clean gear in my locker, I walked the six blocks and took a shortcut through Hair Lane, as I called it, because in summer street barbers would set up makeshift salons and cut people's hair for 10 kuai—under two US dollars. I reached Huaihai Middle Lu and crossed over to my gym on the corner.

The instructors were pleased to see me and, because of the way I was dressed, they assumed I had been on a trip. I guess I had tripped in a way. I smiled, and said hello as I walked past them and into the change rooms. Then it was straight over to the row of running machines. I plugged in my iPod, stood on the treadmill and started walking. After three minutes I turned the dial nearly to the far right and started to run. Fast.

Dates, times and scenarios were flooding my head. I wanted to run faster to outdistance the jumbled mess, but I realised I was going at my capacity and that trying to run any faster could not fix what was broken.

Henry's trips to Europe had been more recurrent in the past year, I realised; his mood swings I had simply put down to exhaustion. Then again, I was probably right with that thought. He and Chrystal had no doubt been spending every waking moment together when he was over there. Bastard.

Seeing eight kilometres on the indicator, I turned the speed to a slow walk, lifted the towel from the front of the machine and wiped the sweat from my face, neck and arms. A couple more minutes to cool down then I made my way back to the change rooms. I was so deep in thought, walking with my head down, I literally bumped into my close friend Ben.

'My god, Eve,' he said. 'I was getting worried about you. Did you get my texts? Are you okay?'

I lied and said I'd misplaced my phone and had only just found it. He clearly didn't believe me, so I said, 'Let's meet in Rehab in, say, half an hour?'

He smiled at our private joke, but his eyes were questioning. He nodded and walked towards the weights room.

We had named the breakout area 'Rehab' when we had first met two years ago. I had dropped a weight on my foot and Ben had been the first to help. I had limped into the breakout area and he had tended to the injury with genuine concern. The swelling was almost immediate and we'd sat and talked while waiting for the ice pack he had placed around my ankle to reduce the swelling so I could ease it back into my gym shoe. When I said we talked, I mean we chatted non-stop.

I discovered that Ben had been living in Shanghai for seven years and had become quite established as a travel and portrait photographer. Our friendship developed quickly and, whenever he was in town and I wasn't travelling with Henry, we spent most of our time together. He had the sense of humour that I adored and was so wickedly funny and cheeky that, in the beginning, I had thought that if he were heterosexual and I had met him at a different time in my life, my attraction to him may have been played out very differently. The more frequent Henry's business trips were (and now I knew why), the more time I spent with Ben and we had become very close friends.

My studies at Jiao Tong University had extended into a journalist course and Ben had landed me a few freelance writing jobs with some of his clients. The first time we worked together he had asked me, on a whim, to accompany him on a photography assignment to Hainan Island in the South China Sea. He told me he was photographing butterflies and he watched my enthusiasm without understanding the meaning behind my smile. The three days in the Jianfengling rainforest there were extraordinary—we saw some of the most rare and brightly coloured butterflies, while Ben captured the magic of it all so beautifully.

On our second night, as we were scrolling through the photographs on his digital camera, I saw the iridescent green in the wings of a butterfly. I don't know if it was the heat or the light, or the whisky that he had placed in front of me, but suddenly, amidst a storm of tears, I told Ben about my love of butterflies, about Tomas—and about our baby, Ezra.

My friendship with Ben was secured in that very second and that's when he decided to nickname me Papi, short for his favourite French word, *papillon*—butterfly.

While waiting for him now and rehydrating on water, I grabbed my iPhone out of my bag to check my email. There were twelve new messages and I saw they were from sites promoting various products that my online buying had linked me to. As I was deleting them, I saw one from my friend Amelia who was living in Beijing with her partner and pregnant with their first child. I touched 'reply' and asked whether winter would be a good time for me to visit, before the birth of her baby. I wrote briefly about my current situation, and that I had left Henry.

I had met Amelia and Tony at a dinner party hosted by a mutual friend a few months before Henry and I were married. Those days seemed a long time ago, when Henry was still in love with me. At the time he owned a boat and Amelia and Tony had joined us on a number of weekends motoring around the canals and barbecuing freshly caught fish on whichever part of Moreton Bay we decided to anchor for the evening. Before we left for China, Amelia told me she and Tony were trying for a baby and I was thrilled when I found out she was pregnant. I knew they both would be fabulous parents.

There was also a long email from my sister Lili in London. This one I wanted to spend time reading a little later, because her stories were always filled with hilarity; I wanted to be able to distance myself, however briefly, from my emotional chaos and to savour her words.

Ben bounded in as he always did, his energy nearly exhausting me. He kissed me on both cheeks and said, 'Now tell me your news. I've felt so miserable not being able to speak to you over the last few days. So, I'm not going to let you out of my sight until you tell me something very bad and devilish.'

I laughed and said, 'Well, how bad would you like me to be? I could make something up and you could continue it. Want to play that game?'

Ben burst out laughing and said, 'Oooo, yes please!'

'Okay. Once upon a time there was a devastatingly drop-dead gorgeous man called Ben. Ben met an even more devastatingly drop-dead gorgeous girl, Eve, at the gym and they became BFFs. They shared so much time together that they could almost second-guess what the other was going to say next.'

I sighed and looked sadly at Ben.

'Oh my god, Eve! Has that bastard done something to you? What happened?'

Ben had disliked Henry when they'd first met; he had apologised to me at the time, saying he didn't like Henry's arrogance. Our meetings had subsequently always been just the two of us, with the occasional guy that Ben had picked up along the way.

'Remember Chrystal? Yep. More's the point, he did something to *her*, and it's been going on for a long time.'

'Whaaaat?! Chrystal? I never did like her. I knew she was trouble when I met her last year. You two are total opposites. I can't believe he's done that to you. She's a moronic ugly toad!'

Even though I was terribly sad, his words made me laugh. I grabbed his left hand and kissed it and said, 'I do so love you. You always say the right thing at the right time. I only just found out. And now for the devilish part.'

I proceeded to describe the scene the previous night at Face Bar.

'Fantastic. Brilliant. How perfect, to say that in front of his old boss. What are you going to do? Apart from staying with me until you decide.'

I sighed and replied truthfully, 'Right now, Ben, I don't know what to do. I might go and see Amelia in Beijing before she has her baby. Then I'm not sure. I might have to go back to Australia, unless I can possibly organise some work here.'

'We'll sort something out,' he said as he hugged me. 'But right now, I'm going to take you back to your place and we can pack up your stuff. I'm cancelling all plans for the rest of today and we're going to nut this out together. You'll be safe with me. Come on, lovely, let's go.'

All of a sudden I lost the anxious feeling that had been making my stomach churn for the past two days. I knew Ben was right: I had to move out straightaway and make some decisions about what my next move was going to be.

We drove across the river and, as Ben pulled up outside the gate of our home, I suggested that I go in first, just to make sure Henry hadn't returned.

Opening the front door, I took off my shoes and stared across the marble floor past the antique Chinese cabinets and silk rugs to my enormous oil painting which filled a third of the wall. I named the painting The Wise Man because of the wisdom depicted in his eyes; I spent a minute staring into those eyes, then I stepped on a splinter from the smashed Ming vase. The rest of the vase had been swept into a cardboard box and placed under the entrance table; Henry's travel bag was missing from its normal place beside the telephone chest. There was a cold feeling in the house.

Feeling by now like an intruder, I tiptoed into the kitchen and, suddenly strangely starving, I opened the fridge and dunked my finger into the honey jar. The smooth sweet taste was comforting, and a contrast to the frigidity I sensed all around me. I texted Ben the all-clear.

We went to the bedroom and I instructed him to place my red suitcase on the bed and what clothes to pack while I sat in a kind of trance on the old chair with my arms wrapped around my bent knees and my hands clasping my elbows. Dragging myself off the chair I walked into the bathroom, picked up a towel and pressed it to my face. I was sobbing into it when Ben walked in. He enveloped my body into his and I let all the sadness fall into the towel. We stood like that for some time before I stopped heaving and my sobbing stalled into little gasps.

'Come on, Papi, let's just go. We can come back and get the other things you need later.'

Feeling like a lost child, I picked up my handbag and followed Ben, pulling my red suitcase out the front door and down the stairs to the laneway.

———————⋇———————

Ben's penthouse apartment was in an old converted Chinese house up one of the tiniest lanes off Maoming Lu in Luwan, not too far from the Face Bar. His charm was reflected in his furniture and his books; his creative brilliance was on display in the origami miniature statues he had made. On every wall he had hung photos taken on his assignments. The large black and whites were my favourites. One photo of me, which he had taken on my birthday the previous year, was hanging in his foyer. I studied it and thought about how much my expression had changed over the course of two days.

There was a pergola over the rooftop garden and Ben had installed a retractable louvre roof that would automatically close when the rain fell on it. I smiled at the red silk embroidered cushions on the day bed, remembering how I had pleaded with him to buy them, even though he had wanted the green cushions instead. To me, Asia represented reds and oranges and butterflies, yet Ben was more inclined to choose the greens and blues that reminded him of the freshness of the rainforests he had photographed all over the world.

We sat there with a glass of wine each and I tried to relax in the sun while Ben plugged his iPod into his supersonic music system. Slow jazz played out of the six speakers that he had hidden around the garden. If it was any other day, I thought, we would have been laughing about Ben's love antics or discussing his next photographic assignment. Today, though, Ben had other things on his razor-sharp mind.

'So, I think the plan for today, my darling, is to work out what you are going to do.' While we'd been driving, Ben said, he'd been thinking about how I could earn some extra cash. 'Do you remember Alice from Malaysia? She's my friend who commissioned me to photograph the devastation in Aceh after the tsunami. I could chat to her and see if somehow you and I could collaborate on my next gig. You could write the words for my photographs. What do you think?'

'Oh Ben, I think your photographs tell their own stories. Words would lessen the power of them.' I was touched by his offer, though, and it sparked an idea. Perhaps, I suggested, he could ask Alice if she had anyone covering the Eurasian Art Exhibition in Beijing in about six weeks. 'It could be good timing,' I added, 'as I might be going up there anyway to visit Amelia.'

Ben immediately picked up his phone and, when she didn't answer, he left a message for Alice to call him. Then he turned back to me. 'What are the dates for the exhibition? I'm wondering if there's a chance I could do something up there as well. We could travel together. *Eeek!*—Watch out Beijing! Perhaps I could shoot the "behind the scenes" of the exhibition to go with your story?'

I gave him the details for the exhibition and having sorted that out in his mind, his thoughts returned to my financial needs. 'My cleaner is useless. I know you won't let me give you any money. So, would you consider doing some light housework in the short term? Helps me, and gives you a salary.'

'Thanks, that'd be great. The whole divorce thing is going to be horrific, and I know Henry will draw it out as long as he can.'

Ben picked up the backgammon board with eyebrows raised. This was our ritual and sometimes we played countless matches well into the night. We always started out with the same moves, Ben protecting his home base while I played a racing game.

At one stage I had two pieces off the board waiting to come back on and then my next throw showed a double four. I had studied a little feng shui and believed that the number four was inauspicious, which it is for some Chinese people, as its pronunciation is similar to the word for death. I looked pointedly at Ben as I placed the two pieces on the fourth triangle in his home base. 'Coincidence?'

Ben laughed and scolded me for choosing to see this as a bad sign. 'Stop it, Eve, you're being superstitious. Four can be a positive number. Anyway, it totals to an eight, so there!'

I didn't care that the double equated to an eight—I was trying to dislodge his competitiveness so I could win the game.

As the afternoon burned slowly into dusk we both got up, leaving the game so we could turn on the lamps and light the candles. Ben changed the music to an upbeat Black Eyed Peas track, and said he would duck down to the wet markets and pick up some fish and lemons.

I closed the front door behind him and walked over to the bookshelf where some of the origami figures were placed. The butterfly he had designed with me in mind was perched on the top shelf. I slid my hand behind it and picked up Ayn Rand's *Atlas Shrugged*. I began to read the words I knew so well—'Who is John Galt?' Now, almost twenty-five years since I first read this book, I felt the weight of my own world on my shoulders. Could I just shrug and see what would happen?

I suddenly remembered the 6 p.m. Skype link I had agreed to with Emma. Damn, I thought, when I realised my battery was completely flat and I had left the power plug for my laptop back at the house. I walked through into Ben's office and moved the mouse next to his iMac to activate the screen. There was a curious website in front of me, but I dropped the window to a minimised state without investigating it further. As Skype was not yet common technology, Ben had not installed the application on his iMac. I downloaded the free application, signed in and initiated a video call to Emma.

'What's up, girlfriend?' she asked. 'Where are you? Is that Ben's place? I can see some origami pieces behind you.'

'Hey, Em. Yep, here at Ben's. How's your new cottage?'

She was cooking a late meal and had placed 'me' on the kitchen table, so I could see her in entirety as she moved around the island bench in her kitchen. Even in such a mundane setting, she looked as gorgeous as ever—statuesque (she's 1.75 metres tall), with long natural blonde hair. A male friend of mine had once described her as being 'God's creation' and I knew that view was shared by many.

Emma and I had met in our early twenties at the Australian Film, Television and Radio School in Sydney, where she was studying production while I was studying design. She and I had worked together on a number of television productions before she took some time off to have kids. Her humour made me laugh out loud and her own laughter was infectious. These days, when she spoke her accent was unique—a mixture of British, American and her native Australian, resulting from the time she spent in Europe and the States when she was still working as a television producer.

In reply to my question, Emma picked 'me' up and walked me through each room of her cottage. She opened the back door so I could see her garden, and the crashing sound of the waves of the ocean beyond reminded me how much I missed the beaches in Australia. Then 'I' was returned to the kitchen and we continued our conversation.

'So what's happening in your lust life?' I asked, winking at her as I tried to keep my tone light.

Emma had been married for fifteen years to a man many years her senior, whom she loved a great deal. When he died he bequeathed a small fortune to her, a modest part of which she now spent on men who were at least fifteen years younger than she was.

Now she walked to the side of the island bench opposite me. Grabbing it with both hands, she slowly pushed her body backwards and down through her hips while she raised her left eyebrow and turned her head sideways at me. She whispered, 'Let's just say, men who are thirty-something have a certain energy, which is all I need.'

I laughed and it felt good. It was so typical of her—somehow we all adored Em for her questionable love life.

'So tell me what's happening in Chinatown. Any cuties I can visit when I come back to Shanghai and stay with you and Mr Boring?'

'I've left him, Em, and I've moved in with Ben for a little while.'

'What? When did this happen? Are you okay?' The concern was in her voice, all over her face.

I tried to keep my face neutral when I replied. 'Thursday, but it feels like a lifetime ago and, yes, I'm okay. Found out he's been screwing Chrystal for at least two years, and god knows who else. I wouldn't care so much if it was someone I didn't know but . . .'

'Unbelievable. Or actually, sorry to say, probably it is believable. He tried it on me soon after you got together. Prick!'

I sat there in shock. 'You never told me that. What did he do?'

'He had the audacity to drop in to my place when you were working on that series in Indonesia. He apparently wanted to show me some earrings he'd bought for your birthday, but his real intent was to ask me to spend the weekend on his boat before you got back. I told him to leave. He did, thank god!

'Probably makes sense to you now, why I've always been so caustic towards him,' she continued. 'Sorry, Eve, but you were just starting out with him and I thought it might have just been a hiccup in his persona. I probably should have told you then or, better still, warned you.'

I didn't have anything to say, so I didn't. She came over to the screen and apologised again. 'Sorry, Evie, I didn't mean to hurt you.'

Looking her straight in the eyes, I smiled as reassuringly as I could. 'Hey, Em, don't worry. It's doesn't matter anymore. Why don't we hook up again in a couple of days, when I've figured out my moves? Ben's going to be home soon and I need to get dinner started.'

'Okay,' she agreed reluctantly. 'You are okay, aren't you? Don't want to chat further?'

Strangely, at that moment the connection dropped out and her moving picture disappeared from the screen. I didn't want to reconnect just yet so I changed my status to 'invisible'.

I scarcely heard Ben return an hour later. I was sitting on the couch, buried in the pages of *Atlas Shrugged* when he walked through the door. I smiled at his thoughtfulness as he handed me a bunch of my favourite flowers—yellow tulips—and kissed me on my forehead. I stood and walked with him to the kitchen to put the flowers in a vase.

'Would you ever fall in love with a character like John Galt?' I asked, holding up the book as reference.

'Of course. Anyone who can force autocracy and corruption into surrender is my kind of guy, for sure. Why?'

'I wish I could have been more like him in my thirteen years with Henry.' My voice had become tiny. I started slicing the bottom of the stems off the tulips.

'Well, Papi, Henry was your nightmare and you've just woken up. Now's the time to be yourself again and not have the burden of a repressive relationship weighing on your shoulders.'

I touched his shoulder and said, 'I guess.'

That repressive feeling was one I was becoming increasingly familiar with. When Henry and I first came to live in Shanghai, we were invited to a cocktail party hosted by the Australian Embassy. I was pleased I went because I met Josie, the Chinese wife of one of Henry's colleagues. One day we were walking through a park on the outskirts of the city after visiting an art gallery, and our discussion changed swiftly into a soliloquy spoken by her. She was espousing Chairman Mao's greatness and I was confused, as I had never heard her speak like this before. It wasn't until we reached the other side of the park and were back on the footpath that she turned to me and said, 'Sorry, Eve, there are lots of microphones in that park, and I wanted to throw off any suspicion that you might be corrupting me or, even worse, spying for your country.'

This constant feeling of repression was always with me in China, so I would regularly escape to Hong Kong. At the same time I would also be escaping from Henry's own form of control—Hong Kong had always seemed to restore my sense of freedom.

After dinner Ben and I continued playing backgammon until very late, when we drifted into his living room to read. There, eventually feeling my eyelids droop, I stretched out on the sofa and fell asleep.

Tomas

You had travelled on tour for a long time and we had no contact in the four years after the last day of school. I always thought about you, especially towards the end of the year, on Ezra's birthday. When we had last seen each other, neither of us knew that we had created a life, our son. You didn't know, and I wondered if there would ever be the right occasion to tell you.

It was by chance that we saw each other again on that Friday afternoon on a street in Rushcutters Bay, Sydney. I was walking home and you were walking on the other side of the avenue with some guy. Remember? We spotted each other immediately and came together in the middle of the road.

As the traffic sped by on either side, you tried to stop us even before we could start again. You told me you were engaged to someone in Queensland, but your face could not disguise your pain and your angled excuses made blunt punctures on my skin.

We knew we were still in love and, although our lives seemed separated by bordered waters, the bridge formed once again between us.

Later, while you were sleeping, I couldn't hear you breathe, even though the contours of your body showed slight movement. The exertions of our lovemaking always stilled you like this, yet the tempest of emotions must have been a roar inside your head.

Because it was in mine.

I woke early, initially unsure of where I was, but faintly aware that I was safe in the darkness. The first thing I saw was the origami butterfly and then everything came flooding back.

Ben had placed under my head a pillow and over my body his favourite angora rug, which he had purchased in Nepal. I stretched my body, wiggled my toes and stretched my arms above my head before I sat up. It was strange being here, knowing that this would be my home for an indeterminate period.

I glanced at my phone and saw a text message from Lili, asking if I had received her email.

Down the hallway I peeked into Ben's bedroom. Seeing his body motionless in a deep sleep, I closed his door softly and continued to the kitchen to get a drink of water. On my way back I stepped into his office, switched on the lamp and sat down at the iMac.

The curious looking website had been re-opened. I dismissed it, opened another tab and logged into gmail.

The first was an email from Henry. The subject read 'Your things'. I nearly hit delete, but I knew I had to read it.

'I have had your things packed up and put in the spare bedroom. Please remove the boxes and your artwork over the next 10 weeks while I'm in Europe. I have changed the locks so you will need to contact my secretary Maxie to get access.

'Your behaviour at Face Bar was insulting and how dare you try to embarrass me in front of a work colleague. You didn't succeed as per usual.

'By the way, Chrystal wasn't my only comfort although the sex was some of the best I've had. There have been many over the years because you could never give me what I wanted.

241

'That's it. I want no more communication with you. Neither does my family.

'My lawyer will be in touch.'

I was surprised at the level of anger I felt as I printed the email. This last piece of cruelty was typical of the toxin Henry had contaminated our relationship with for years. Good riddance.

I scrolled down to find Lili's email for light relief. I always looked forward to reading her words, with their crisp vitality and astounding wit. Except this email was serious. Lili had suspected Will's infidelity for a long time, but she had just discovered his affair with a Russian girl whom she had nicknamed Slutski. My sister's black humour always made me laugh. As I read about a scene at Heathrow Airport where she dressed in a *hijab* to spy on her husband, I gasped at the lengths she was prepared to go to.

'Outstanding, darling,' I replied, 'but heartbreaking all the same.'

I felt the depth of grief in her words and made sure my own emotions were invisible in my reply, promising a longer email in the next few days.

I thought about Zara, Lili and me, and how much our worlds were intertwined. I always relied on their resilience when I was going through a dark time. Except right now I didn't want to say a thing. Didn't know what to say, actually; or, more accurately, I felt I had lost my voice.

Closing the email tab, I was back looking at the strange website Ben must have been reading when I was sleeping last night. It took a minute or two for me to understand what I was looking at. There was a male figure in leather gear holding a whip and standing in front of a chair. The photograph was angled to show part of another male body sitting on the chair with a chain wound around one ankle and attached to the leg of the table.

I glanced at the address line and saw a bunch of numbers and letters. I clicked the 'back' button a couple of times until the Home page displayed a masked woman holding a leash overhead, almost in a frozen pose. The words Dominatrix and Submissive flashed around the page, intermixed with black and white pictures of men and women in various poses of restraint. I had always been curious about this sexual world, and rather than repulse me I knew deep down that it was enticing to me. I zoomed the screen to enlarge the photos.

Ben touched my shoulder and I jumped, feeling as if I had intruded on his personal life.

'Oops,' he said. 'Not quite the website you would normally be looking at, hey?'

I thought he sounded annoyed. I turned and spluttered that I had just emailed Lili, and had returned to this site as it was already open. I apologised.

Ben giggled. 'This is probably not the way I would have wanted you to discover my other life, Papi. But, now that you have, this is my relationship with the BDSM world. You either dominate or be dominated. It's a game, and a rather powerful one at that.'

He lifted the hard copy of the email off the laser printer. 'What's this?'

'Read it,' I said as I drew my knees up to my chest.

'Jesus, he's a jerk. Throw it away, Eve—you don't need this kind of crap in your life. Why did you print it out?'

'It's called ammunition, Ben,' I replied, but really I wanted to change the subject. 'Anyway, tell me more about this other world of yours.' I grinned. 'I'm guessing you would want to be the one in control.' I felt a slight increase in my pulse and shifted my body in the chair to get more comfortable.

'You know me well,' he said and laughed. 'Yes, I am the Dominant. I get to choose what my submissive can and can't do for me. In fact, I've discovered a whole universe of people right here and all over the world who play this game, and make it very much a part of their lives. Are you shocked? Come on, let me enlighten you.'

I wasn't sure how to feel about it. Did I want to be educated in this field? I felt uncomfortable thinking about Ben in this light. However, curiosity got the better of me and I followed him into his walk-in wardrobe. He opened a door at the end of the passageway and we entered a space of leather and chains.

Ben's mobile rang. As he walked out, I heard him talking to Alice. I picked up a strange-looking chain with two small metal clamps on either end; wandering out with it, I sat on the sofa, waiting for him to end the phone call. My interest in this world, I began to realise, was becoming more attractive to me, in a sexual way.

'Good news!' he cried. 'Alice hasn't got anyone covering the art exhibition in Beijing and she's keen for you to write a piece. It's only a small job, but at least it'll be your first for her magazine. I've invited her over for dinner tonight so you two can discuss what you need to do.'

Then he saw what I was holding. 'Ah, I see you've found one of my toys.'

'What is it?' I asked as I stretched the chain to its full length.

'They're nipple clamps. I think you and I should pay a visit to one of the clubs off Huaihai Lu. You'll get a better idea of how the whole thing works, if you want. It's pretty full-on, but maybe you need to step out of your comfort zone and get something that Henry was never able to give you.'

All of a sudden my anxiety returned. It was something in Ben's words.

'Hey, Eve. You've gone white. Are you okay?'

'Oh my god, I've just remembered something. Chrystal confided in me once that she had contracted herpes when she was twenty. Fuck! And I bet they didn't have safe sex.'

Caged in my own mental space, I stood up and started to pace. I felt like a wild cat waiting to pounce on unsuspecting prey.

'Jesus! Look, I'm sure you'll be fine. It's Monday tomorrow. We'll go down to that clinic across the park from Xintiandi first thing in the morning.'

'Do you know what? Damn her. I'm going to call her now and ask if they had unsafe sex. This is unforgiveable.'

It would be night-time in Australia and no doubt she would be putting her son to bed. I didn't care anymore. It could have been two o'clock in the morning and I would still make her wake up—to herself.

I picked up the phone, found her number and punched 'call'. Ben was watching me carefully. I hit 'speaker' so he could hear the conversation.

When she picked up, her voice was hesitant. 'Eve, is that you?' I knew instantly that Henry had updated her on our use-by date. I wanted to throw the phone across the room.

'Not interested in having a conversation with you. I just need to know one thing and you'd better be honest, for once in your life. Did you practise safe sex with Henry or not?'

She started to try and apologise.

'Stop it! Just say yes or no.'

'No, but . . .'

I hung up, and Ben and I stared at each other. Hot tears were forming and I quickly blinked them out.

The trouble with the truth is, when it is laid out bare, it becomes impossible to lose sight of what lies beneath. And there were many lies.

'When I think about it, his filthy escapades certainly didn't foul my body before we arrived, because we had to take a medical test to get our visas validated. I was okay then, but that was two years ago.'

'Shows how resistant you are, Papi. I think it's improbable that you have herpes but you will need to get tested just in case. I have to get tested every year, regardless that I was virus-free seven years ago, when I arrived.'

Ben, dear sweet Ben. I had forgotten that he'd had to live with HIV every day of his life for the past three years. Feeling selfish, I walked over to him and put my arms around him. 'I'm sorry, darling. It's been all about me, and now we should stop about me. Because you are so energetic and healthy, I always forget that you have to live with this solicitude. You are okay, aren't you?'

'I'm fine. Hey, Eve, this is too all-consuming. Let's not think about it until we get you tested tomorrow. Let's cook a feast. Alice is going to be here in a couple of hours. Giddy up, my lady.'

I knew him well. It was time to stop peeling back the layers of his life because I could see he was erecting a barrier and retreating behind it fast. I realised then that I was, too.

A quick shower and I was refreshed and dressed in a short red dress with thin straps over my shoulders. When

I looked in the mirror I looked starved, betraying my state of deprivation. I added an apricot-coloured angora wrap drooped over my shoulders and belted loosely around my waist to hide the evidence. Note to self: eat more.

Alice arrived and we reintroduced ourselves. It never ceased to surprise me how beautiful the skin of some Malaysians was, and Alice was definitely one of the lucky ones. She had the same sort of upbeat energy and humour as Ben, and during dinner our conversation had an easy flow. Afterwards Ben excused himself, headed into his office and left us to chat.

Alice handed me the latest copy of her magazine, *Budaya*, as a reference for the style of writing required. I loved the sound of the name *Budaya*, and when I later translated it into English via Google, I discovered it meant 'culture'. We exchanged ideas easily, discussing our interests in art and switching between the classics and the postmodern. The exhibition was five and a half weeks away and I knew I had to do a lot of research on the exhibiting artists, but Alice told me she would forward me links to various websites, to help my study of the artists and their creations.

It was 11 p.m. when Alice left. I thanked her for the opportunity she was giving me. I also silently thanked her for making me forget about Henry for a little while.

I had called Ben out of his office, so he could say goodbye, and, as I closed the door on her, I turned to see him looking at me with a cheeky smile.

'What?' I asked.

I was staring at two masked men with bare chests, dressed in leather pants. They were looking up at a naked woman, whose wrists were tied together up above her head. Her forearms were sheathed, to stop her shoulder blades from popping out, Ben explained, and these sheaths were hung from a chain secured to the ceiling. Her toes were pointed downwards as she tried to stretch them to the ground. It looked uncomfortable, but I could clearly see the struggle was for everyone else's enjoyment, particularly the two men standing looking up at her.

We had caught a taxi to a club at the other end of Huaihai Lu, about eight kilometres from Ben's place. From the outside it looked like a derelict house, as there were no lights on and the garden was untended. Ben flicked the miniature torch on his keyring and shone it down a passageway beside the house. I followed him until he stopped at the back of the house. He directed the light onto a metal staircase and I held the handrail carefully as I walked down the twenty steps into the cavern below in my stilettos.

We were in The Dungeon, a small bar with a stainless-steel mesh wall that separated us from the BDSM scene that was being played out on the raised platform on the other side. The music was metal and the throb of the beat was in perfect unison with the choreography being performed before us. We had paid 100 kuai each—about fifteen US dollars—to get access to this private area of the house.

Ben now took my hand and steered me towards the next room. We looked through an opening on the side and saw a man straddling a wooden plank, facing the wall behind him; his wrists were handcuffed in vertical hanging chains that dropped to the side of his body. This was the whipping seat, Ben said, and the 'client' could sit facing the back of the seat and be lashed across his or her back, as was happening at the moment. Alternatively, if he leant back against the wall, there were lashings of pleasure to select from.

I was giggling when we left the room. Not that anything was very funny, but I just felt a little out of place.

The next room was pitch black and I waited for my eyes to adjust before I saw it. In the middle of the room was a pit, eight feet deep, and it was empty except for a long pole concreted into the ground. Ben explained that some subs— submissives—were lowered into the pit and were only allowed to climb back up the pole when commanded by their Master. This game would be played out over a couple of hours, and if the sub was too tired to climb the pole, the Master would assist by pulling on the leash attached to their collar.

I shuddered at that level of submission. But then I realised that, in a way, during my relationship with Henry I had been in a dark pit for a long time. Except in my case I hadn't been able to see the way out, until I discovered his infidelity and that flicked my switch into this new world. It occurred to me that my attraction to a form of BDSM had started all those years ago with Tomas when he had restrained me and made me wait for my pleasure. It was also attractive because it was an experience I had *never* shared with Henry.

Ben and I retraced our steps to the front door and walked down another long hallway to a bar with a gas fire at the front of the house. I was admiring the red and gold decor when I felt a hand on my lower back. I turned to see a tall man with jet black hair standing behind me and watched as he moved his hand to shake mine. His name was Alex, his accent unmistakably Canadian—and therefore familiar— and he appeared very comfortable in this scene.

He asked if it was my first time in the club; I nodded, but added that I had experienced a form of BDSM. He didn't have to know it was with a mentally abusive partner and had occurred many times over a thirteen-year period. The difference was that it was *without* my consent.

We chatted for a while and when he asked if Ben was my partner, I simply said, 'No, no. I'm as free as a butterfly.'

We both felt an attraction and could read it in each other's eyes as we talked into the night. Finally he told me that he had to leave, because he was flying down to Hong Kong early in the morning for two days. While he said this, he handed me his card and asked me to call him towards the end of the week. He vanished through the door and into the night, and I was reminded of Anne Rice's *The Vampire Lestat*. I slid his card into the back pocket of my leather pants. As I did so, I could feel my body temperature rise.

I couldn't find Ben so I texted him, asking where he was. There was no reply, so I gathered he was otherwise engaged, and might be for a while. I left the club and had to take the hour's walk home, as there were no available taxis. I didn't care, because I was thinking about Alex and what new disciplines I was about to experience.

I was wide awake when I walked back into Ben's apartment, so I went straight through to the iMac and typed in the website address on Alex's card. His front page was black, with a picture of a door slightly ajar in the centre of the screen with a flicker of light beneath. I thought instantly of my *hutong* door in the garden of my old home. To attract butterflies.

All of a sudden a window appeared over the top, requesting a sign-in or join up. Knowing he would be able to find out the dates and times when members had joined, I decided to leave an identity that he would instantly recognise.

I typed 'Butterfly' for my user name and 'chaos' for my password and found the Chinese character for 'butterfly' on a calligraphy site, which I pasted as my ID.

I felt like I had flown through an invisible wall and into a secret garden of human insects, all clambering for some light. I scrolled through the long list of members, most with a symbol or cartoon character as their identification, along with their user names.

Alex was easily identifiable by his photo, the only apparently true identity in the entire list. I private-messaged him to say I was looking forward to his return.

The next morning I waited inside the medical clinic in Xintiandi and was lucky to see a doctor after a short time. I explained the situation and she repeated Ben's words, that she thought it was unlikely that I had contracted herpes. She gave me a PCR blood test, examined me and told me that there didn't appear to be any sign of abnormality but that I would need to wait for the results from the medical laboratory.

I received a call from her a few days later and she confirmed I had tested negative for herpes. I breathed a long sigh of relief and texted Ben the good news. But despite my all-clear I would never forgive Henry for this. I would make sure he would feel my wrath in time.

A week later, I was dressed in a strapless bodice with an orange push-up bra, leather leggings and impossibly high stilettos. I had called Alex, as promised, and we had arranged to meet tonight. I had given him my address and a box containing the outfit had been couriered to Ben's address yesterday with an attached note: 'Looking forward to the vision.'

Ben wolf-whistled as I walked out of my room.

'What is The Fountain Bar like—is it actually a normal bar, or naughty?' I asked him.

'It's not what you call normal, Papi, but it's nowhere like the BDSM bar we went to last week. You look great and would definitely not feel comfortable if you arrived in one of your normal evening outfits, that's for sure!'

Alex arrived. I put on my silk coat and when I turned back to wave at Ben as I closed the door on my way out, he winked at me and gave me a thumbs-up.

The bar was jam-packed with people as we made our way to a cushioned alcove that Alex had reserved for us. He slid his hand around my lower back and drew me close, into a fervent kiss. There was an urgency about him and I was enjoying his attention, realising that Henry really hadn't given me this kind of attention for a long time.

Alex asked me what I wanted to drink and disappeared towards the bar into the crowd of people there. I leaned back against the cushions and studied the outfits of those in front of me. Ben was right, it wasn't a normal bar. In fact, there were many cushioned alcoves and everyone was in various states of undress; however, there was a certain style about them and it didn't seem sleazy.

Alex reappeared all of a sudden and handed me a glass. We clinked each other's drinks and I took a sip. I choked. He laughed.

'What is this? It's definitely *not* wine.' It had a very sweet taste, but I couldn't identify what it was. I had never tasted anything quite like it before.

'I know. Thought we should have some fun. You've never had a Hurricane before?'

I looked at him and wondered if this was wise—to accept a drink I had never had before—but his innocent look put me at ease so I shook my head in reply and took another sip.

'Whoa, go easy on it! It's a mixture of spirits and liqueurs. To be honest, I've never known the exact recipe, but it certainly lives up to its name if you're not careful.'

He sat beside me and we kissed; his hand felt hot as he touched my cheek. Actually, I was starting to feel very hot and strangely fuzzy, yet I hadn't felt this good for such a long time.

I was taking another sip of my Hurricane when he asked me, 'So, tell me, Eve. What is it about bondage sex that you enjoy the most?'

I nearly spluttered my drink back up, swallowing hard to try to stem a coughing fit. Okay, I thought, that's direct and to the point. I struggled for an answer, trying to remember what Ben had told me, except I was muddled. Then I shocked myself with my reply.

'Well, in my experience, I'm definitely *not* the Dominatrix. I'm more into being submerged . . . I mean, submissive.' My voice had taken off like a locomotive train, and my brain was trying desperately to catch up with it.

Alex was laughing. I was laughing. And then, to my horror, the train was wobbling on its tracks, and heading straight towards a dark tunnel. I couldn't see what was on the other side.

'The nipple clamps are one of my favourite toys.' What was I saying? Jesus, where had that come from? My voice was now out of my control, and I listened horror-struck as it continued, 'Have you got some toys back at your place? I would take you back to mine, but it isn't really mine. It's my friend, Benz. Do you like him? He's my best friend.'

Alex was smiling. I noticed he had very white teeth, a nice nose and a gold fleck in his right eye. He leant over and took my hand in his and clasped it tight. I was trying to smile back, but my jaw felt locked. There was a rosy glow in my peripheral vision.

Then he pulled me up and put his arm around me; we walked across the bar, out of the club and into the fresh air. Well, it wasn't really fresh but it certainly cleared my head a little.

Alex said, 'Let's go back to my place, because I want to do things to you that I can't do here.'

I was ready to do anything with Alex and couldn't wait to get back to his place, if only the fuzzy blur in my vision would go away. At his apartment block I stripped in his lift and we were laughing. Alex was probably more aroused than me—he was excited by the prospect that someone might get into the lift on the way up. Me? I wasn't sure where my head was, but I was feeling great.

The only thing I remember about his place was that it was very Zen. Minimal. One large bed in the middle of an empty room. I started to lie back on the bed, and then he turned the lights off. I remained still, waiting for him.

All of a sudden I heard his voice directly behind me, or was it above me? And then he was right beside me. We were on his bed, and then on the floor beside a fire. He picked me up and we were on a tree branch under a burning sun, and then the next minute in the freezing cold snow and there was a snow leopard ready to pounce.

He climbed on top and slowly moved inside of me. It was fast and made me think about the heat inside a volcano. When the lava decided to flow I came back to earth and to the bed we had lain down on initially. And then we must have slept for a little while.

When I woke, Alex was asleep beside me and our clothes were strewn all over the room. I tried to get up, but my muscles weren't working—they felt like lead.

And that's when I knew I was in trouble.

My hands were bound behind my back and my feet had been tied down to something at the end of the bed and on the floor. My head was pounding and my lips were parched.

I realised then that my drink had been spiked. Had Alex spiked it? I wasn't sure, but was starting to feel the beginning of a panic attack. If I had been drugged, what if my body had a latent adverse reaction? I concentrated on taking long slow breaths until I felt a little calmer.

But then I scolded myself. 'You idiot, Eve. You meet this guy once and now you're tied down in his place with god-knows-what chemicals running through your body. What on earth were you thinking?'

Alex woke and looked at me with a crooked smile. There was something unusual about his eyes, and his skin colour was sallow. I knew I had to tread carefully with him.

'Good morning. Did you enjoy your trip last night, Eve?'

Something told me not to answer, so I nodded slowly instead. His smile got wider.

'Bet you felt out of this world. Man, that stuff is powerful. It makes sex so much more surreal.'

I was furious, but scared at the same time. I asked to use the bathroom.

Suddenly he was back to being the charming Alex who had appeared to be a regular guy when we first met in the BDSM bar. The change in him was dangerously quick and I knew I had to get out of there, and fast. He untied my feet and then unbound my wrists, and pointed me in the direction of his bathroom with a slap on my bottom.

I was washing my hands in hot water because my body had broken into a cold sweat. He came to the bathroom door and said, 'Would you like something to eat? I'm starving. I'll duck downstairs and get us something from the bakery across the road. Any special requests?'

'No, nothing for me, I'm fine.' I knew that wasn't true, but I couldn't wait for him to leave so I could get out of there, too. Perhaps he was giving me an opportunity to flee his place while he was gone because he felt my discomfort, but I didn't care about how he felt. At all!

The sound of the front door closing had me on my feet, throwing on my clothes and grabbing my bag. I didn't bother to put my shoes on because I needed to be able to run, fast. I took the fire escape instead of the lift.

When I reached the ground level, the fire door exited into a laneway on one side of the building. I ran as fast as I could towards the back of the building and kept on running until I reached a main road. I was in unfamiliar territory, but I knew there would be a taxi rank not too far away—there are taxi ranks everywhere in Shanghai. Before I knew it, I was in a taxi and heading across the other side of town to Ben's place.

I sent Alex a text. 'I had to leave. I can't believe you drugged me. Please don't contact me again.'

⸺ ⋙ ⋘ ⸺

'Oh my god, Eve. You poor thing. He didn't seem to be that kind of person. But then again, how could I tell? He was only here for a second.' Ben was wearing his 'worry' look and I knew I was in for a little lecture. 'Okay, from now on you need to keep me up to date by text when you go on another date like this. Deal?'

'There won't be another date like this, Ben.' I felt embarrassed. It was the next day, about lunchtime, and the first chance we'd had to talk.

'Eve, I hope you believe me. It doesn't have to be like this. BDSM can be a lot of fun, as long as your partner and you completely trust each other. Did he give you a safe word?'

'I have no idea what really happened—only snippets, and I'm not sure they're real,' I said, thinking how lucky I had been, how much worse it could have been. 'What's a "safe" word?'

Ben sat down heavily on the sofa beside me. 'A safe word is a word you use for your own protection. BDSM is fun as long as it is consensual and you say the safe word when you want to stop the scene immediately.'

I wondered what safe words I could have said to Henry that would have stopped him from hurting me. *Ming vase?* Perhaps not.

'Come on,' said Ben, suddenly perking up as if he sensed my thoughts had fallen darkly on Henry. 'Let's search for some interesting sites. I want you to experience this world properly. I don't want you to be afraid of it. But next time, Eve, promise me that you'll spend some time getting to know a guy before you allow yourself into that kind of situation again.'

I promised.

For the next couple of hours Ben and I surfed through some interesting BDSM sites. As we made our way through the sites, I giggled and said, 'Can you imagine how many Google robots are working overtime to send your information to the relevant authorities as we do this? They might come knocking at your door, Ben.'

He laughed and said, 'I know. It has crossed my mind many a time. Ah well, we aren't committing a crime. Yet.'

Ben landed on a site which he was already a member of. It had categories for every kind of BDSM. He clicked on the 'DS for Heterosexuals' tab and we scrolled down the page, looking at various links to videos and stories which members had posted.

Then he got bored and left me to it, saying, as he walked out the door, 'Remember, Papi, you'll have to sign up if you want to make contact with anyone. And, please, make sure you get to know your next contact.'

'Yes, Ben, got it!'

Despite my unpleasant experience and new-found caution, I had to admit it was a great distraction reading some of the posts members had written about themselves. Wow—some people could be very explicit as to what turned them on.

I decided to join up but to *not* use the name and password I had created for Alex's site. As I wondered what to call myself, I thought, 'What the hell, why not just use Eve as my user name?'

I then set the password as 'Ezra' and posted the same picture of the butterfly in the profile. It then requested an email address, which I initially baulked at. Then I thought: too easy. And I logged onto gmail to create my new address, evetomas@gmail.com.

Now I was a member. Scrolling up and down through the list, I always returned to the same spot but didn't really concentrate on why. Obviously something had caught my eye, but I was distracted by the ache in my neck. I stretched my arms above my head; my body felt very heavy. I wondered if the effects of whatever Alex had drugged me with were still wearing off.

I left myself signed in to the site and walked through to Ben, who was talking to someone on the phone. I put my palms together, pointing to the sky and along one side of my face; then I tilted my face onto this 'pillow' and momentarily closed my eyes, letting him know that I was going to go to sleep for a little while. He nodded and gave me a little wave.

I stretched out on top of my bed. I felt exhausted.

Tomas

I went travelling four weeks after we had seen each other in Rushcutters Bay. I needed to get away. My final destination was on the Yucatan Peninsula of Mexico, but this was in an era before it had become overrun by tourists.

It was autumn, and I slept in a cheap hotel in Cancun on a single bed on a linoleum floor surrounded by dirty walls. I didn't care, because I spent my days either walking on the long deserted beach in front of the hotel, or letting my mind lose its way while I swam in the turquoise water of the Caribbean Sea.

I rented an old battered red Volkswagen car and drove south to the Toltec site of Chichen Itza, one of the Mayan ruins in the area.

This site was you, to me.

In earlier times the Mayans had played a form of football on the pitch in front, which always ended in a ritual sacrifice. Historians could never agree as to whether it was the winners who were beheaded as an honour, or the losers.

As I sat there in the ruin I thought of us, Tomas, and what we'd sacrificed.

And I wondered if there was any honour left between us.

❦

When I woke there was complete silence, so I went to find Ben because I suddenly felt lonely. He had left a note to say he was out for the night and to have a look at the iMac. I found a note stuck to the screen.

'Check out Member 32 in the list, Fox—interesting user name. By the way, I know you'll be taken by his eyes—or what you can see of them.'

I scrolled through the site and stopped. This was exactly the place I had kept returning to earlier, without knowing why. Member 32, or Fox, was wearing a mask, yet the image couldn't hide the deep green of his eyes. Ben was right—those eyes captured me.

What is it that attracts us to some people, and not to others? Instinctively we might react to a physicality: hair, eyes, neck, smile, ankle bone, ear lobe. And the list goes on. Equally our intrinsic natures are threaded with sensory stimuli, knowledge and experience—good or bad. And these are the pieces we place together in our jigsaw of desire—for someone.

I knew that what I desired in someone at this moment was not what I needed, but looking on the surface, and not beneath, was easier for me to cope with at this stage. Nor was I ready to inspect the damage caused by the sledgehammer Henry had slammed into our relationship, but I was aware the cracks were growing deeper and wider every day.

⋯⋰⋱⋯

And so I wondered what it was about this masked man, apart from his eyes, that had caught my attention. Even stranger was that, while I was looking at his image on the screen, he pinged a message to me.

'Hello there.'

'Hello. Curiosity kills the cat and not sure if I want to be taken by a fox, yet. Why "Fox"?'

His reply was immediate. 'Speed and agility. And you, why "Eve"—first woman?'

'It's my name.'

'I see you've just signed up to this site. What is it that you're after?'

'Some fun. Nothing specific, just an escape, really. To be honest, I'm not really sure how this whole thing works.'

'It works the way you want it to. If you want to be in control, then take control. Otherwise be controlled. It's your choice—entirely up to you.'

And there they were again, those words: 'your choice—entirely up to you'.

I brought my hands together in front of my mouth, almost as if in prayer, and stared at the screen. They were Tomas's words from years ago, and now a complete stranger had brought them back to life. I looked down at the white circle around the fourth finger of my left hand, which showed clearly where the sun had not been able to reach for all of time.

But I had chosen to marry Henry. I had chosen to stay with him and remain faithful to him till death do us part. He had chosen to remain faithless to me instead. And now it was entirely up to me to have faith in myself and the choices I was to make from here on in.

I replied to Fox. 'Not sure I have the energy to be in control right now. Maybe I'll leave it up to you for now.'

'Sounds like we could get along well. Does the butterfly have any significance?'

'Just something that I love as I don't really want a photo of me on the site. Not something that I really want to advertise that I'm doing.' Not that I was doing anything anyway.

'Fair enough, but there are lots of ways to disguise yourself. I like my mask because it gives an idea of what I look like, but stops me from being identified. Have you got a mask?'

Thinking about Ben's wardrobe, I replied, 'I do.'

'I'd like to see you in a mask. Would you like to take a photo of yourself in a mask for me?'

'Hang on.' I ran through to Ben's walk-in robe. There were a number of masks on the lower shelf and I took them all through into his bedroom. I chose the red one, because I had that exact colour in a lipstick. I pulled my hair up into a high ponytail, secured the mask around my head and put my red lipstick on.

I sat in front of the camera lens on the iMac screen and kept on taking photos until I was happy that no one would be able to identify me from the shot. I retrieved my profile from the site and replaced the picture of the butterfly with the masked shot.

Switching back to the text window I typed, 'Do you like what you see?' I knew I was being flirtatious, but I thought what harm could it do? After all, I wasn't married anymore and was free to have some fun.

'I do. Very much! Where do you live? I'm based in Hong Kong.'

'I live in Shanghai. Do you travel to the mainland much?'

'Mostly to Beijing. I've only been to Shanghai a couple of times. How do you find living there?'

'I love it, but have to admit it's good to get out occasionally, away from the "eyes and ears". I usually escape to Hong Kong, funnily enough.'

'Well, we might just need to organise something. I'm going to have to sign off as I have some work to finish. Do you want to send me some more shots? I'd love to see *more* of you. Send them to e_fox@hotmail.com.'

'OK, I'll find some for you to enjoy. Let's chat soon.'

After writing down the email address, I signed out of the site, signed into my new email account and added his address to my contacts list. His was the only contact here, I noted.

I felt strong, and good about myself. I liked the sound of Fox, and the fact that he was interested in getting to know me. Ben's words echoed: 'promise me that you'll spend some time getting to know a guy.' Well, I was, and I have to admit, it was thrilling.

I woke up refreshed and felt great for the first time in weeks. I changed into my running gear and ran out of the apartment and all the way to Fuxing Park. After watching my favourite show on earth, I took off again and ran all the way to The Bund and across the Garden Bridge to the Old Town for a cup of tea.

Exhausted from my run, I checked email while I poured my third cup of tea. Alice had sent me a whole lot of links to help my research for the art exhibition. 'Oops—need to do some work, Eve, and better get started,' I said to myself.

There were things in the house I needed to get, and I knew that I had to call Henry's personal assistant, Maxie, and organise a meeting. It was 7.30 a.m., but she was always at work by seven. She answered within three rings and was very cool when I said who it was.

'Oh, hello, Eve,' was all she said.

'Hello, Maxie.' I couldn't be bothered with any niceties as I knew Henry would have poisoned her mind with lies so I just told her, equally coldly, that I hadn't organised a removalist yet, because I was waiting for Henry's lawyer to contact me regarding our divorce settlement. 'In the meantime, I need to get some of my things. So can we organise to meet at the house today or tomorrow?'

She replied, 'I can't tomorrow. It will have to be today. The only time that suits me will be 8.30 this morning.'

I glanced at my watch—it was nearly 7.45. The traffic was already very heavy heading into the tunnel that ran underneath the river to Pudong, but if I caught a cab immediately I'd be able to make it.

'Alright, that will have to do, I suppose.'

I hung up and my phone buzzed with a missed call from Ben, followed by a brief text. 'Where are you? I'm going to the gym, shall I meet you there?'

I texted back and asked him to meet me at my old house, to lend me some moral support.

The house felt like a cold stone as Maxie let us in. She guarded the place as if we were thieves. I felt like telling her that Henry had stolen something from me that was far greater than any object in his house. Instead, I just took my laptop charger and my tape recorder, as they were the only things I needed right now. I looked at Ben, and he knew the meaning behind my words when I said, 'Let's fly.'

———❖———

I spent most of the next three days concentrating on the links to websites that Alice had emailed me, reading about the exhibiting artists and reviews of their work—with Fox in the back of my mind. All the time.

Finally, when I had exhausted any retention ability I had left, I linked back to the DS site, and saw a message from him.

'Sex is the consolation you have, when you can't have love.'

The words were familiar to me, something I had read once. And then I understood. It was a test, and a good one at that. I liked the quote he used and replied with another to make sure I was on the right track.

'There is always something left to love.'

I waited for his reply, to see if I was correct.

Henry would never have been drawn to the narrative brilliance of one of my favourite authors, Gabriel Garcia

Marquez. Fox, however, was coaxing me on a level that I loved, and he was definitely luring me into his den.

I was just about to sign out when the reply came. 'I see we like the same author. Am beginning to like you, even though we haven't met. By the way, where are the photos? I need to whet my appetite.'

'I will, I promise.'

As our conversations became more frequent, I found that we shared quite a lot in common; I was starting to like the sound of Fox. I mentioned my upcoming Beijing trip and we decided to meet there for a couple of days at the end of my stay.

Neither of us had said anything more about sending photos of ourselves so we could recognise each other when we met. Instead, we had sent each other tokens for identity purposes. I sent mine to a private box in Hong Kong, and had given him Ben's address so I could receive his token there.

'I'll email you the hotel details. By the way, what does the "e" stand for in your email address?'

'Edward.'

So he had a name.

———— ✸ ————

My leather boots were tight around the toes as I waited in the baggage collection area at Beijing Airport. I had bought the boots in Bangkok on one of my shopping trips with Ben, but I had never worn them, even in the winters of Shanghai, and was now desperate to take them off.

Waiting for my suitcase was when I saw him for the first time. He was tall and casually dressed, in a dark brown leather jacket, white T-shirt, faded jeans and La Sportiva hiking boots. He let his dark blond wavy hair fall just above his shoulders and I noticed a white scar above his right eyebrow.

But I was more absorbed in the way he tapped his mobile phone on his other wrist, because it revealed a rare Armani Chronograph wristwatch—my token to him.

He glanced up, sensing my look, and raised his eyebrows questioningly before seeing me eyeing the watch. I smiled directly into his deep green eyes and opened my jacket just enough for him to see the diamond-encrusted leather choker clasped with a key, before dropping my hand back to my bag. He nodded with a knowing smile as I walked over to him.

'You must be Eve. Hey, the watch is very unusual but stunning. And I see you are wearing my token on your neck.'

I could feel the electricity between us and said, 'I've booked the room for three days and have emailed all details to you. Did you receive it?'

He nodded as he took my wrist and moved it to his mouth, grazing it with his teeth. He then dropped it to my side as he walked forward to retrieve his suitcase. I glimpsed the nametag on his hand luggage—'E. Sutton'.

Without turning back he disappeared into the crowd and I was left knowing I had to wait a little longer.

———— ≫•≪ ————

Everyone talking on their mobile phones reminded me to text Amelia to let her know I had landed. Her reply was immediate. She told me her driver, Mr Kim, would be waiting with my name on a board in arrivals.

I saw the board held by a very tall Chinese man with a worried look on his face, standing in a maze of black hair and placards at the back of the arrivals hall. When I headed towards him, his face clearly showed relief as he realised his quarry had arrived safely. He smiled and we exchanged *ni hao*'s before he scooped up the suitcase and we headed out into the bitter cold towards a black car.

It was snowing as we drove through the Chaoyang district; I had forgotten how beautiful the capital was in winter. I remembered Beijing's nickname, 'City of Bicycles'—even in the snow a large number of people were riding bikes, wearing yellow rainproof ponchos. When we stopped at some lights, I watched a woman glide gracefully past on her bicycle; she had a chopstick holding her hair in a bun and wore a business suit underneath a see-through poncho, plus stockings and high-heeled shoes. Across the road two men were pushing a wooden wagon loaded with steel blocks up the right side of the road, in front of an alleyway full of people eating steam buns bought from a street vendor.

We passed the Lido market and I looked at my handbag, remembering a bartering episode in the previous year. Henry had brought me along on this business trip; while I'm sure now he was having his 'fun' time, I had spent my days going back and forth between Hongqiao and Lido markets, buying presents for the following Christmas.

Mr Kim spoke in broken English and said he had to make a quick stop in the city before taking the fourth ring road out to Amelia's place. The snow had stopped and the city lights were starting to glow.

I stood in front of the fire and looked across at the photo of Amelia on her bookshelf. She was the star of a ballet and she was about sixteen years old. Her face hadn't changed in the seventeen years since that photo and, apart from her now being pregnant, neither had the basic structure of her physique.

She walked into the lounge room with a tray holding two cups of green tea, a bowl of hummus and thin bread sticks, placing it on a coffee table before lowering herself, in that pregnant way, onto the couch. I sat next to her and warmed my hands around the delicate teacup.

'It's so lovely to be here, darling. To finally see you after—how long?'

'Nearly two long years, I think. Now, just what did happen between you and Henry? I can't think why he would do something so revolting, especially with that friend of yours—what's her name again?'

'Ex-friend. Her name is Chrystal, and I don't think anything just happened. It's been happening probably since the day we started. He couldn't keep his grubby hands to himself, or rather just for me.' I told her about having to be tested for herpes.

'Oh my lord, how disgusting. What a worry for you, you never said a word to me.'

'I know. Sorry, Amelia. What could I say? "Hello darling, just in the hospital getting tested for an STD. Want one? Because they're going for nothing so you don't need a loyalty card." It doesn't matter now—it's all in the past.' There was no point in talking any further about Henry and I didn't want to dampen the mood, so I switched topics.

'Anyway, on a happier note I've just started to enjoy myself and I'm seeing someone. Kind of, well, we've only met briefly. It's casual. Nearly all the communication so far has been electronic. I like the way he thinks.'

Amelia was quite traditional in relationship matters and I knew I had to tread carefully. She would have been shocked about the BDSM route I had taken. I told her that his name was Edward and he was younger than me, and that I was just toying with a little fun.

'I'm so pleased, darling. You're so lovely, and deserve to be happy. How much younger is he? What does he look like? Tell me about him.'

I replied airily, 'Actually, I don't know how old he is, but not that much younger than me, I think.' I described, vaguely, his blond hair, green eyes and whip of a mind. I said that we were meeting up at the end of the exhibition for a couple of days, which should be fun. And then I added hastily, 'Not ready to introduce him to anyone yet, you understand, don't you?'

'Of course I do,' Amelia said and I knew she wouldn't speak a word of it to anyone. 'You two should go to Dali— it's such a romantic restaurant. Or is that not appropriate?'

I laughed and said too quickly, 'No. Romance would be out of context.'

Amelia raised her eyebrows, so I covered with, 'Too soon.'

'So when does the exhibition start again? I know you've already told me, but lately I have the memory of a sieve. Pregnancy will do that to you.'

I knew too well, but just smiled and gently touched her 'baby' stomach before reminding her of my plans. I had to be in Da Shan Zi by ten the next morning. The official opening started at noon, but because it was my first story for *Budaya* I wanted to be there at least two hours before to be prepared. 'Do you have time to walk around the exhibition with me?' I asked Amelia.

'I'd love to, but I'm having my twenty-week ultrasound at eleven. At least we can drive in together—I'll get Mr Kim to drop you there, and then he and I can go on to the hospital.'

Later that night in bed I connected to their wifi stream and Googled 'Edward Sutton'. There was a story about an old guy shooting what he thought was a burglar but nothing else. I tapped Facebook and tried to search him there. No luck. My final search on LinkedIn resulted in the same. I was starting to like the anonymity of Edward; it made me more curious to get to know him.

Even more curious was an email with the subject line 'Settlement' waiting at the top of my inbox when I logged in. There was a cover note from J.H. Samson with a title under his name: Divorce Lawyer.

I opened the document and read that Henry had decided my total worth after our eight years of marriage was $150,000, except that he intended to subtract any purchases I had made on my Amex card during the two-year period we had lived in Shanghai. This meant I would receive $100,000.

I was shaking with anger, because most of the $50,000 he'd subtracted he had asked me to spend on airline tickets for our holidays together or to pay bills or for gifts he had asked me to buy for myself on the card. He also knew that I didn't have any money to contest the settlement, given that my savings account had only a couple of thousand dollars left. Plus, I knew he would employ one of the best lawyers available, who would orchestrate a strong case against why I should receive anything more. I decided to put my emotions aside, because right now I had to be practical.

I phoned Ben, who said, 'He's a complete bastard, Papi. What are you going to do?'

'Nothing. I can't afford to fight it.' I then explained that my first priority was to move my things out of the house, and I planned to use the same removalist who moved us into the house two years ago. Ben, as always, was only too willing to help; not only did he have a storage unit where I could leave my belongings, but he would also contact the removalist and oversee it while I was in Beijing. I sent an email to Maxie about organising access to the house to pack my old life away.

<hr />

The exhibition was being held in one of the old factories in 798 Art District. This district had been slowly de-industrialised and over time transformed by the migration of artists who had gradually changed the factories into stunning art galleries and cafes.

I walked into the Xi Xi Gallery while they were still washing the floor and making sure everything was perfectly placed for the crowds of people who would be visiting over the next three days. The concrete floor had been painted in a beautiful deep blue-red and the white walls were spotlit and hung with art by both international artists and Chinese artists from throughout the country. The entrance had a large painting of a Buddha in greys and black, with gold-leaf-painted bodhi leaves scattered in the background. They were a spiritual representation of the name of the exhibition, 'The Awakening'.

I met with the curator, Jan Gwo, a petite Chinese girl with a long thin face and eyes that sparkled with the passion of youth. Her knowledge of the artists was impressive and I was glad I'd brought my tape recorder for accuracy because she spoke quickly and I would not have been able to memorise, nor write in my notebook, at the speed of her knowledge.

The lacquer pieces from Vietnam were within my area of special expertise and I asked her if there were any pieces from the Vietnamese artist Dinh Quan, because I owned six of his paintings. She pointed me in the direction of one of the rooms off to the side at the back of the gallery. His painting style had changed. Instead of beautiful women with long thin necks, painted in lacquer on wood, as in his earlier works, there was anger and brutality in the scary faces of his recent work. I thought darkly that Henry would be a perfect client.

I picked up a copy of the program, put on my jacket and gloves, and tied my scarf around my neck; then I walked through the back door and out into the mid-afternoon winter sun. The sky was darkening and some snow clouds were approaching.

I called Amelia. 'Hi, gorgeous girl. How did the ultrasound go?'

'All good, thank goodness. I've just emailed you a copy of it. Makes it more real now, seeing a tiny baby inside me. What time should I get Mr Kim to pick you up? By the way, is it snowing there?'

'It looks like it's about to start. Maybe get picked up about 4.30?'

The next two days fell into the same pattern, with Mr Kim driving me to 798 Art District each morning and picking me up again late each afternoon. It would snow intermittently and occasionally there was the prospect of black ice, which would cause us to crawl along at snail's pace.

On the last day of the exhibition I phoned Ben to check on the removal of my things from the old house.

'Papi! How's Beijing and the exhibition?'

'I wish you were here, Ben, it would be more fun. It's a constant work in progress, this place. Wonderful. Think I've got enough information for my story. Were you able to organise my things out of Pudong?'

'Yes, all safe in the storage unit. By the way, there was a pile of mail for you as well.'

'Thanks, Ben, I really appreciate it. Obviously the storage unit was big enough?'

'Just. I can't wait to hear about your encounter with Mr E. When are you back?'

'On Sunday, but I'll text you in the meantime. Talk then.'

I watched the snowflakes drift through the air before they disappeared on the ground. The temperature had dropped below zero. There was just one more day before I would see Edward for our first encounter.

I was looking forward to the heat it would create between us. And my surrender.

─────────◦━━━◦─────────

I am waiting for Edward in Room 363, as I have done for the past two days. It is our last day together and I am wearing the clothes he has given me as gifts: a black corset that sits tightly underneath my breasts, lace thigh-high stockings and high-heeled leather boots. Today there is no leg-spreader, but I have put my blindfold on and buckled the red ball gag around my mouth to the back of my head. I am ready to give in to his demands.

I hear the door handle turn and my heart rate increases as I hear him walk into the room and close the door. I feel his body directly behind me, and he moves his hand over my stomach and up across my breasts. I shiver with lust, breathing heavily through my gag. He pulls hard on my nipples with both hands before he trails them down to my thighs and slides one finger into my wet pussy, and suddenly moves it out. This is the way we like it, that we stop every now and again, to maximise the sexual tension.

We have played our BDSM roles well over the past two days and I can tell he is enjoying it as much as I am. There is an apparent lack of emotion as he orders me into various stages of submission, but it is titillating and I find it sexually rewarding. There is also an emotional closeness when he whispers into my ear on a regular basis that I only have to mention our safe word and he will stop. I haven't had to use the safe word yet, and doubt that I will need to, but I feel comfort knowing that it is there if required.

'Today, we are going to do some posture training, Eve,' he says as he swishes the cane through the air.

'I want you to stand up straight and remain nice and still while you balance this book on your head for me. Every time it falls you get two canes, do you understand?'

I nod, knowing I don't have a choice, but I am ready to obey. I feel him place the book carefully on my head and I stand still like a statue, willing the slight cramp in my tired calf muscles to disappear.

He tickles the inside of my upper thighs and I struggle to remain still, but the book doesn't fall and he rewards me with a compliment.

'Very good, Eve. Now we need to make it a little harder for you.'

I feel the nipple clamp as it tightens on my left breast and then I groan because, as he places the second clamp on my other nipple, I shift my feet slightly and the book falls to the ground. I receive two whips from the cane.

He places the book back on my head and says, 'Now, this time I want you to make a perfect turn for me.'

I whimper and start to slowly turn 360 degrees, shuffling carefully in my boots, my tired thighs quivering from the physical demands of our three-day sexual marathon. I manage to turn the full circle without dropping the book.

'Very good,' Edward says as he pulls on the nipple chain, forcing me to bend forwards. I focus on keeping the book on top of my head as he runs his hand from my calf muscle up my inner thigh and expertly slides his finger inside me. I groan and my body trembles as I move my hips in unison with his hand. The book falls again and he retracts his fingers. I feel the cane again.

The chain from the nipple clamps strains as he pulls it down towards the floor. I am held in this position because he ties something between the chain and my right ankle. It is an awkward position, but I am determined to fulfil his needs and make him happy. He places the book back on my head as he says, 'This will be more difficult. I want you to do one more turn for me. This is the last thing I want from you today and, if you do it well, I promise you will receive some pleasure.'

I whimper in disbelief and think about using the safe word. My muscles are aching and the strain from standing in my high heels and balancing the book on my head is starting to wear me down, both physically and mentally. It is close to torture, but not close enough to make me give in and stop our erotic play.

Edward taps me on my bottom and says, 'Need some motivation?'

This rouses me to move and I begin to shuffle around in a circle once again. I finally make it, my legs shaking from exhaustion, and I moan against the mouth gag.

He picks me up and I circle his hips with my legs as he carries me to the bed. He asks me to sit, takes off my blindfold and tells me I can open my eyes. I watch his muscular biceps as they reach behind my head to unbuckle the gag. He moves in front of me, undoes the rope around my ankle, slowly releases the nipple clamps and gently sucks both nipples, giving me some long-wanted relief.

I am now lying on my back with my head on the pillow. He unzips my boots and slides them off my legs and finally unlaces my corset until I am completely naked except for the stockings.

He takes his mask off and his eyes are iridescent green, like the butterflies in the Jianfengling rainforest two years ago. He smiles at me and bends down to kiss my lips before saying, 'Your performance has been excellent, Eve, and now I feel you have earned some pleasure.'

He pushes my thighs apart and climbs on top of my body, moving himself slowly inside me while watching my eyes the entire time. I know I have to wait for his command before giving in to an orgasm, and that will be hard to control. He starts to move at a faster pace and I am concentrating on moving my hips at the same rate as his. All of a sudden it is too difficult and, as I start to move my hips faster against his, he grips my wrists and pushes them down beside my head on the pillow.

His tongue is in my mouth and he knows I am ready, so he tells me that I am allowed to come. I feel the pleasure and pain release themselves through the tightening of my muscles, and then with the eventual shudder through my entire body.

He pulls his cock out and moves up towards the pillow, and I take him into my mouth. I know he won't last more than a minute, and so I work hard and fast to give him his final pleasure for the day. He ejaculates to the back of my throat and I release his cock from my lips. He moves beside me and lies on his side, stroking my lips before finally telling me that I can swallow.

This is our last day in Beijing together and I close my eyes, feeling his fingers stroke the skin on my stomach. His touch is sensual and this action tells me he feels more intimate towards me, closer than the BDSM roles that we each act out together. I, too, am starting to want more intimacy between us, and I like our erotic connection although I remind myself that I'm not allowed to let my emotions influence me anymore.

———————— ✖✖ ————————

Ben was home when I walked through the front door. He looked at me with a naughty smile and said, 'And? Hmmm?'

I laughed at his cheeky reference to my sojourn and replied, 'Hot!'

'So, in person, what's he like—apart from being hot?'

'Think he's around thirty, as he certainly has the energy for it. He has a steady gaze which I find sexy. The DS stuff is fun and I feel safe doing it with him. He's quite tender as well which I like, but I'm trying not to like him, if you get my drift. The strange thing is that I Googled his name and *nothing* came up. Well, it did, but it was about an eighty-year-old guy in London who shot someone.'

Ben laughed. 'Really? Did you try LinkedIn?'

'Yes, nothing. Oh well, I have his mobile number and his email. It's probably not a good idea to find out too much about him at this stage.'

'You're probably right. When are you seeing each other again?'

'I told you he lives in Hong Kong, didn't I? Anyway, he said we should get together soon either there or here in Shanghai. I can't wait.'

When I got to my room I saw the pile of mail with an elastic band around it on my bed and sorted through it, flicking most of it into the bin beside the dresser. Then I saw an official-looking envelope addressed to Henry. It must have accidentally been included amongst mine.

I opened the envelope and unfolded a three-page document and started to read. It was dated six weeks ago. Then I started to laugh. Ben came in and took it from my hand. As he began to read it, he started to giggle and then we were both crying with laughter. It was so ridiculously funny that we couldn't stop.

Eventually, while wiping our tears away, Ben said, 'Herpetic Henry,' which started us off again.

I gasped. 'I know. It's *perfect*. Who said karma doesn't have a deadline. I bet it was Chrystal who gave it to him. Is your printer a scanner as well?'

Ben nodded and I followed him to the office. He scanned the medical report and I copied it onto the same memory stick where I had stored Henry's email database file.

'I've just thought of something brilliant,' I told him. 'Think I'll call Kaz to help me as he's a whiz at this stuff.'

Kaz had been living in New York, building his incredibly successful IP company, and had stayed with us on his way home back to Australia. He was a genius with technology and had helped me synchronise my email accounts.

I sat at the iMac and called him. I could hear the smile in his voice when he picked up. 'Eve! I've been thinking about you a lot lately. How are you?'

'Do you want the long version? Actually, there's too much to tell, so I'll fill you in properly a little later. Right now, I need to break into Henry's email account and send an email on his behalf with a couple of attachments.'

————◦⊷✦⊶◦————

It was six weeks after my Beijing trip and I had just returned from a long run. I had lots of energy these days and had just been remembering my encounter with Edward two weeks ago, which had given me extra zest.

My mobile vibrated on the entrance table. I walked over to it and saw I had a missed call while I'd been running. There was a voicemail message from Zara to ring her and my mouth was dry and I heard panic in her tone as I listened to her message about our other sister. 'Lori is in an induced coma, but is stable and in intensive care. A hit and run. She has serious internal injuries and her arm is broken, poor darling. She's covered in bruises and cuts and looks like hell. Please call me as soon as you get this message. Sorry that I had to let you know on voicemail, sweetheart.'

I called her immediately and she repeated the contents of her voicemail. My mother's voice was shaky and when my father took the phone from her he told me not to be frightened; I didn't know what to say.

Lori was older than Zara, Lili and I and had chosen to form a more conservative approach to life. We used the eight years' difference as the reason why we didn't have anything in common. The fact was, she disagreed with the way I conducted my life and, for that matter, how Zara and Lili handled theirs. But in that one phone call our history became insignificant and all I could think about, regardless of the past, was that she needed our love and support.

My bags were packed before I knew it and Ben drove me to the airport. I went online as we drove and booked a one-way ticket on the next available flight to Sydney. One way, because I didn't know when I would be returning.

I wondered if I should call Zara while I waited for my flight, but didn't really think there was any point. What could I say to make things better? I called Lili, but only reached her voicemail. No doubt she was organising to make her long journey home as well. I left a silly message and hoped it would make her smile.

I thought about Edward but was very worried about Lori, so I decided instead to message his mobile phone instead. I wrote that my sister was unwell and that I was flying back to Sydney to take care of her.

We flew through the dark evening sky and I fell asleep looking down at the disappearing lights with Evanescence's *Bring Me to Life* playing through my earphones.

My sleep was intermittent and my dreams scattered.

Lori. Edward. Tomas.

Tomas

It was the middle of spring and I had jogged to the North Sydney Council to pick up my renewed car registration.

Although I didn't know it, it was your green BMW bike that caught my eye because the colour was my favourite and it was shimmering in the sunlight. As I started to cross the driveway I forgot to look to my right but the sound of your bike engine stopped me running. You had seen me.

For some unknown reason I stood and watched as you parked the bike and took off your helmet.

And there you were right in front of me, and my heart skipped a beat. I released a long sigh, a calming technique I had been taught in yoga, and waved to you with small movements in my fingertips. I felt as if I was melting from the heat in the ground beneath my feet, and from seeing you.

You ran to me and I stood still, afraid that if I fell you wouldn't be able to catch me, again.

Your words were rushed. You said you had broken off your engagement soon after seeing me two years prior. You had come back to the apartment a few weeks later and had knocked on my door, but when I didn't answer, you peeked through the window on the garden side and saw that the apartment was empty. You didn't know that I had needed to vacate, because I couldn't get the scene of you and me together in that place out of my head.

You took me back to your apartment in Kirribilli and there was no stopping the physical want. We breathed a renewed rhythm into our old so-often-played melody while listening to the slow groove of Vandross in the background. I was twenty-three and you were twenty-four yet I felt at that very moment that we had spent a lifetime together.

Afterwards, you got up and disappeared into the other room, returning with a tiny box and asked me to open it. Inside was a gold butterfly designed as a hair clip. You took it out of the box and clipped my hair back from the side of my face.

I wanted to tell you then about Ezra, but it was the wrong moment.

And three days later you died.

Three days, Tomas, was also the time it took for Ezra to be taken from my arms and placed into someone else's world.

The boundaries that divided our worlds back then had forced us along different paths, which only crossed those few times in our lives. But I will forever treasure them.

In the first couple of years that followed, whenever I went running, you always walked across my sky.

The plane landed heavily and I woke with a start. Yesterday seemed a long time ago, and now that I was here it was time to take care of Lori and forget about my own situation.

As I walked out into the arrivals hall, Zara was holding a bunch of tulips, which were almost crushed in our hug. Her eyes had dark circles beneath and her skin was tight around her mouth. She took my hand and walked us out of the terminal and into Sydney's harsh sunlight.

We went straight to the hospital and I was shaken by how tiny my sister looked in the hospital bed. Her body was hooked up to a number of machines that were beeping; the sounds were cold and robotic. I stroked her forehead and her skin felt thin and fragile. We sat and watched Lori as she struggled to breathe through the tubes connected to her nose and mouth.

Our parents arrived and my father looked older. I held his hug as if I was going to lose him if I let go.

Zara handed me her mobile and I heard Lili on the other end. She was in Dubai waiting for her connection and sounded very worried and alone. I tried to calm her by making a joke and, even though she laughed, we both knew our sister's situation was far from humorous.

The nurses gently let us know that it was time to leave so Lori could rest for the night. My father drove us back to their house and the four of us ate without appetite and without conversation.

Dad looked grey as he stood and let us know he was going to bed. He was so exhausted he left the room without kissing us goodnight. I saw Zara's sadness and asked if she was okay.

'I'll tell you tomorrow, Eve. I don't have any energy to talk. We'll have a better chat tomorrow. Night, darling.'

I was relieved, as I, too, couldn't face talking about anything outside of my family's circle of love, but then again I didn't know if I could face what was happening inside the circle either.

———— ✖ ————

Papa was making a pot of coffee when I wandered into the kitchen at 6.30 in the morning. Zara was sitting with her feet tucked up underneath her, reading yesterday's newspapers.

I poured myself a cup of coffee and sat with Zara. 'How's Sergei? I can't wait to see him.'

Zara looked quickly at Dad, who was oblivious to everything going on around him, before she said very quietly, 'I think I might be losing Sergei to someone else.'

I was about to ask 'To whom?' but the telephone rang and Mama walked in and picked up the phone. We heard her say, 'Thank you, thank you very much for letting me know.'

Zara and I stood up as Mum smiled across to Dad. 'That was the hospital. Lori is showing some positive signs. She is still in a coma but they're talking about bringing her out of it in the next few days.'

I hugged Zara who was also endeavouring to smile.

'What time does Lili arrive?' I asked.

'She lands at 1.30 p.m. That's if Turkish Airlines is on time, of course. I didn't even know they flew to Australia.'

We spent the day at the hospital and at one point the nurses asked Zara and me to take a break while they re-dressed Lori's bandages. We sat in the cafe and I asked Zara about Sergei. 'Who are you losing him to?'

'Someone I have suspected for a long time. Did Lili ever tell you about that time in the gym when she saw a woman, and the feeling that she got?'

'Yes, she emailed me about it. But really? Sergei is so in love with you.'

'Yes *really*. There is so much more to tell you, but it'll have to wait until later. Come on, we need to get back to Lori.'

That afternoon we picked Lili up from the airport and drove straight to hospital, updating her on Lori's progress—or lack of it—on the way. As we walked into ICU, Zara said she would wait in the cafe downstairs because they didn't allow more than two visitors in the room. One of the nurses overheard and said that they would allow the three of us to be in the room together, just this once.

Mum and Dad arrived a little later and we told Lili she needed to go home, unpack and rest. She left with Zara while I stayed with my parents in the ward and watched them watch Lori. I could see the desperation in their eyes. Desperate for her to wake up. Desperate for their daughter to come home.

The same desperation was visible in Lili's eyes that evening. Mum and Dad had gone to bed, and she and I sat outside with a glass of wine while she told me about Will, the spy software and Slutski. It was a brief respite from our present situation and we laughed about the emails, and the brilliance of the 'set-up'.

I told her briefly about Henry and Chrystal, about Henry's medical report, and about the copy of Henry's email file on my memory stick. I giggled a little as I revealed that I had sent a copy of his medical report and his cruel email to me to every female he had on his business contact list, purportedly from him of course. I had also cc-d the lot to Chrystal and sent a copy to Henry's personal email address. Lili was suitably impressed, and we chuckled at our retributive justice and how much Will and Henry had deserved being the beneficiaries of our mischief-making.

But I couldn't bring myself to tell her about Edward, as it would force me to take a closer look at what I was doing, and why, so I closed the conversation with a kiss on her forehead and told her I needed to sleep.

I stretched my body out on the bed in the small spare room. I loved this room at my parents' house as there was a long window opposite the bed through which I could watch the blinking light from the lighthouse on the cliff face at the end of the beach.

I was thinking about Lori in the ICU ward when without warning my nightmare came back again . . .

Tomas

I didn't return to work that afternoon when you reappeared in my life outside North Sydney Council. We spent the rest of the afternoon in bed instead.

Later, you told me you had football practice but would only be gone for a few hours. You said you didn't want to leave, and I didn't want you to leave either.

A noise woke me up much later that night and I found you sitting at the kitchen table with an ice pack around your shoulders. I sat on your knee, stroking the top of your head; you told me you had been tackled head-high and had fallen awkwardly. Because you said you had no memory of what happened directly after that, I reached for the phone while holding your head close to mine to check your pupils. Immediately you placed your hand over mine and took the phone from me and placed it back on its cradle.

You kissed my ear and said, 'Don't worry, baby, I saw a doctor in the club afterwards and he told me I need to take it easy. So let's take it easy and go to bed, instead!'

I tried to stop you two days later, but you told me you felt perfectly fine and were excited to be playing the last club game for the year. You didn't know it would be the last football match of your life. We kissed and I watched the sun fall on a blond wisp of hair across your forehead. Our eyes locked together as we said goodbye.

You were prone to concussion, I was told later, and head injuries, especially accumulative head injuries, will eventually take their toll. Apparently the kick to your head on that last Saturday afternoon, coupled with the head-high tackle two days before that, proved to be the deadly game changer.

By the time I heard about the accident on the Saturday evening, you were already in a coma.

And you never regained consciousness.

———✦———

Lori did regain consciousness, eventually. Her gradual steps towards us were her tiptoes back into our lives and we watched her every move with relief. When her eyes opened, it was a blessing to us—a corner turned.

With her awake, we could now pretend that everything was fine, even though we knew there was a long path ahead—in all of our lives. The time had come for me to journey back to China.

Sitting in the business centre at Sydney Airport I tried to distract myself by looking at news bulletins on the internet. It was another hour before my flight back to Shanghai was due to take off, so I logged in to gmail and sent a message to Edward, asking if he was going to be around on the weekend. I missed him and realised how quickly my life had taken yet another path since I met him.

Lori's accident had also taken *us* on a path to recovery—and even though I knew it would be a slow process, it was obvious that her accident would gradually fill the years of disconnect between her and us three sisters. I also knew that I needed to visit Sydney more frequently to ensure she was fully aware that we were all here for her, and for our parents as well.

I added to Edward's message that I would be back in Shanghai the following evening and asked him to call me around that time. I thought it would be great to meet up with him in Hong Kong for a couple of days and hoped that he didn't have anything planned.

———※———

Ben was away on an assignment for a few days when I arrived home. I unpacked and was preparing dinner when my mobile rang. I flicked my hair back as I answered, not looking to see who it was as I knew it would be Edward.

However, the voice was unfamiliar on the other end. 'Hello, is that Eve? Is that Ezra's mother, Eve?'

'Yes. Yes, it's Eve. Who is this?'

'My name is Sophia. I'm Ezra's wife.'

I gasped for air. Ezra's wife? I didn't even know he was married, I thought wildly. Of course I didn't know—I haven't spoken to him for an age. Why is his wife calling me, and why isn't he?

All of a sudden the adrenalin kicked in and I was fully alert. There was silence and I thought I heard a sob before Sophia said, 'I'm so sorry to have to tell you this on the phone, but I didn't know how to do it any other way. I'm just so sorry . . .' Her voice broke.

I froze and instinctively placed my hand over my heart and clasped the phone so hard in my other hand I thought I was going to crush it.

Sophia continued in a faltering whisper between sobs. 'Ezra died in a bike accident two days ago. I have only just found your number on his phone. I never knew he had it. I mean, he told me about you, a little, I knew your name, but I didn't know he had your number . . .' Her words tumbled out. 'I'm sorry . . . we've been married for six years, and you didn't know . . . I wish you had. Even though our marriage has been strained of late, he is . . . was . . . my heart.' She stopped talking then and cried uncontrollably for a few moments. 'Sorry, sorry . . . I am so very very sorry, Eve, to have to share this terrible news this way . . .'

Nothing happened for a second and then my heart stopped beating regularly. My body began to shake involuntarily and a wave of nausea made me fall to my knees. I dropped the phone.

A black bird landed on the windowsill and I gazed at its enormous beak. It looked back almost intently at me before opening its wings to dry off the rain that had soaked them.

I saw the crucifix it represented.

I stood up slowly and walked through to the bedroom and sat on the bed. I didn't want to breathe in case I was swept away into a void. I blinked and two heavy tears flowed down my cheeks and dropped to my chest. I grabbed the pillow and held it tight against my face, against my fright.

Sometime later I picked up the mobile phone from the floor. There was a missed call from Edward. 'Well timed,' I thought blankly. It would be too hard to call him back and explain about Ezra and what had happened. My head felt light and I lay back on the bed and closed my eyes.

The sadness crept into my heart silently, remaining still like frozen ice. Waiting for its time to crack and seep through my body, breaking it down with the severity that only grief can.

To nought.

———⊶�✖⊷———

There was a bell tolling in the background, a kind of time-keeper. I drifted back to consciousness and realised it was take my hand, and together we walked up the steps and into their house. She guided me into the bedroom that she had shared with Ezra.

She held my hands and apologised again for having to tell me about Ezra's death over the telephone and added, 'I'm lucky in a way that I found your number, so I called you immediately before realising I was making the call from my dead husband's phone. That call was the last time I used his phone. Actually, it was the second last time because I called you back to make sure you were okay, but when you didn't answer, I thought it would be best to leave it until a little later. I've locked the phone away in a drawer until such a time that I can bear to look at it again.'

She released my hands and picked up an oblong box from the bed and handed it to me before continuing. 'Two days ago I found this box among Ezra's things. It's locked and I don't know where the key is. Your name is inscribed on it, and I think he did it himself. He must have saved some things to give you at some stage. I don't think he knew he was going to die so soon. I also have this for you, as I thought you might like to see your son as a man.'

She pressed a photo into my hand, and moved to the bed and started to cry.

I lifted my sunglasses to the top of my head and held the photo at arm's length to see the man who had once been my baby, Ezra.

A face stared through the camera lens and straight at me.

The dread started growing like a poison through my body and the words came stalking through a ghostly whisper, before I realised they were mine.

'Oh my god, what have I done?'

The man in the photograph had green eyes and blond hair.

But it was the white scar above his right eyebrow that had a terrible familiarity.

⚬────❦────⚬

Two years have passed since Ezra's funeral and I have moved to a small fishing town in the Marlborough Sounds at the top of the South Island of New Zealand, partly to be able to visit my parents and Lori on a regular basis, but mostly because I have taken on a role as a theatre designer for the local drama club. The job pays a pittance but I invested the money from my divorce wisely and am able to live a simple life. I swim in the water every morning in summer and run the running tracks in the mountains around my home after work in the evenings.

No one asks me about my life, which is the beauty of this small sleepy town. I am thankful for their discretion.

Ben and Emma came to stay with me six months after the funeral and we spent two weeks sailing around the Sounds and sharing secrets. I finally admitted to them about Edward, and who he really was. They didn't take the information well at first, but of course they realised that I hadn't known from the start who Edward was either. It was a shocking revelation, but I knew I had to share the story with them, no matter how hard it was for them to hear the words, or how hard it was for me to voice my bitter truth.

I was busy working on a set design on my Mac one evening after my run when I received an email from Sophia. We had tried to keep in contact, but she had been getting on with her personal life while I had hit a full-stop on mine once again, and we had gradually lost regular contact.

She wrote that she had met someone and wanted to tell me about him. Her words were cautious but I read happiness and responded to her email with encouragement. I was pleased for her, but I wondered in my heart what Ezra would have done, if he had still been alive and they had not remained married.

The choker he had given to me as a token had sat on a windowsill in my bedroom since I first moved in. Every morning I looked at it with sadness, and shame. It signified a tomb to me and I knew I would never wear it again. I thought I should probably have the diamonds removed and styled into another piece of jewellery. As for the collar, I needed to surrender it to the water at the bottom of my garden so it could float and gradually break down in the drowned valleys beyond.

As a postscript Sophia had asked me in her email if I had been able to break into the box she had given me after the funeral service.

I didn't answer that question, nor did I tell her that I didn't have to break into the box because one morning, when I moved the choker to dust the windowsill, it had dropped to the floor and its key had fallen out.

That's when it occurred to me for the first time that the key that had clasped the choker might fit the lock.

And it did.

<hr />

I had resisted opening the lid for three days and took a deep breath when I saw what was inside.

You know *that* moment when you fall in love and you can't fathom a basic thought because what's happening seems too out of reach? I felt that moment when I lifted a letter out of the box.

The words were written in blue ink, on a piece of rice paper, with a picture of a butterfly as a watermark—slightly faded in the background.

And the last line read, 'There is always something left to love.'

my phone. I looked at the screen and didn't recognise the number. I answered because I realised that I needed to let the outside in, even if it was from someone that I didn't know.

It was Sophia. She let me know the details for the funeral. That was it, really. I knew I wouldn't remember so I gave her my email address for her to send me everything I needed to know.

It was a brief conversation. Even though we both knew there was so much more to say, neither of us could bear to go there.

The trip to Hong Kong for Ezra's funeral was without consequence. Without consequence because I was unaware of anything except Emma and Ben. My darling friends who had booked my ticket, packed for me, dressed me for the trip, and sat on either side of me on the plane as my protectors.

I was in a fog in the departure lounge but somehow logged on to gmail and sent Edward a brief message to say I would be out of contact for a little while. It didn't seem important to say why. But what was important was that I kept in contact, as my feelings for him were starting to grow into something deeper. Our connection had started to peel my layers back a little and, if I was true to myself, I wanted to get to know him more, get a little closer.

But right now, I didn't want to be close to anyone.

For the service I dressed carefully, selecting a black silk suit with a cream lace camisole and cream-and-black shoes. Emma brushed and pinned my hair into a loose bun with my gold butterfly clip and I found some drop-heart earrings which I threaded through my ears.

At some time, while all this was going on, I found myself staring at a little white tablet that had suddenly appeared in my hand. I looked at Emma who explained it was Valium. 'It's okay, it will soften the reality a little and keep you calm.' She handed me a glass of water, and I put the tablet on my tongue and washed it down with the water.

'How long does it last for, Em? Will it get me through the day?' I was shaking and had to sit down quickly on the kitchen stool in the hotel apartment.

Nothing seemed real. This was the day my son would be buried. This was the day I would meet Sophia for the first time. This was the day I didn't want to be alive for.

The cathedral was stark in its beauty. I held Emma's hand tightly and leaned into Ben's right side, his arm around my waist as the three of us walked through the entrance and turned left into the west wing.

A striking woman walked towards me and I realised it must be Sophia. We embraced and I kissed her on the cheek, introducing myself. Sophia took my hand and we walked to the front pew with Emma and Ben. We sat. I felt incapacitated and heavy beneath a black weight.

My body was numbed from the Valium that Emma had given me and the sunglasses, thankfully, made everything dark. I sat with my eyes closed throughout the entire service listening, but not listening.

When we arrived at Sophia's house, Ezra's house, my heart was beating fast and my vision was impaired. Their garden was a mass of wildflowers and I saw a waterfall to the left. There was a fishpond full of goldfish and waterlilies. And there were butterflies, everywhere.

Sophia was talking to people at the top of the stairs when we approached. She walked down the three stone steps to